"Someone was in here while I was sleeping."

"Son of a bitch," he muttered again, fury coursing through him. He pushed open the door and stepped inside. A slight breeze blew through the flimsy curtains over the window and chilled his skin.

In her thin gown she had to be freezing. She reached for the cape she'd worn earlier that night, which was lying across a chair near the king-size bed. While she wrapped that around herself, he checked out the room and the adjoining closet and bathroom.

"It's clear," he said. "Now lock yourself in and also call the police."

She nodded.

But when he started for the door, she grabbed his arm. "Don't—"

"I have to see if I can catch them," he said. If they hadn't gotten away yet, he had to try to stop them and retrieve that gun. He just wasn't certain how he could manage that without getting shot.

"Be careful," she whispered.

He nodded, then headed out into the hall. A crazy thought jumped into his head that he should have kissed her.

Dear Reader,

Happy holidays! I love this time of year with all the twinkling lights, the scents of pine trees and cinnamon-glazed roasted almonds in the air. As enjoyable as they are, the holidays are also a lot of work. Shopping, decorating, and getting everything ready for the social obligations and family parties can be stressful. Those issues are the least of heroine Dr. Priscilla Pell's concerns this Christmas, though. She just wants to finish the research she started with her late husband, and she doesn't want to lose the baby she's carrying via her last IVF treatment. But someone is trying to kill her. So it's the Payne Protection Agency to the rescue, or so she hopes when hunky bodyguard Blade Sparks moves in to her mansion.

Bachelor Bodyguards is my longest-running series, and I'm so excited to bring you another installment featuring more heroic bodyguards as well as cameos from the Payne family and Chief Woodrow Lynch. All these characters are so real to me that they're like my family, too. So it's extra fun getting together with them for the holidays.

Hope you enjoy the book and your holidays!

Happy reading!

Lisa Childs

CHRISTMAS SECURITY

LISA CHILDS

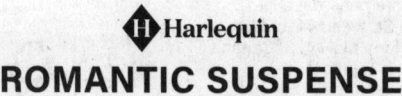

ROMANTIC SUSPENSE

If you purchased this book without a cover you should be aware that this book is stolen property. It was reported as "unsold and destroyed" to the publisher, and neither the author nor the publisher has received any payment for this "stripped book."

Recycling programs for this product may not exist in your area.

ISBN-13: 978-1-335-47169-7

Christmas Security

Copyright © 2025 by Lisa Childs

All rights reserved. No part of this book may be used or reproduced in any manner whatsoever without written permission.

Without limiting the author's and publisher's exclusive rights, any unauthorized use of this publication to train generative artificial intelligence (AI) technologies is expressly prohibited.

This is a work of fiction. Names, characters, places and incidents are either the product of the author's imagination or are used fictitiously. Any resemblance to actual persons, living or dead, businesses, companies, events or locales is entirely coincidental.

For questions and comments about the quality of this book, please contact us at CustomerService@Harlequin.com.

TM and ® are trademarks of Harlequin Enterprises ULC.

 Harlequin Enterprises ULC
22 Adelaide St. West, 41st Floor
Toronto, Ontario M5H 4E3, Canada
www.Harlequin.com

Printed in Lithuania

MIX
Paper | Supporting responsible forestry
FSC® C021394

New York Times and *USA TODAY* bestselling, award-winning author **Lisa Childs** has written more than eighty-five novels. Published in twenty countries, she's also appeared on the *Publishers Weekly*, Barnes & Noble and Nielsen Top 100 bestseller lists. Lisa writes contemporary romance, romantic suspense, and paranormal and women's fiction. She's a wife, mom, bonus mom, avid reader and less avid runner. Readers can reach her through Facebook or her website, lisachilds.com.

Books by Lisa Childs

Harlequin Romantic Suspense

Bachelor Bodyguards

Close Quarters with the Bodyguard
Bodyguard Under Siege
Hostage Security
Personal Security
Christmas Security

Hotshot Heroes

Hotshot Hero Under Fire
Hotshot Hero on the Edge
Hotshot Heroes Under Threat
Hotshot Hero in Disguise
Hotshot Hero for the Holidays

The Coltons of Owl Creek

Colton's Dangerous Cover

The Coltons of Alaska

The Unknown Colton

Visit the Author Profile page at Harlequin.com for more titles.

For all the members of my Between the Covers readers group! I appreciate your support and friendship so very much! Love you all!

Chapter 1

The number that lit up the screen of his cell phone wasn't in his contacts, but Blade Sparks knew who was calling him. He reached for the phone that lay on the top of his desk, and he clicked to decline the call just as he had the other times she'd tried to reach him.

For what?

Not that he was actually curious about her reason for trying to contact him. He couldn't imagine she would have anything nicer to say to him than she had in court all those years ago when she'd testified against him.

When she'd lied.

Even if she'd told the truth, he probably would have gotten prison time. Maybe.

But none of that mattered now. He couldn't undo what he'd done. But he'd found a way to move past it with the help of the Kozminski brothers. He had a job that he enjoyed, working for and with a great group of people.

Milek Kozminski was so tall that Blade could see him over the wall of his cubicle. The blond-haired guy gestured for Blade to join him and his brother. So Blade hopped up from his desk and walked into Garek's office. Milek closed the door behind them, shutting him inside the room with its glass walls that looked out into the open area of the old warehouse that had been converted into the office of the newest franchise of the Payne Protection Agency.

The Kozminski brothers looked like a set of blond bookends while he looked like the odd man out. Both of the brothers were tall and thin with longish hair and really pale eyes. Blade was tall like they were but much broader, to the point that it was hard for him to find clothes that fit his muscular build. His hair was dark. His eyes were blue, but a darker blue than theirs. And he definitely didn't have their perfect profiles. His nose had been broken more than once even before he started boxing.

"Okay, let's try this again," Garek said as he dropped back into the chair behind his desk. "Maybe we can brief you on your new assignment before anyone else nearly gets killed."

Since the agency opened, it seemed as if the bodyguards of this franchise had been in constant danger. But that was part of the job.

Blade didn't mind at all. He was used to being in danger; at least now it was for a good cause. To protect others. And this time, protecting someone else wouldn't send him to prison. Or so he hoped.

"The subject you're being assigned to protect is Priscilla Pell, the widow of Dr. Alexander Pell, who's famous for creating vaccines and medicines to treat all kinds of ailments," Garek said.

"So the widow inherited a boatload of money," Blade said, making a probably correct assumption. "But I thought this franchise focused more on protecting things than people." That was probably because when they were younger, people hadn't been able to protect their things from some of them. The Kozminskis were the sons of a notorious jewel thief and had been forced into stealing themselves when they were kids. The same man, the godfather of River City, Michigan, had forced a couple of the other bodyguards into stealing in their youth as well.

Blade had also done some stealing himself as a kid, but he hadn't been forced to do it. He'd just been trying to support himself and his single mom. It was better than her hooking up with the losers she had. But theft wasn't why he'd gone to prison. He'd been a lot better at getting away with stealing than he had been with murder. Actually manslaughter. He hadn't meant to kill the brute.

"We are being hired to protect the valuables she inherited," Milek said. "As well as being a biophysicist, Dr. Pell was also a collector of beautiful things. He has an extensive art collection and jewelry and antiquities from all over the world."

Blade nodded. "Oh, okay." Now he understood his mission. "I need to set up a security system to protect the valuables." During his training at the original office of the Payne Protection Agency, he'd quickly caught on to which systems were the most effective at keeping out criminals. The part of his job that he enjoyed most was testing the clients' current security systems to prove how accessible they were. And he always insisted on going into those tests blind, with no knowledge beforehand of the system or even much knowledge of the client.

He was going to check out Mrs. Pell's system this evening before meeting her in the morning at the appointment his bosses had scheduled with her. Then he would be able to tell her where the deficiencies were and what needed improvement, and he would get filled in more thoroughly on his assignment and the client's particular needs.

"You're also going to have to move into her mansion to ensure that she and that collection stay safe," Garek said.

Blade struggled to make sense of the necessity for that. "But why? A great security system will protect her and the house."

Milek and Garek exchanged a look. Despite how much they looked alike, they weren't twins, but they still seemed to share that twin thing, the intuition.

"Is there something I'm missing?" he asked as his own intuition kicked in with a warning that something wasn't quite right with this assignment. Then he shook his head. "Never mind. I can get filled in more tomorrow during the meeting."

Garek shrugged. "There's not a lot more to fill you in on, actually. Hull, the CEO of the insurance company, who's hiring us for these assignments, hasn't told us much either. That makes me feel like there's something we're all missing. That there might be more going on than we realize."

"With Hull and why he's making his policyholders hire us for protection?" Blade asked. He didn't trust the guy either. But then he'd learned long ago to never trust anyone. Despite the break they'd given him and his coworkers, Blade wasn't even sure he trusted the Kozminskis completely.

"But I still don't get why I have to move into the mansion," Blade said, but then he shrugged, too. "I can wait though to figure it out." And he hoped he would be able to prove his moving in was unnecessary once the estate had the correct security system.

"I don't know either what the CEO is so worried about," Garek admitted. "Maybe he's concerned about another inside job going down, like what happened at Croft Custom Jewelry."

Blade sucked in a breath. That case had been a doozy with an innocent child and his grandmother being kidnapped. That was how Blade's coworker Josh Stafford had learned he had a child; unbeknownst to him, his fiancée had been pregnant when he'd gone to prison for a crime he hadn't committed. Blade felt a pang of sympathy for his new friend, for having to do time for something he hadn't done and for losing those precious years with his young son because of it.

At least Blade had done the crime he'd served time for. And despite how it had all turned out, he wasn't sure even now that he would do anything different from what he'd done back then, a decade ago.

"A lot of people live in that house with Mrs. Pell," Milek said. "Several Pell family members as well as around-the-clock staff and a personal assistant who's always on call."

Blade released a soft whistle. "So that's how the rich live..." With staff and assistants and all the family under one roof. It sounded like a nightmare to him. After the eight years he'd spent in prison, he didn't want to live with anyone else ever again. In the couple of years since his release, he'd managed to keep that promise to himself. But for this case, for the Kozminskis, he was willing to suck it up. They had given him a second chance, and he would not let them down.

"I'm not sure that's really the reason Hull wants a bodyguard in the house, though," Garek said. "But he did mention all those people living there. And he wants a bodyguard in residence for a while to make sure that the new security system is sufficient. I guess he really doesn't want to pay out on any of the valuables he insures in that house."

"All those people there, all those possible thieves," Blade remarked. It was going to be damn hard to protect valuables from the people they potentially belonged to, though. He blew out a breath and nodded. "Sure, I'll bring some stuff with me tomorrow at the meeting, so that I can move into the mansion then."

He actually had an overnight bag in his vehicle now, but if this assignment lasted a while, he was going to need more than the toothbrush and the change of clothes that he had packed in his duffel.

"Theft might not be all that Hull is worried about," Garek said.

"What else could he be worried about?" Blade asked with curiosity.

"Considering how our previous assignments for him have gone, Hull has a lot of reasons to be worried," Garek admitted.

Croft Jewelry had had the inside job. Their last assignment, at an art gallery, had once done some money laundering but only under its previous ownership. What could be the CEO's concerns about this case?

"You just need to be extra careful," Milek said.

Every assignment for Midwest Property and Casualty had nearly caused some casualties for the Payne Protection Agency. Maybe that was Hull's real agenda; maybe the CEO wanted to get rid of some of the bodyguards. But since they had no proof of that, the Kozminskis kept taking his assignments. At least they had jobs for other clients that were much easier and safer, just installing security systems.

He nodded. "I'll be careful." He knew what happened if he wasn't, if he got too involved or too emotional: somebody could wind up dead.

Blade did not want that to be him or the widow he was supposed to protect. Priscilla Pell. He was going to do everything within his power to make sure that they both survived this assignment.

***

Priscilla tried to insert the key into the lock of the door of the den, but it didn't slide in smoothly. Something seemed to stop it. She pulled out the key, held it up to the dim light in the hallway and studied the metal teeth on the side of it. Had she grabbed the wrong key?

She'd been so tired lately that maybe she wasn't thinking clearly. But she didn't have enough keys to confuse them. This was the one for the home office; she knew it because she used it so often.

Or she once had.

She had to force herself to go into the office at all lately. But she had a promise to keep: a project to finish. And to finish it, she had to get into the den where all the notes and computers were.

She looked from the key to the lock on the big mahogany door. The pewter was scratched. She leaned closer to it. No. It was gouged. Deep grooves marred the metal and distorted the keyhole. Someone had tried to jimmy it or, from the crudeness of the gouges, maybe they'd tried to chisel it. She would probably need a whole new knob and lock.

Damn.

The insurance company CEO was right: she needed better security than Dr. Pell—Alexander had installed in the house. He'd figured the gate and the wall around the estate would keep out intruders. So he hadn't had cameras installed. Not even a doorbell one. Maybe it had been secure enough when he was alive, but it wasn't safe now.

She wasn't safe now.

Because for someone to try to jimmy the lock like this, they would have had to be inside the house. Had they gained entry through an exterior door, or had they already been inside—living with her?

Now that Alexander was gone, everybody in this house hated her. She knew that, and she probably would have walked away if not for those promises she'd made.

And for…

She pressed her hand over the slight swell of her abdomen. She couldn't feel the baby move yet. If not for the morning sickness and fatigue, she might not have believed that she was still pregnant. She would have worried that she'd lost it just like she'd lost the other embryos over the course of her IVF treatments.

This was the last one. Her last chance to fulfill one of those promises, to bring to life this legacy of her late husband's. Despite it being night now, she felt a morning sickness wave of nausea that she had agreed to all these promises.

But she would make sure this child was more than a reflection of his father. He was hers, too. Only hers now. Protectiveness gripped her, making her tighten her hand against her stomach. She would ensure that her son had a normal and happy childhood. If only she knew what one of those was…

Tears stung her eyes. Damn hormones. She'd been struggling with them. The fatigue. The brain fog. And something she hadn't experienced before…erotic dreams. Very explicit fantasies, which were something she'd never had before.

She'd always been so busy with school and then with work for Dr. Pell—Alexander. She had trouble remembering to call her late husband by his first name because he hadn't ever been a real husband to her. He'd been her mentor and her employer and her best friend and maybe even her salvation.

She'd had relationships before him, but she'd always given more in those than she'd received. And even though she'd never had sex with her husband, she might have given him more of herself than she had anyone else. So, for once, she wanted to take. She wanted to experience things she hadn't experienced before.

Pleasure. Real sensual pleasure. Christmas was coming. Could she ask Santa for that as a present? She hadn't believed in Santa even when she'd been a kid, though. She certainly didn't believe in him now.

She sighed and leaned her forehead against the door to the den. The hardwood was cool against her skin. She tried to clear her mind, to focus on what really mattered. She had to finish the book Alexander had started, but all his notes were in the office. And she had to finish the research, too. They'd been so close to a breakthrough in the drug for Alzheimer's. She was certain she could figure out the correct formula. But not tonight. It was late.

So in the morning, she would call a locksmith to change out the lock. She also had that meeting with the Payne Protection Agency in the morning. Maybe they could install cameras and sensors inside the house to catch whoever was trying to get into the den. She didn't need to worry about anyone else getting in there tonight since she couldn't unlock the door even with the key.

While the insurance CEO was worried about the art and the jewelry and the antiques, Priscilla knew that the real valuables were in that office, in those notes, and in the book and the research that she needed to finish for Dr. Pell—Alexander.

But what was the most valuable to Priscilla was the baby she was carrying. She couldn't lose him. And she was afraid that once the people in this house, the ones who all hated her, realized she was pregnant that neither she nor her unborn child would be safe. They might be concerned that another heir, a biological one of Alexander's, would reduce their share of the estate. And they had reason to be concerned with the way that Dr. Pell had drawn up his will.

But she had a plan to protect herself and it didn't involve the Payne Protection Agency that Mason Hull had convinced her to hire. Out of necessity Priscilla had learned long ago how to protect herself.

Blade had left a while ago, but Garek found himself staring at the open door to his office with a sudden longing to call him back. But it was too late; the bodyguard had probably already arrived at the Pell Mansion, as the place was known in River City, Michigan.

"We should have gone with him," Garek said. "Assessed the place ourselves for the necessary improvements to the security system."

Milek glanced up at him; he'd been staring at the screen of his cell phone. "Blade knows how to do his job. And he loves this part of it, testing the current system, finding the weaknesses. And he does it well. He'll find out everything we need to know before we all meet with her in the morning."

"I don't know. I'm worried. You and Ivan thought you were just taking a quick look around at that art gallery a few weeks ago, and you nearly caught someone trying to break into the place. If Blade stumbles across an intruder tonight, he's unarmed. He's not even allowed to carry a gun yet," Garek reminded him. A convicted felon, even though he'd been released early from his sentence, wasn't allowed to own or handle a firearm.

"Amber is working on it," Milek said, referring to his wife, who was the River City district attorney. "She's trying to get his conviction overturned."

"She thinks that's possible?" Garek asked. "He admitted to killing the man."

"But it was an accident," Milek said. "He didn't mean to kill him. Just to stop him from hurting someone else."

"It didn't help that that *someone else* testified she wasn't in any danger," Garek said. Before hiring any of their bodyguards, he and Milek had discovered everything they could about them to make sure that they were indeed worthy of a second chance.

Blade definitely was.

Milek snorted. "Despite her bruises and crudely healed broken bones." He sighed. "I feel for Blade. He stepped in to help someone and wound up spending years in prison for his act of heroism."

Garek nodded. He'd done that himself, taking the blame for something he hadn't done to protect his family: Milek and their sister, Stacy. "Yeah, it sucks," he agreed wholeheartedly. "Fortunately it didn't stop him from wanting to help anyone else." And putting his life on the line once again to do it. Garek hoped he wasn't doing that tonight.

"Yeah, people like that, who sacrifice everything for someone else, are the real heroes," Milek said, and his pale eyes glistened a bit as he held Garek's gaze. "Blade's a good guy. I know he likes to go into these tests blind, so he doesn't know more about the current system than any other outsider would know. But I feel like we probably should have warned him about the widow Pell."

"About the rumors?" Garek asked and shrugged. He hated gossip; his family had been the subject of it all too often over the years. "I'm not sure we should put that much credibility in them. It wasn't as if any of them have been proven."

"Yet," Milek said. He sighed. "We have time to fill him

in on everything tomorrow morning before the meeting. He's going to be surprised that she's not the old lady he thinks she is."

"I've heard the rumors about her," Garek said, "but I have no idea how old she is." And he had been so damn busy with their other recent assignments and trying to keep his team alive that he hadn't had much time to research her yet. "I haven't met her personally. You have?"

Milek nodded. "Yeah, I guess it was close to a year ago. I met her and Dr. Pell at an alumni event, for a holiday party, for the university Amber attended. He'd once been her professor."

"Amber's?"

Milek nodded. "And Priscilla's. I don't even know if she was married to Dr. Pell when I met her last year, or if she was still just his research assistant. She's a young and beautiful blonde."

"Oh…" Now those rumors made a hell of a lot more sense to Garek about her being a gold digger and worse. Why else would a young woman have married a man so much older than herself except for his money and his power? And how had she made certain she inherited everything?

"Do you think that will be a problem for Blade?" Milek asked.

"No, but it probably explains what people have been saying about her," Garek said, "and it might also explain why Mason Hull is so concerned about her. Maybe he has a thing for her."

"She is beautiful," Milek said.

Garek considered the CEO for a moment, then shook his head, rejecting the notion. "No. I think the only thing that man cares about is money." Hull certainly didn't want to pay out any claim money on the policies he carried for his clients' valuables. Or so that was the way he made it seem, but Garek didn't trust the guy.

Something was off about him.

And it wasn't just Garek's cynicism and suspicious nature making him think that anymore. Every case they'd handled for the guy had been exceptionally dangerous. And even though they'd identified the threat and dealt with the people responsible, Garek wasn't convinced that Hull hadn't at least known about the dangers ahead of time.

His gut tightened with concern again. "We shouldn't have let Blade assess the system on his own."

Milek tensed and stared across the desk at him, concern on his face now. "Now you're making me nervous, too."

Garek was the cynical one. Milek wasn't. So now he scrunched up his forehead and studied his brother. "What are you worried about? Those rumors?"

Milek shrugged. "I don't know what to believe. I only met the widow once."

"Hull just claims that he's concerned about the current security system not being good enough," Garek said. "There's just the gate and the stone wall to keep people out, and inside there are no cameras or alarms. I don't know if he's worried more about the inside, about the people living there, or about someone accessing the house from the outside. Whatever his concerns, it sounds like the place definitely needs a better system."

Milek nodded. "Sounds like it. Blade can figure out what it needs. And he agreed to move into the mansion, too. So he'll make sure nobody steals the valuables and that nothing happens to the widow either."

"Do you think she's in danger, though?" Garek asked. "Or do you think that she *is* the danger?"

"Do I believe she killed her elderly husband for the money?" Milek asked. He shrugged. "I don't know what to think."

"There was no investigation into his death, as far as I could tell," Garek said. Despite how busy they'd been with their previous cases, he'd taken the time to make a few inquiries about the widow. "Or as far as Detective Dubridge or Chief Lynch would admit." Which didn't mean there hadn't been one or there wasn't one currently ongoing. Dr. Pell hadn't died that long ago.

"But even if she did, that wouldn't mean that Blade would be in danger," Milek said, as if he was trying to convince himself.

"Unless he figured it out," Garek said. "And he's smart. He catches on fast."

"Is that why you're worried about him?" Milek asked. "You think he's in danger from the widow? Tonight?"

Garek shrugged now and sighed. "I don't know what to think. I just have that *feeling*."

Milek groaned. "Me, too."

The infamous Penny Payne-Lynch sixth sense. The woman was the mother of the original founder of the Payne Protection Agency, Logan Payne, who was also Garek and Milek's brother-in-law. And she had this almost supernatural ability to sense when someone was in danger.

Or so it seemed. But maybe her sixth sense was just common sense. Because being a bodyguard was a dangerous job, one in which the bodyguard put themselves between the subject they were protecting and the threat against them.

But in this case, who was the threat to Blade?

Some person trying to steal from the Pell estate or the person who had inherited it all: Priscilla Pell?

Chapter 2

Avoiding the glow of the streetlamps, Blade slunk in the darkness. He was most comfortable there for so many reasons. He could hide in the dark, hide from people who gawked and stared at his size and his tattoos, and he could hide from himself as well. He could forget all about his past and focus only on his job and using it for a fresh start.

Out of appreciation for the second chance the Kozminski brothers had given him, he was determined to be the best damn bodyguard on their staff. And given how tough and smart his coworkers were, that wasn't going to be an easy task. So he needed to be prepared for that meeting in the morning with the widow and his bosses. He had to figure out the weaknesses in the current security system. From how worried the CEO of Midwest Casualty was, Blade figured there were probably quite a few ways to get into the estate and to the valuables Hull was so damn concerned about. But Blade would be careful, so that he didn't bother the widow until tomorrow, until they showed her where the weaknesses in her current system were.

He had his cell phone to record how far he got into the estate. Right now he was slinking between the sidewalk of the street in the affluent neighborhood and the tall stone wall that encircled and protected the Pell property from outsiders. He'd been careful to avoid the camera and the alarm at the wrought iron gate that crossed the driveway. But he needed to find a place where he could get over the wall and onto the estate. A few places where tree limbs, bare of leaves and lightly dusted with snow, hung over the high stone wall. But he had to make sure that no cameras from other properties would catch him climbing the trees. Or catch sight of him at all.

He'd shucked off his bright-colored parka, leaving him in just his long-sleeved black T-shirt, so that nobody would notice him in the dark. He even held his breath, so that no puffs of frozen air were visible in front of his face. But he was definitely freezing. Despite not having much snow yet for early December, the temperature dropped low at night.

Ignoring the cold, he rounded the corner onto another street, one with fewer streetlamps and properties. Oblivious to however rough the bark might be, he wrapped his hands around a branch and pulled himself up, climbing the tree like it was a rope ladder. Once he was above the stone wall, he swung himself over it. His feet sank into the light snow that covered the thick grass, and he hunched down, frozen in movement as well as temperature. He listened and waited.

Were there any dogs?

The client on their last job, at an art gallery, had a dog. While the Rottweiler loved the primary bodyguard on the case, Ivan, the dog hadn't been as enamored of Blade. But the beast of an animal hadn't been trained as a watch or guard dog. As far as Blade knew, the widow Pell didn't have any watchdogs either, but he waited another moment, with his breath held, and listened.

An owl hooted and a soft breeze rustled some bare branches that sent snow wafting down onto the grass. But there was no barking, not even from another property. Maybe he would recommend that she get some watchdogs; he would just make sure that they liked him like Angel the dog liked Ivan. But maybe Angel liked Ivan because Angel's owner really liked Ivan.

Ivan was happy and so was the client, Blair Etheridge, so Blade was happy that they'd found each other in the most unlikely and dangerous of situations. But he didn't want that for himself. He didn't want the complication of a relationship. He just wanted to focus on his job.

He blinked a couple of times and waited for his eyes to adjust to the darkness of the shadows on this side of the high stone wall. And there were a lot of shadows. The property was heavily populated with trees and various tall sculptures, raised flower beds, with only bushes in them now, and a fountain. He was surprised it hadn't frozen, but water trickled through it while a light glowed from beneath where it pooled, casting an eerie hue around that section of the yard. The house was farther away from the area where Blade stood, but he could see the enormous three-story structure. Lights glowed from just a few of the many windows.

It was late but not that late. Was everyone else asleep already?

According to his bosses, the widow didn't live alone. She had an extensive staff, a personal assistant and assorted family members in residence, too. And tomorrow Blade would become the bodyguard in residence when he moved into that huge house.

As he drew closer to it, he could tell that the exterior was stone like the wall around the estate. And over the tall windows on the main level, there were bars. The wall, the bars, the enormous building reminded him of prison, and that memory sent a chill racing down his spine.

Or maybe it wasn't the memory at all that turned him cold but the fact that he wasn't alone. He could feel someone else out in the shadows, watching him. He physically froze for a moment and listened again.

But all he heard was that trickle of water through the fountain. Whoever was out there wasn't moving either. Maybe they weren't even breathing. He held his breath, too, and waited for some telltale sign of their whereabouts. Because he didn't doubt himself.

He trusted his instincts. If he hadn't learned to do that, he wouldn't have survived his time in prison. As it was, he'd had a hell of a lot of close calls with other prisoners taking him on because of his size and his reputation. And they hadn't fought fair like the bouts he'd fought professionally.

But then he'd learned long ago that most people didn't fight fair, especially when desperate. His fellow inmates had been desperate just to survive, like he'd been, and they'd figured that taking on and defeating the biggest guy in prison would guarantee that nobody else would mess with them. He'd understood that, and he'd been careful to only defend himself and nothing more, nothing that would take another life and give him more time behind bars.

Whoever was hiding in the darkness was hiding because they didn't want to be seen any more than he wanted to be seen. But what was their reason? What were they up to? And were they watching him or the house?

He turned his attention back to the house for a moment, and in one of those lit-up windows, a silhouette appeared. A curvy silhouette that made his pulse leap. And he'd thought he wouldn't have any complications here that his coworkers had had, that there would be nothing to distract him from doing his job. Like Josh's fiancée had distracted him and how the beautiful gallery owner Blair had distracted Ivan.

Those guys had nearly died. The stakes for a bodyguard were too damn high to allow for any distractions. Josh and Ivan were lucky enough that they'd survived the danger they'd faced despite the distractions of falling in love. But Blade knew that wouldn't be the case for him. The only luck he'd ever had was bad luck.

And he'd never had any kind of love. Nobody had ever loved him, and he didn't expect anyone to fall for him. He just had to make sure that he didn't fall for anyone because he instinctively knew that would be his ultimate downfall.

Her late husband hadn't been the only Dr. Pell. Priscilla also had her doctorate in biophysics. She understood in exact detail how and why hormones were affecting the cells in her body. But understanding and handling the surge of hormones were two entirely different things.

She knew why she was so damn exhausted, and it wasn't just because she was pregnant. She couldn't sleep through the night because of the erotic dreams. Hormones caused the dreams that woke her up and then kept her awake longing for that physical connection with another body.

And not just any kind of body.

She wanted a particular body. A big, masculine, heavily muscled body. Every time she tried to sleep that was what she envisioned when she closed her eyes: bulging biceps wrapping around her, pulling her tight against a heavily muscled chest so that her skin pressed against his.

Heat flushed her face, making it burn. She reached for the sash of the window she stood in front of and pushed it up. A soft breeze ruffled the sheer curtains, but despite how cold the night air was, it didn't cool her off. Her blond hair stuck to her head like the nightgown stuck to her body.

Behind her the tangled sheets on the king-size bed were

damp, too. She hadn't been able to sleep because of that image, of a man's muscular body, that kept flitting through her mind, making her burn up.

Damn hormones.

She had always concentrated on her studies and then the research she'd worked on. She had never focused on herself, on her needs. But then she'd never really had needs before. While she'd had a few relationships in high school and college, she'd never been madly in love.

She wasn't even sure that emotion existed. It was probably just the rush of pheromones some people felt when they met someone they considered attractive. She'd never felt that rush before.

Except when she closed her eyes and saw the beauty of that man's body, the smoothness of his skin stretched taut over his impressive muscles. She didn't understand her obsession with that kind of physique. She'd never been attracted to brawn before. She wasn't even sure if she'd been attracted to brains even though she respected anyone of intelligence.

She'd respected her late husband, but she certainly hadn't been attracted to him. She'd married him because he'd made a compelling case for it, because he'd trusted her to continue his legacy. And she'd been flattered and happy to do that for him and for science because she knew how many people his work could help, how many lives it could save.

Science, and using it to save lives, was what used to consume her time and her thoughts. But now...

It was some muscled man whose face she didn't even see when she closed her eyes. She was losing her mind. Pregnancy brain. That was another phenomenon related to the influx of hormones that involved the extra cells she was carrying, that were becoming a life. A person of their own.

Of hers and Dr. Pell—Alexander's. And what would that combination of their DNA create?

That was perhaps their most important experiment. But Priscilla hadn't thoroughly considered the side effects of that experiment, of how being pregnant would affect her. Of how she would be so unlike herself.

So needy and emotional after being so independent and levelheaded her entire life. She had to figure out a way to deal with this, to ignore her crazy, demanding hormones and clear her head and her heart, so she could focus again on what was really important. Finishing the formula, making a drug that could save lives or at least greatly improve the quality of them. Unlike what had happened to her parents...

But she couldn't let herself think about that either. Not right now.

She leaned down, so her face was closer to the window screen, and inhaled some of the frigid air. But then in the faint glow cast from the stone fountain, she noticed something moving in the shadows of the garden. Something tall and broad. *Somebody.*

A man was down there.

Men lived in this house with her. Her stepson, who'd also been Alexander's stepson from his first marriage, was older than she was. But Bradley wasn't that tall and broad. His son, Kyle, who also lived in the mansion, wasn't that tall and broad either. The only man who was that big, the gardener, Fritz, wouldn't have been working this late.

So who was that, if not someone from the house who'd stepped outside to enjoy the peace and quiet of the gardens at night? Was there an intruder on the property? And for what reason? To steal the valuables Dr. Pell had collected over the years?

None of that stuff mattered as much to her as his research did, and with bars on the windows and that lock jammed, nobody was getting into the den tonight. So she wasn't particularly afraid of an outsider.

But she would have called the police if she knew for certain that the person wasn't someone from the house, someone who had a right to be here. Who thought they had more of a right to be here than she had.

Then she would only create more chaos and drama than her marriage and Alexander's subsequent death had already created. So instead of reaching for her cell phone, she moved away from the window and walked over to the safe on the bedroom wall. She entered the code to unlock it and opened the door. The safe held some jewelry, cash and documents, but she pushed them aside and reached for the weapon.

If that person in the garden was someone from the house, she might not need to protect herself. Or, given the way the people in this house felt about her, she might need it even more if it was one of them.

And if it was a stranger, an intruder...

She would be able to defend and protect herself and her unborn child. Because the baby was most important to her.

While she grasped the Glock in one hand, she touched her nearly flat stomach with the other. For the first time in her life, she understood the instincts of a mama bear. She would do anything for her baby.

Even kill...

From listening to gossip and, when that failed, prying for information, the person standing in the shadows of the garden knew that Priscilla had a meeting in the morning with a new security company. Time was running out. If

Priscilla was finally going to get what she deserved, she needed to get it tonight.

Or it might be too late or too damn hard to get to her without getting caught. But she had so many enemies now that it might be easy to pass the blame for her demise off onto someone else.

Like whoever had dropped so quietly over that wall moments ago. The person had easily discovered one of the weaknesses in the current security system, which was pathetically just the wall and the gate.

The person moved so silently through the garden that they had to be a professional of some sort.

A professional killer?

Had someone hired an assassin to get rid of Priscilla? To get her out of the way?

That seemed too risky. An assassin, if caught, might turn on the person who hired them. That wasn't a risk this person was willing to take.

But that wasn't the only reason why they wanted to take care of Priscilla themselves. They wanted the pleasure and the personal satisfaction of taking her life away from her, of taking back control.

Priscilla thought she was so smart. But in that moment, as she recognized her killer and realized why she was dying, she would also realize how stupid she was. But by then, it would be too late because her life would be over. Soon.

Chapter 3

Somebody else was definitely slinking around the shadows on the property besides him. And Blade needed to focus on finding out who that was. Now that the silhouette had disappeared from that upstairs window, he turned away from the house and peered into the shadows.

Someone was out there.

And they weren't moving at all. He waited to see if he could catch a glimpse of their breath, white in the cold. But they might have been holding theirs, too. Or had he seen it and mistaken it for the light snow that was beginning to fall again?

That person was definitely out there; his every instinct warned him that he was not alone. Were they waiting for him to leave? Or for him to find them? If that was the case, they were probably armed.

That was the problem for him as a bodyguard. Because of his felony conviction, he couldn't legally carry a weapon. But he hadn't needed one when he'd killed a man. He was that strong.

And he was probably even stronger now than he'd been back then. Physically and even more so mentally, because now he was better able to control his emotions. At least he had been until the woman in the house had caught his attention. Then he'd been a bit distracted, and he might have stayed that way had she not stepped away from the window. Maybe he'd been too careful about not getting involved with anyone; maybe denying himself even a physical relationship was making him more easily distracted instead of less so.

That was something he would have to think about later, when he wasn't trying to find the other person hiding on the property. He wanted to yell, "Come out, come out, wherever you are…" like he'd done as a kid playing hide-and-seek with other kids in the old neighborhood.

That had been a long time ago, though. Like his coworkers and bosses, his childhood had been cut too short. He'd had to grow up fast to help support and protect his single mom. But in the end, he hadn't done enough; she'd passed away a long time ago, leaving him on his own at sixteen. If not for his boxing coach taking him in, he would have had to live on the streets like some of his coworkers had.

He had to do a better job protecting Dr. Pell's widow. To make sure that person didn't get to the house, he had to stay between it and that area of the yard where he'd felt someone watching him. He moved slowly, staying away from the glow of the fountain as much as he could, toward the property where there were more trees and sculptures. Someone could easily hide in the deep shadows the statues cast or behind the trunks of the trees.

He placed each foot softly, and despite his size and weight, he made no noise, not even on the gravel walkways that wound through the property. But finally, as he neared the garden, he heard a noise. A twig snapped, and a branch rustled, sending more snow onto the ground. Whoever had been hiding there was moving. But toward or away from him?

He had to make sure that they didn't get to the house, so

he stepped back toward it. As he did, something dug into his flesh right behind his heart. He'd been arrested and had also been mugged before, so he instantly recognized what that something was: the barrel of a gun.

But how had someone snuck up behind him?

The noise he'd heard had come from the other direction. Were there two intruders?

He drew in a deep breath, then released it in a shaky sigh. "You don't want to do this."

"Do what? Shoot you?" a female voice asked, a very female voice with a sexy throaty tone to it that had Blade's pulse quickening even more. Instead of lowering the weapon, though, she pushed the barrel harder into his back.

"Yes, don't shoot," he said. "I'm a bodyguard with the Payne Protection Agency."

"Before you concocted that cover story, you should have checked your sources," she replied. "They have not been hired yet."

"Oh, you clearly have some sources, too," he said. "Is that why you're here tonight? You know that it's your and your partner's last chance to break into the mansion before Payne Protection takes over tomorrow morning?"

"Me and my partner?" The woman uttered a husky chuckle. "If you really are with Payne Protection, you're pretty sure of yourself, that you'll get hired and that nobody will bypass the security system you'll install."

"Payne Protection is the best," he said. Ever since Logan Payne had opened the first branch of the security business, the company had worked hard to be the best and remain the best and not just in Michigan but in the entire country.

"It's not tomorrow morning," she said. "So what are you doing here now, in the middle of the night?"

"Checking out the current system before the meeting,"

he said. "Figuring out what the weaknesses are. That way we'll know what has to be changed. And since you and your partner got onto the property, it looks like there will be quite a bit that needs to be addressed."

She chuckled again, and as she did, the pressure of the barrel against his back eased a bit. He whirled around, caught the woman's wrist of the hand holding the gun and jerked the weapon from her grasp.

She was a woman; he could tell that from her voice and from the delicateness of her wrist. Despite the cold, her skin was warm to his touch. She wore a big, hooded cloak that concealed most of her face and her body. He'd seen more of the silhouette in the window on the second story of the mansion than he could see of the woman standing in front of him.

She tried to wrench her wrist free of his grip, but he firmly held on to her, preventing her from running away. Then he raised his voice and said, "Now tell your partner to come out of hiding, and then we'll call the police."

"Yes, let's call the police," she readily agreed. "Right now."

She was either very bold and not worried about the consequences of trespassing or confident that she was not the trespasser.

He was.

And what consequences would he suffer when the police were called?

A ticket?

Or a trip to jail? The place he'd vowed to never return. But hell, jail was better than a bullet in his back.

Chief Woodrow Lynch awoke with a start at the buzz of his cell phone vibrating against the surface of the bedside table. Blindly, he reached out in the dark for it and brought it to his ear. "Hello?"

It continued to vibrate.

His wife emitted one of her sexy chuckles. "You need to accept the call first."

He groaned and swiped his finger across the screen. "Hello?"

"Chief Lynch?" a female voice remarked. "I hate to bother you..." But the amusement in her tone implied she was actually enjoying it.

He groaned again because he recognized that voice all too well. "Officer Carlson, then why are you calling me?"

"I've responded to a trespassing call at the Pell Mansion, and I figured you would want to know about it," the ambitious young officer replied.

"A trespassing call?" he asked, and now he glanced at the time on his cell phone. "Why would I want to hear about that at two o'clock in the morning? Is the wealthy widow demanding special attention?"

The young officer snorted. "She's not the one I'm calling you about."

Though the chief could understand if Carlson had called because of the widow since Dr. Alexander Pell had been one of River City, Michigan's most successful, affluent and influential residents before his death six months ago. "What's this about, Officer Carlson?"

"The Payne Protection Agency strikes again," she said. "And I just wondered if you wanted to vouch for this particular bodyguard like you have some of the others."

With four branches of the Payne Protection Agency, there were a lot of bodyguards on staff. But the only ones Woodrow found himself having to vouch for were the ones from the recently opened branch, the one the Kozminski brothers ran, which they'd staffed with people like themselves, who had criminal records. Some had juvenile records that had been sealed while others had committed more serious and adult offenses. "Which bodyguard?" he asked.

"Blade Sparks."

Of all the bodyguards, Blade was the one who'd served time in prison for killing a man. Obviously, Officer Carlson was well aware of his record and didn't trust him because of it. But she hadn't read the police report and trial transcripts like Woodrow had.

"I'll definitely vouch for Sparks," he said.

The young professional boxer had been trying to do the right thing all those years ago. But as Woodrow knew from his years in law enforcement, sometimes doing the right thing could go very wrong.

Once the police car had appeared with sirens wailing and lights flashing, the man who claimed to be her bodyguard had returned her weapon. Actually he'd pressed it back into her hands as if it was a hot potato. Or stolen goods that he didn't want in his possession when the police arrived. Like he was a criminal.

And the young female officer had treated him like a criminal. Even as he'd identified himself and explained his reason for being on the property, the officer had frisked him and read him his rights for the trespassing offense. Either she hadn't believed his story, or she hadn't cared what his story was.

Priscilla cared. Was it possible that he was really a bodyguard? When she'd called the police, she and the man had moved closer to the house, onto the well-lit patio. The minute she'd been able to see him clearly, she'd wondered if he was real or if she'd conjured him up in her hormone-driven dreams. He was so heavily muscled, like the man she kept envisioning when she tried to sleep.

And it made more sense that she was dreaming due to the way he was dressed in the December cold. He wore no coat, hat or gloves. And his biceps bulged out the sleeves of his black shirt, and his chest strained against the thin fabric. His faded jeans were loose around his lean waist but tight around his heavy thighs. Just the sight of his body had her heart pounding fast and hard, even faster and harder than when she'd come up behind him in the yard and pressed her gun into his back. And when he'd taken that weapon from her, his huge hand wrapping around her wrist, she'd been struck with both fear and lust.

Even now she wasn't completely able to focus, she felt as if she was dreaming.

But people had come out of the house when the officer had arrived. While the butler, Thomas, had escorted Officer Carlson through the house to the patio, the others had followed them out. All of them were bundled up in coats over pajamas or clothes; she just glanced at them when they'd walked out, her total attention on the man she'd found on the property. But she'd seen that Bradley and his wife, Sally, and their son, Kyle, as well as Priscilla's assistant, Monica, had come out to see what was going on.

She and this man weren't alone on the patio. But he was the only one she was able to see. Maybe that was just because he was so big, well over six feet tall and so broad. There were tattoos on the sides of his thick neck, or maybe it was one tattoo that wrapped around his neck; it looked like a thin cord or rope. She couldn't discern exactly what it was because it disappeared inside his shirt. His dark and thick hair hung nearly to his shoulders. While his face wasn't handsome, it was interesting. His square jaw had dark stubble on it. His nose must have been broken at one time; it wasn't straight but not unattractive either. And his eyes...

They were beautiful. A deep cool blue that did nothing to cool off Priscilla despite the low temperature of the cold December night. She pushed off the hood of the cloak she'd thrown on over her nightgown, but the heat wouldn't leave her body, making sweat trickle down her back and between her breasts. Then she caught him staring at her, at her face and at the blond hair that tumbled down around her shoulders. And her pulse quickened even more.

"Officer Carlson," the man said to the woman who was talking on her cell phone just a short distance from them now. "You need to verify this woman's identity."

"I'm Dr. Pell," she said. Either the officer had already recognized her, or Thomas had identified her to the young woman once he'd led her through the house.

But this man laughed. "Dr. Pell is dead," he said. "You didn't do your homework very well before breaking in here. You need to frisk her, too, Officer."

"Dr. Alexander Pell is dead, unfortunately," she said with that twinge of pain she always felt over the loss. "I'm Dr. *Priscilla* Pell."

One of the people standing behind Priscilla, closer to the house, snorted derisively. "Yeah, Dr...."

"We all know how she earned that doctorate," another chimed in.

She recognized the voices of her *family*. Family by marriage, as they always reminded her. But unfortunately they were the only family she had. They were the only family Alexander had had, too, after his first wife died. So he'd officially adopted her son even though he'd admitted they hadn't been particularly close. And they certainly weren't close to Priscilla.

Her stepson, Bradley, had made the first comment about her, her stepson's wife, Sally, the second one. Priscilla imagined their son, Kyle, was standing somewhere behind her, sneering at her with his usual resentment. While her assistant said nothing, Monica tended to lurk around, watching, waiting…

Was she waiting for Priscilla to ask her to do something or was she waiting for something else to happen? Something that she could report to someone because sometimes Priscilla suspected the woman was a spy. And while she could have fired her, she wanted to know for sure if the young woman was actually spying and if so, for whom.

At this moment, she ignored them, as she usually did, and addressed the man instead. "Blade Sparks?" She repeated the name he'd given when he'd identified himself to the officer. "You couldn't come up with something more believable than that as your alias?"

He laughed again. "Once Officer Carlson hands back my driver's license, you can look at it. That's also what's on my birth certificate because it's my real name."

"Was your mother obsessed with romance novels or Hallmark movies when she came up with that?"

"My mother's obsessions were drugs and men who mistreated her," he replied matter-of-factly.

A gasp of sympathy and remorse escaped Priscilla's lips. "I'm sorry," she murmured. While her childhood hadn't been idyllic, with older parents who'd forced her to focus only on her education and not friends or having fun, there had been no drugs or violence in her upbringing. And, in their own way, they had loved her.

He shrugged those impossibly broad shoulders. "She's at peace now."

Despite his dispassionate tone, she knew that he didn't mean his mother had recovered but that she'd passed away. So Priscilla whispered again, "I'm sorry."

He opened his mouth as if about to reply, but the officer joined them then, passing Blade's driver's license back to him. She held her cell phone in her other hand. "Would you personally like to speak to the chief of police?" she asked Priscilla.

She shook her head. "That's not necessary." She believed Blade Sparks was who he claimed. A bodyguard. And not a figment of her hormone-driven dreams. "I don't understand why you called him and not the Payne Protection Agency."

"I trust the chief of police more than I trust the Payne Protection Agency, or at least this branch of it," the officer replied. She glanced at Blade Sparks and then looked back at Priscilla. "You would be wise to do the same."

"Why would my insurance company recommend I hire them as my security company if I can't trust them?" Priscilla asked because the young woman wasn't making sense. Clearly the CEO of Midwest Property and Casualty did not want to pay out any claim settlements for theft or anything else.

"Good question," the officer replied. "If I were you, I might look into changing insurance companies, too."

"See, I told you it was a mistake to change," Bradley, her stepson, said. "You never listen, though, because you think you're so smart."

His wife and son made noises more than words that conveyed their agreement with him. Since his adoptive father's death, Bradley told her that everything she did was a mistake. And he didn't even know about...

Priscilla closed her eyes and drew in a breath. And as she did, a sudden wave of dizziness washed over her. She swayed on her feet, unsteady and off-balance. Then a big arm slid around her waist, holding her upright.

"Are you alright?" Blade Sparks asked.

She wasn't. Heat streaked through her, almost scorching her skin. But it wasn't the heat that had put her off-balance. She was exhausted. Too exhausted. This kind of fatigue wasn't good for her or for the child she was trying to grow inside her. But she nodded.

"Yeah, yeah, I'm fine. Just tired." Which was one hell of an understatement. She opened her eyes and found Blade staring intently at her, probably at the dark circles and bags beneath her eyes. "It's late. My appointment was in the morning with the Payne Protection Agency. Not tonight."

"I told you that I was assessing the current system, such as it is," he reminded her. "And it definitely has holes in it." He turned now, with his hand still on her waist, to the yard. "There was someone else out there."

"You saw someone else?" she asked. Because she'd seen only him. He was the big shadow she'd noticed moving in the yard. But had there been someone else?

"Well, I didn't see them," he admitted. "But I know they were out there. And just before you came up behind me, I heard them moving." With his free hand, he pointed toward the area of the property with more trees and sculptures.

Officer Carlson headed in the direction he indicated. She held her gun that must have had a flashlight attached to it because a bright beam illuminated the area in front of where she walked. When she reached the spot he'd pointed out to her, she shined the light around the trees planted close together in that section of the property. She studied the ground for a while before slowly walking back to the patio.

"Well?" Blade asked. "What did you find?"

"There are footprints in the snow out there. Looks like someone was standing in the trees." The officer glanced beyond Priscilla at the people hovering behind her, like they usually did, probably waiting to put a knife in her back. "Were any of you outside tonight?"

"Not until we heard the police vehicle roll up with sirens blaring and the lights flashing," Kyle replied.

The others muttered out noes. But Priscilla didn't trust any of them enough to believe them.

"Could the tracks have been from another time?" Priscilla asked.

The officer shook her head. "I don't think so. The snow has been falling on and off all day and these prints were fresh and sank pretty deep into the snow and into the grass and soil beneath it."

It had been a warm December so far with the temperatures rarely dropping enough for the ground to freeze.

"So someone was standing there for a while," Blade said. "They weren't walking around like they were going for a late-night stroll in the gardens. They were standing and staring at the house."

Despite how hot she'd been earlier, a sudden chill rushed over Priscilla. She'd been standing, too, in front of her bedroom window. And while she'd been staring out, someone had been staring up at her.

"You were," Priscilla reminded him. She knew that he was the person she'd seen out her bedroom window. The tall, broad, heavily muscled man. That had to have been him.

"Yes, I was out here," Blade said. "But the difference is that it's my job to protect you. I don't think that is why that other person was standing out there, watching the house, watching you."

Despite the cloak still being wrapped around her, she shivered. "If someone was out here casing the place, like you're implying," she said, "I'm sure they're only interested in the valuables inside." Hopefully just the art and jewelry and not the research.

"I'll have a tech come out and take pictures and make casts of those footprints," the officer said, and she was reaching for the radio on her collar.

The man was studying her face, though. "You think this is just about the valuables?" he asked, as if he'd realized she was worried about something else.

"That's why the insurance company wants me to hire the Payne Protection Agency," Priscilla replied. She'd already realized, when she'd noticed the gouged lock on the office door, that the current security system, such as it was, was woefully inadequate. But she wasn't worried about the valuables like the artwork and jewelry like the insurance CEO was.

She was worried about Alexander's research notes and about the book and the formula she needed to finish for him. But she was worried the most about the baby she was carrying. She had to make sure that nothing happened this time. That she didn't lose him like she had the others. But worrying was probably what had made her lose the others. She needed to feel safe, to not have any stress.

But that was unlikely even if Payne Protection was as good as this man had claimed.

Blade glanced back to that corner of the yard and then to the people standing on the patio behind her. "I think it would be a good idea for me to stay here tonight," he said. "Then in the morning we can install more cameras and extra sensors to keep you safe."

The insurance company had insisted on hiring his company, so he should have been concerned about the same things they were, about the valuables. But he seemed more concerned about her.

Did he realize what she had long ago? That her late husband's family hated her so much that they probably wished she was the Dr. Pell who'd died and not him.

And maybe they intended to make their wish come true...

Chapter 4

As a boxer, Blade had learned to anticipate where the next punch was coming from, so that he could either deflect it with a quick sidestep or a raised arm, or just brace himself for the impact. Nobody had ever been able to sneak in a sucker punch on him until tonight. He'd been "struck" twice, first with the gun barrel pressing into his back and then again when the woman who'd pressed that gun into his back had lowered the hood of the heavy black cloak she wore.

And all that blond hair had tumbled out. Even in the dim glow emanating from the patio lights and the house, her hair had shimmered like gold dust. And her face...

He didn't know if he'd ever seen anyone as beautiful as Dr. Priscilla Pell. At least he hadn't in real life, just on movie screens and in magazines. He'd assumed the widow would be elderly like the man who'd died of natural causes after a long and illustrious career. Blade should have known better; that just because the man had been old, it didn't mean that his wife had been as well. Some of the men his mother had dated had been old enough to be not just his grandfather but hers as well. He grimaced at the thought, then caught his reflection in the rearview mirror of his old Chevelle. Unlike hers, his was not a pretty face. It showed the scars and bumps and bruises of a life that had been lived hard.

Maybe the widow had changed her mind about letting him inside the gate that guarded the only opening in the tall stone wall. The gate did not open when he pulled his vehicle up to the wrought iron.

He'd told her what he was driving and that it would only take a couple of minutes for him to retrieve his car from where he'd parked down the block. So she should have been watching the monitor connected to the camera that hung just on the other side of the wrought iron. She should have seen him drive up and opened the gate, if she actually intended to let him in.

He'd thought she'd agreed a little too readily to his spending the night. Maybe she'd just been playing along to get rid of him, just agreeing for him to stay but having no intention of actually letting him drive his vehicle onto the estate once he retrieved it. But at the time that she'd agreed, he'd wondered if she'd been more scared of the people living in the house with her than with whoever might have been outside trying to get in or even of him.

And he was used to being the most feared. A lot of people crossed to the other side of the street when they saw him. Maybe because of his size, or his tattoos or his face, they instinctively feared him. She hadn't seemed to, though. Priscilla Pell hadn't had any problem confronting him in the dark, but she'd been armed.

He wasn't.

But still, he was able to do his job. He could protect her. Just his presence alone might keep her family from harassing her like they had on the patio with their petty comments. But what was worse than the things they'd said was the way they'd looked at her. With such hatred on their faces.

She hadn't made any introductions. She hadn't really even acknowledged the people who'd stood behind her, glaring at her, so he didn't know who was related to her and who just worked for her. But she wasn't respected or cared about by any of them. She needed him in that house to diffuse the tension. At least the tension between her and her stepfamily and the staff that she must have inherited after her husband died.

But there had been more tension than that. There had been some tension between the two of them. Or maybe that had just been in his head or another part of his body. Because a woman like that, so beautiful and smart and wealthy, couldn't be attracted to a man like him. And he couldn't be attracted to her because he couldn't afford such a distraction for both their sakes.

The gate creaked as it slowly began to open, and he drove his Chevelle through it. Then he followed the driveway that curved around the front of the mansion to a parking space off to the side next to a carriage house. He parked there near the vehicles that must have belonged to the staff because they were as inexpensive as his beater. He'd bought the Chevelle years ago with the intention of restoring it, but he hadn't gotten the chance before he'd ended someone else's life as well as his own as he'd known it. Nothing would ever be the same after that; he would never be the same. But he was going to do his damnedest to be better than he'd been.

To *do* better.

And that meant keeping his focus on protecting the estate, its valuables and the woman who had inherited it. Dr. Priscilla Pell. When he stepped out of his Chevelle, she was standing there in the dark. The hood was over her head again, casting shadows onto her beautiful face. He acted startled, as if she'd surprised him again. But he'd somehow known that she would be waiting for him out front and out of that house.

"Do you always dress like the grim reaper?" he asked.

She chuckled. "This isn't mine. I grabbed it from the hook by the back door."

So someone else in that house was the grim reaper. Or at least wanted to look like one. Did they want to act like one as well? Did they want to take a life? Hers?

"What about the gun?" he asked.

"That is mine."

"I'm surprised you're not pointing it at me right now," he admitted.

She smiled and her teeth glinted in the shadows of that hood. "I still have it on me."

"So you don't trust me even though you agreed to let me stay the night?" he asked. Then he reminded her, "The chief of police vouched for me." He was a little surprised himself that Woodrow Lynch had done that. But the man was related to the Paynes by marriage so the chief was close to the Kozminskis, who were also related to the Paynes by marriage as well as by a shared tragedy.

"I don't have this gun because I don't trust *you*," she said.

"Ah…" She must have purchased it after she'd come to live in this house, with people who clearly resented her presence. "That's why you agreed to let me stay tonight."

"I'll show you why. Come with me." She reached out and grasped his hand in hers.

As her soft skin touched his, he felt a jolt. A sizzle almost as if heat arced between them despite the cold December night. She sucked in a breath as if she'd been jolted, too.

He hadn't imagined the tension between them; it gripped his body now.

He swallowed the curse trying to slip out his lips. Damn. He'd thought he could be better than his coworkers, that he could stay unaffected and uninvolved. Hell, after what had happened all those years ago, he needed to stay uninvolved. His freedom depended on it.

He cleared his throat. "Where?" he asked since they just stood there on the driveway in the dark with her hand holding his.

She dropped it now as if it had burned her. "Uh, into the house. Do you have an overnight bag?"

He reached into his vehicle and grabbed his duffel bag. As a bodyguard, he always had a go-bag packed in case he had to stay with a client to protect them or leave town with one for their protection. A few months before the Kozminskis had opened their own branch, he'd worked with them at the original one, Logan Payne's office. And they'd trained him well. "Yup, I'm all set," he said. "I won't have to borrow any pj's."

"That's good. I don't think there are any pajamas in this house that would fit you," she said, and her gaze moved from his face down over his body. Slowly. Like she couldn't make herself look away from him.

Or so it seemed that way to him and had his heart skipping a beat with the attraction that gripped him so tightly now it hurt. "I don't wear pj's anyways," he said to see how she would react.

A soft sound escaped her lips. Maybe a sigh or a gasp.

"Just my boxers," he said.

She drew in a breath now and seemed to stand taller. And she was already pretty tall. Most of the women he knew came about to his elbow. But she made it to his shoulder.

She brushed it as she walked past him toward the house. But when she got to the front door, she stopped and hesitated for a moment.

"Let me," he said, and he reached around her to open the door. Then he stepped across the threshold first. Maybe that wasn't the gentlemanly thing to do, but it was the bodyguard-ly thing to do. Clearly she was afraid of something or someone in this house because she was reluctant to walk inside her own home. And she'd been willing to let him stay even before she had her official meeting with his bosses in the morning. So technically the Payne Protection Agency hadn't even been hired yet.

She remained outside while he stood on the marble floor of the two-story foyer. A chandelier hung over his head and another one near an elaborate staircase that led up to the second story and, from the way it wrapped around, it must have continued up to the third story, too. Several doors and hallways opened off the huge two-story foyer.

"Big house," he commented. Making this place secure was going to be a lot of work. What he'd thought when he'd first seen the three-story structure flitted through his mind again and out of his mouth. "Kind of reminds me of prison."

"Me, too," she murmured as she finally stepped inside and closed the door behind herself.

"You've been?" he asked even though he was pretty sure she hadn't. Not a woman who lived in a house like this and had earned a doctorate degree, no matter how the other people in this house figured she'd earned it. She also knew how to handle herself and carried a gun.

Priscilla shook her head, and that hood fell back again, exposing all that gorgeous blond hair and her beautiful but very pale face. "I haven't, but I imagine that an inmate has to feel trapped and out of control and always in danger."

That was exactly how an inmate felt, or at least it was how this inmate had. "But this place is not really like prison," he said, "because you can leave anytime you want."

She shook her head. "No. I can't."

He tensed and moved closer to her. Then he lowered his voice to a whisper and asked, "What's going on here? How much danger are you in?"

He wasn't sure he was the right bodyguard for this job. From what he'd understood of the assignment, he'd thought he was just going to be making sure nobody could break into her place and steal all the valuables she'd inherited. And a lot of thieves weren't violent. He hadn't realized how much danger she might be in, and even though she had a gun, he couldn't carry one. Yet. Supposedly Milek Kozminski's wife, the current River City district attorney, was working on getting an exception for him. He wasn't holding his breath.

Blade knew better than to think that good things ever lasted. His previous promising boxing career had been over much too soon. And he was worried that this gig as a bodyguard might be, too. If he lost the client on his first solo assignment, he was definitely going to lose his job as well.

But losing her wasn't an option. He had to do whatever necessary to protect Dr. Priscilla Pell. But what did he need to protect her from?

He knew his wasn't a face that inspired confidence. People were afraid that he was going to hurt them, so they weren't likely to trust him with their physical safety, let alone their secrets. But he stepped even closer and lowered his head to whisper into her ear, "Talk to me."

She shuddered and stepped back.

Had he repulsed her that much?

Then she took his hand and led him, not toward the

stairs where the guest room probably was, but toward one of those hallways leading off the foyer. A few short steps down the corridor, she stopped and pointed at a heavy mahogany door.

"What's in there?" he asked.

"Dr. Pe—my late husband's office," she said, and her pale face flushed a bright pink.

Had she almost called her own husband Dr. Pell? He would have asked her why, but she already seemed embarrassed and upset. And he remembered how she'd seemed shaky and weak out on the patio. Or maybe just exhausted; it was late.

She pointed at the fancy pewter doorknob. "Someone tried to break into it."

He leaned down and studied the gouges in the lock. "Somebody who didn't know what the hell they were doing." He pulled his lockpick set from his back pocket, and with a few clicks of a couple of tools, he opened the door.

And she gasped. "How do you know..."

"Trained by the best," he said. "My boss Garek Kozminski. You'll meet him in the morning." Or should he have called them tonight?

Maybe. But he'd wanted them to think that he could handle this assignment on his own. That was what he was supposed to do. They had other cases, other clients. She was supposed to be his. Something primal leaped in his chest, something that almost felt like possessiveness, which was weird because he'd never really felt that way about anything.

Not even the old Chevelle his former manager had kept for him while he'd been in prison. He could have let the car go. Part of him had wanted to let go of everything from his old life. But yet he'd stayed here, in River City, even after he was released from prison.

Why did Priscilla Pell think she had to stay here? That she couldn't leave of her own free will? He wanted to ask her again and get an answer out of her this time.

But she walked into the office and was moving quickly around the room, checking drawers and filing cabinets, the wall safe and many computers that occupied several desks and tables in the big space. Then she pulled out a key ring and unlocked one of the desk drawers. After pulling it out, she released a sigh of relief. "It's here. It's all here."

"Whoever tried breaking in didn't get inside," he assured her. The damage to the lock made it clear they hadn't known what they were doing. But that didn't mean they wouldn't try again.

But since Priscilla had the keys, it would be easier to get them from her and get inside the office. "What's in here?" he asked. "What was someone after?"

"Notes," she said. "Research."

"And given what your husband was, those things could be worth a lot," he assumed.

She nodded. "Far more than any of the artwork or jewelry the insurance company is worried about."

"That's why you want me to stay?" he said. "To protect this stuff?"

She nodded again. "And that's why I can't leave."

"Because of this stuff?"

Her head bobbed in another quick nod. "Because I promised to finish it." She touched her stomach then as if the thought made her nauseous.

"You promised your husband, right?" he asked.

She nodded yet again, and her mouth with its full lips pulled down into a tight frown.

"He's dead," he said, wincing a bit over how insensitive he might sound to her. But maybe she needed to hear it, to release herself from whatever hold the guy seemed to still have over her. "He won't know you broke your promise."

"No," she agreed. "But I will know. And I can't do that. What he was working on... It's too important." Tears glistened in her eyes, and her voice was even huskier with emotion. "It could save lives."

And in that moment, hearing those words and seeing her intensity and sincerity, Blade realized that the other people living in this house, the ones who'd glared and sniped at her out on the patio, were wrong about her. She wasn't some manipulative gold digger.

She was just gold. Solid and pure.

Honest.

He hadn't met too many people like her. Even more reason to protect her. But she clearly didn't care about herself as much as she cared about this research.

And her late husband. Just his legacy or him? Or the lives she wanted to save?

Blade didn't really care what meant the most to her. He would do his best to protect it all. He dropped his duffel bag on the floor next to the couch. "I'll sleep here."

"You're too big for that couch."

He shrugged. "I can sleep anywhere. And I sleep lightly, with one eye open. Nobody will get in here and get anything out of this place with me in here. And in the morning, I'll work with the Kozminskis and make sure that nobody gets in here and that we catch whoever tries."

She released a ragged sigh, and more tears sparkled in her very pretty green eyes. "Thank you."

He shrugged again. "Just doing my job." But then he stepped closer to her again because he had a feeling someone was hovering around, listening to them just as they had out on the patio. Or maybe the other person who'd been standing out on the property watching the house was watching them now. That could have been someone who lived in this house and had snuck around them when Priscilla distracted him with the gun in his back.

He lowered his voice and advised her, "You need to protect yourself tonight. Lock yourself in your room and keep that gun close."

"I'm not worried about myself," she said but touched her stomach again, as if she felt sick.

"Please, just do it," he implored her.

She didn't argue with him. She simply nodded once again, and then turned and left him. He could have followed her up to her room, checked out the place and made sure it was safe for her. But she had the gun.

And this room wasn't secure. With the damage to the knob, he wouldn't be able to engage the lock again now that he'd opened it. She was clearly more worried about this stuff than herself. Research like this, that could save lives, was probably priceless. But who could figure out what it all meant, let alone how to use it?

He looked at some of the sticky notes stuck to the dark computer monitors. The equations made no sense to him, so she wasn't concerned about him stealing any of her late husband's secrets. She knew what all these equations were, though. She was smart, maybe even brilliant. And beautiful...

And totally out of his league. He had to remind himself that he was just her bodyguard. And that was all he would ever be. A woman like her, that rich, that smart, would never be interested in an ex-con like him.

* * *

"Talk to me..." the deep voice of her lover rumbled in her ear.

She shivered now like she had when Blade Sparks had first whispered those words to her. Her skin tingled, and her pulse quickened.

"Tell me what you want, Priscilla," he continued, his voice gruff now with the passion that also gripped her. "Tell me where to touch you..."

"Here," she murmured. And she brushed her fingers across her lips, yearning for his kiss. "And here..." She cupped one of her breasts that ached for his touch. Then she shifted against the sheets as her body pulsated with desire. She needed him to kiss her, to touch her, to release all the tension that gripped her.

"Blade..." she murmured, imploring him to give her what she needed.

Him...

He'd asked her what she wanted, but he hadn't kissed her, hadn't touched her yet. What was he waiting for?

She was sick of waiting, of wanting...

But when she reached out for him, to pull him close, she felt...nothing. The sheets were cold, the bed empty except for her aching body. She opened her eyes to darkness. It was just a dream.

Again.

But this time the man in her dream had a voice and a face. And a name.

Blade.

He wasn't here, though. At least not in bed with her or even in the room. Blade was downstairs, guarding the den. And that must have made her feel better on some level or she wouldn't have fallen asleep as easily and quickly as she must have since she'd already been dreaming.

But it also made her resentful. The research and the book had become more important than she was; no, it had always been more important than she was. It could save so many lives and stop so much suffering. That was why she'd made the promises that she'd made and why she was determined to finish the research and the book. Not just for Dr. Pell or even for herself but for all the other people it would help.

But now, even though she'd told Blade that it was more important for him to protect the den, she wished he would have come upstairs with her. That he was with her.

In her...bed.

The door rattled, and she glanced over at it. Faint moonlight shone through the curtains and glinted off the doorknob as it turned. Someone was trying to get into her bedroom.

And she had a feeling that it wasn't her bodyguard but instead someone from whom she needed his protection. Someone who wanted to hurt her.

Chapter 5

Garek grabbed his cell and walked out of the bedroom before accepting the call. He didn't want to wake his beautiful wife. She was pregnant with their first child, and she needed her rest. He did, too.

But with the assignments the agency had had since opening, he hadn't had very many restful nights. His team had been in nonstop danger pretty much since they'd opened their doors, or at least since they'd started taking assignments from Midwest Property and Casualty CEO Mason Hull. But other people had been responsible for the attempts on the lives of his team, not the CEO, so Garek really had no reason to refuse to take any more assignments from Hull.

And he also wanted to find out more about the guy, so he needed to keep in contact with him. He'd also put another plan into motion, too.

So even before Blade's call came in, Garek had been lying awake, worrying. "Hey, everything okay?" he asked as he picked up. But he didn't know why he bothered with the question; everything was not okay or Blade wouldn't have called so late.

"Chief Lynch or Officer Carlson didn't call you?" Blade asked a question of his own.

Garek groaned. "No. What happened?"

"Nothing," Blade replied. "Yet."

"I don't think the chief or Carlson would be calling me if nothing had happened," Garek pointed out.

"True," Blade said. Then his sigh rattled Garek's cell speaker. "The widow got the jump on me."

"What?"

"Yeah, exactly," Blade said. "You know, one of you could have warned me that she wasn't the little old lady I thought she was."

Garek chuckled. "Well, you are always adamant about going in blind to assess the current system. And we've been so busy that I'm not even completely up to speed yet on this assignment. I take it that your assessment didn't go well? Is the morning meeting going to be canceled?"

"No," Blade replied. "And I thought I could wait until the morning to fill you in, but I don't think that's a good idea now."

"Why not? What's happened?" Garek asked, his heart beating heavily with dread.

"I think we need to act tonight to increase the security on this place, that it can't wait till morning now. Someone already tried to get into the late doctor's den where some pretty important notes of his are kept," Blade said. "I'm in here now. But that leaves the widow…"

"Where?" Garek asked.

"On her own…"

"And unprotected," Garek finished for him.

Now Blade chuckled. "I wouldn't exactly say that. She has a gun, and she didn't hesitate to shove it in my back."

"Ah, that's how she got the jump on you," Garek said. Another man might not have admitted that, but Blade Sparks had no ego.

"Yeah, I was trying to sneak up on whoever else had

made it over the wall like I did, and she was sneaking up on me," he said.

"Someone else got over that high stone wall around the estate?" He wasn't surprised that Blade had; the man had been a professional athlete.

"Well..." That sigh rattled the speaker again. "They could have come from inside the house, but I don't know why they would have been standing out in the cold except..."

"Except what?"

"Maybe to watch her bedroom window," Blade said, "which makes me worried about her safety. It just feels like tonight might be the night they would try something, especially since it seems pretty well known in this house that we're overhauling the current security system, which is pretty much nonexistent, in the morning."

"Ah..." Even though Blade couldn't see him, Garek nodded. "That makes sense, then, that someone would try something before we change the system. Good thinking to catch that."

"So you'll send out a team tonight?" Blade asked. "We're going to need a lot of cameras and sensors and a really good lock for the door of the den. At least there are bars on the windows."

Garek could almost hear the other man shudder. He could imagine what those bars reminded Blade of because they would remind Garek of the same thing: prison.

"Sounds like you still managed to assess the current system despite getting caught," Garek said. "So she knows that you're bringing us in tonight?"

"Uh..." Blade sighed again. "No. She went up to bed. But I should tell her."

"Yes," Garek said. But he could tell that Blade clearly

dreaded disturbing her again. "She let you stay tonight. She must know she's in danger."

"She knows," Blade said. "She's smart."

Cunning was the word that Garek had heard used to describe her. How cunning? Enough to set up a bodyguard to take the fall for whatever might be going on with the insurance company CEO? He hadn't quite figured out what that might be. Setting up this new branch of the Payne Protection Agency to take the fall for thefts?

Or...

Garek didn't know, but he didn't trust Mason Hull. And after what he'd heard about the widow, he didn't trust her either. Learning that she had a gun made him even more concerned about Blade. Garek had learned long ago to trust no one. Or at least he hadn't trusted anyone but his family until the Paynes had become family, too.

Blade had no family, though. He was completely on his own. Did he trust anyone? Even his bosses?

"Be careful," he advised.

"That's my plan," Blade replied. "Just get the team out here as soon as you can."

Blade Sparks was a former boxer. A man who'd fought for a living. Garek had considered him fearless until now. Now he sounded, if not scared, at least extremely cautious. Something was definitely going on at the Pell Estate.

And Garek hoped nothing bad happened before he could get a team together and get there as backup for Blade. But that horrible feeling was gripping him again, that premonition that something bad was about to happen.

Blade had learned to trust his instincts and as he'd tried to relax on the leather couch in the den, those instincts had kept jabbing him to stay awake. This was the last day before the new security system got installed, therefore the perfect day for someone in this house to go after Priscilla. They'd already tried getting into the office.

While she was more concerned about it, Blade was more concerned about her safety. Getting rid of her would probably give access to this den to whoever wanted it either through their inheritance or just because the new heir would fire the Payne Protection Agency. So Blade needed to make sure she was safe.

Since she was worried about the den, though, he did his best to secure the door behind himself, jamming his lockpick tools into the lock to jam the tumblers inside it. But if someone wiggled them around enough, they would probably be able to unlock it. But if they did, he'd set up an extra camera he'd found in his duffel bag, and it would catch an image of whoever walked into the office.

Now he had to find Priscilla. But the house was enormous. He knew where her bedroom was from the outside, on the second floor, but he couldn't remember how many windows from the end of the house. He also had to make sure that the team would be let inside the gates the minute they arrived, so he should probably find the housekeeper or butler. A butler had shown Officer Carlson out to the patio earlier, so he had to be around here somewhere.

Blade retraced his steps from the den back to the two-story foyer. The chandelier had been dimmed to just a soft glow that reflected off the highly polished marble floor. Feeling like a rat choosing a direction in a maze, Blade started down another hallway, hoping to stumble across the butler quarters. Wouldn't his room be on the main floor near the kitchen? But then everything Blade knew about rich people he'd just seen on television or in the movies. He'd never been in a house like this before, one so massive.

He found the kitchen that was big enough, with its endless counters and enormous appliances, to service a restaurant or a hotel. It was cold in there and not just because of the tile floors and stainless steel surfaces. There was air wafting through from somewhere. He pushed through a swinging door into a formal dining room. While there were bars on the windows, the patio doors didn't have any, and one set of the three sets in the room were wide open with the wind swirling snow across the hardwood floor.

"Damn it!" He pressed the door shut even as his stomach plummeted. He didn't believe someone had left that open earlier, at least not on accident. Someone had used that door to gain access to the house, to Priscilla.

His instincts were right; she was definitely in danger.

Priscilla lay in the dark, holding her breath, as the knob turned again and rattled. Was someone trying to do the same thing to the lock that they'd done to the one on the office door?

Would there be deep gouges in it?

If it was the bodyguard trying to open it, it would have already opened. He'd been so quick with those tools that it wouldn't have taken him this long to unlock the door. This wasn't Blade trying to get into her bedroom no matter how much she wished it was.

But still she called out, "Who's there?"

And she hoped he would answer her with his strange but sexy name. But total silence greeted her. The knob even stopped turning. Had they thought they could break in while she was sleeping?

And do what?

Smother her with a pillow?

She reached under the pillow next to hers and pulled

out the gun she'd stashed there per the bodyguard's advice. That was damn good advice because she might have locked it away again in the safe. Despite owning it, she really didn't like handling it. But Dr. Pell—Alexander had insisted she learn to use it. He'd known how much danger marrying him might put her in, but she hadn't realized it until after he died.

His research alone was worth killing for, even more so than the artwork and jewelry he'd collected. And his family, adopted family, hated her because she'd inherited more than they had. While they had trust funds, she had the majority of the estate and she had something even more important than that: she had control over all of it—the money and the property both physical and intellectual.

And for another heir to gain control, she had to die. Would someone try to kill her themselves or would they hire someone?

That hadn't been just the bodyguard hanging around outside earlier tonight. The footprints on the ground in the grove of trees proved someone, besides Blade Sparks, had been out there tonight.

Had they gotten inside?

Was that who'd been trying to unlock her bedroom door?

Or had it been someone who was already inside the house? Who lived here with her?

Then they would have to head to their bedroom from hers. Could she catch them?

Should she try?

She tightened her grasp on the gun and slid out from beneath her blankets. The air seeping through the window she'd left cracked open chilled her but not as much as the fear already gripping her.

But she hated being afraid, feeling victimized. That was

not going to happen here, not in her own home. And no matter how much the Pell family protested, it was her home. With her free hand she touched her stomach that barely swelled against her satin nightgown. Her home and this baby's home.

And she wasn't going to let anyone hurt either of them or drive them away. She had too much work she needed to finish here that was too important for her to walk away. Too many lives could be saved. But first she had to protect her own life.

She moved around the king-size bed toward the door. It wasn't rattling now. Had the person left? Or were they just waiting out there somewhere for her to open it?

She was armed, though. She wasn't going to get hurt. Or so she told herself as she reached for the knob. It turned easily beneath her grasp. Whoever had been messing with it had managed to unlock it.

If she hadn't called out, they might have already been inside the room with her. But the fact that they hadn't opened it proved to her that they didn't want her to see them, which made her even more determined to discover who they were.

She drew in a deep breath and pulled open the door. Then she peered out into the hall. Dim light emanated from a wall sconce that had been turned low. That sconce was between her room and the stairs, but she could see just beyond it, to the shadows near the stairwell.

Was there someone standing there?

She couldn't tell for certain, so she stepped farther into the hall and called out, "Who's there? Who are you?"

And that shadow moved, shifting away from the steps and down the hall running on the other side of the open stairwell. That was where the Pell family's rooms were.

It had to be one of them who'd messed with her lock and

the one on the office door. But for what purpose? None of them would understand Dr. Pell's notes.

But they were smart enough to know that they were valuable and probably intended to sell them. They wouldn't get to those notes tonight. Despite just meeting Blade Sparks, she trusted him to keep the den safe. He seemed like a man who took his job seriously, so seriously that she could have shot him when she'd found him outside in the yard.

The others didn't realize that she hadn't just inherited the majority of the estate from her husband but also the gun he'd purchased for her as well. They didn't know she was armed. So she started down that hall toward where the shadow had gone.

"Come back here," she said. "I know you were trying to get into my room." And they had very nearly succeeded. "What do you want from me?" she asked, raising her voice louder in the hope of drawing attention from others in the house. If there was an intruder, the others should know. But nobody else moved, at least that she could hear.

Knowing how everyone in that house felt about her, they would probably ignore her even if she screamed for help. But maybe she didn't need any more help than the gun she grasped in one hand and that bodyguard protecting the real valuables in the den.

She couldn't see that shadow now.

Had they opened a door and slipped into their own room? If so, it had to be one of the family. Bradley or Sally or Kyle. Monica, her assistant, and Thomas, the butler, both had rooms on the main level of the house. And Fritz, the gardener, stayed in the pool house. But any of them could have come up to the second story either via the main stairwell or the back one at the end of the hall.

As she neared the main stairwell, she glanced down, but

she was pretty sure that shadow had slipped away down the hall instead of down the steps. Yet she caught a glimpse of somebody moving up those stairs.

Somebody big and muscular. And her pulse quickened a little. Her bodyguard hadn't stayed in the den. He was coming up to her. But as she focused on Blade in the darkness, hands pressed against her back and shoved her toward those stairs.

She opened her mouth and screamed.

Blade was coming to her rescue, but he was probably going to be too late to save her and the baby he didn't even know she carried.

Chapter 6

Blade had known she was in danger the second he found the patio doors standing open in the dining room. He'd rushed back through the house to the foyer and that grand staircase. But as he'd started up the runner covering the steps, he'd noticed movement in the hall above him. And he'd stopped for a second, midflight, to peer up into the shadows, trying to figure out what or who was moving around.

Then he'd heard her voice calling out to someone. Whom was she talking to? What the hell was going on?

He opened his mouth to call out himself, to her, but then she came into his view at the top of the stairs. She wore something silky that hit near her knees and clung to the curves of her body. And he lost all reason for a second until he heard her scream.

Then her body lurched forward, as if someone had pushed her, and she started to fall.

He vaulted up the steps separating them and reached out, closing his arms around her. He staggered back a bit as her body hit his, and fear struck him that he was going backward and taking her with him down all the steps below.

But he twisted his body, while holding hers tight, and managed to slam his back against the wall to stop his descent to the marble-floored foyer. But his feet were still slipping and sliding, and he had to scramble to keep from falling down the rest of the flight. Finally he was able to plant his feet on two stairs a couple of steps apart and lock his legs.

She was still struggling to find her balance, her feet dangling, as he held her tightly against his chest.

"I've got you," he assured her, his breath shuddering out of his lips from his exertion and the close call. "You're okay."

Her body relaxed then, her breasts pushing against his chest as she gasped for breath. Then she leaned her forehead against his shoulder, and a soft cry slipped out of her lips. "Thank you. Thank you so very much."

"What happened?" he asked. Because he was pretty damn sure she didn't take a tumble like that on her own, not with the way she'd screamed and with the way she'd looked as she'd been standing at the top of the stairs. The fear. It shone now in her bright eyes as she looked up at him.

"Somebody pushed me," she said.

Blade glanced up at the top of the stairs, but he couldn't see anyone. Sure, the person who'd pushed her had probably run. But where was everybody else in the house? How could he be the only one who'd heard her scream?

"Go down to the foyer," he said. "A team from Payne Protection is on their way. Let them through the gate." Then, with his hands on her bare shoulders, he eased her away from him.

She clutched the banister behind her but then steadied herself. "Where are you going?" she asked.

"To see if I can catch the bastard who pushed you." He started up the stairwell.

She grabbed his arm. "Wait."

"They're getting away," he said. Or they probably already had. But he needed to look for them anyway.

"But..."

He turned back to her. Was she scared to be alone? Which was understandable after what had just happened. Or was she worried about the damn den?

"What?"

"They got my gun," she said, holding up her empty hands.

"Son of a bitch..." But that was even more of a reason, to him, to find who the hell had pushed her before he tried again. And now he or she had a gun. "Go back to your room and lock yourself in." He didn't wait for her to comply. He hooked his arm around her waist and half guided, half carried her up the stairs.

Any member of his team could get over the stone wall like he had, or even hotwire the security panel at the gate to get it open. They would get in, but he wanted to make sure her assailant was gone.

What if the bastard had gone into her room?

"Which way?" he asked at the top of the stairs.

She pointed, her hand shaking. Then she started off down that direction. He stayed close, using his body to shield hers. Just in case the person tried again to kill her and this time used the gun.

She stopped outside her door and pointed at it. Just like the knob on the door to the den, this one had gouges in the metal. "Someone tried to get in while I was sleeping."

"Son of a bitch," he muttered again, fury coursing through him. He pushed open the door and stepped inside. A slight breeze blew through the flimsy curtains over the window and chilled his skin.

In her thin gown, she had to be freezing. She reached

for the cape she'd worn earlier that night that was lying across a chair near the king-size bed. While she wrapped that around herself, he checked out the room and the adjoining closet and bathroom.

"It's clear," he said. "Now lock yourself in, and also call the police."

She nodded.

But when he started for the door, she grabbed his arm. "Don't—"

"I have to see if I can catch them," he said. If they hadn't gotten away yet, he had to try to stop them and retrieve that gun. He just wasn't certain how he could manage that without getting shot.

"Be careful," she whispered.

He nodded, then headed out into the hall. A crazy thought jumped into his head that he should have kissed her. It would have been wildly unprofessional. But he was worried that he might have missed the only chance he had of ever kissing her. Because if he found the armed person, he might not survive the night, let alone his entire assignment to protect Priscilla Pell and the estate.

Priscilla stared at the door that closed between her and her bodyguard, locking her inside while leaving Blade Sparks out in the hall and unprotected. She'd warned him to be careful, but it wasn't enough.

Not to keep him safe.

As those hands had pushed her forward, she hadn't even realized that the gun had been slipped from her grasp. She knew she hadn't dropped it because her fingers had been clenched too tightly around it. And she hadn't heard it drop to the ground. The person must have grabbed it from her when she'd started falling, and she'd been too stunned to react.

At least the safety was engaged on the gun, but she was sure the person who'd taken it from her would probably be able to figure out how to slide that safety off. And if cornered by her muscular bodyguard, that person probably wouldn't hesitate to use it. To shoot him...

She shuddered at the thought. And she reached out for her cell phone with a trembling hand. She had to call the police like he'd advised. But she couldn't help but worry that they wouldn't get here in time, not if her bodyguard found the person with the gun before the police arrived.

Or his team from Payne Protection.

She was just getting ready to tap the emergency call button on her cell screen when alarms started going off inside the house. The blare was certain to awake everyone now even if her scream hadn't.

Was that the fire alarm or the security alarm that had been set off? The only security alarm was at the gate in the wall and was only tripped if someone was trying to get it open. She hadn't heard it go off before, so she wasn't sure if it was that or the smoke alarms. Damn Dr. Pell for not upgrading his security system before now.

Should she exit the house or stay inside like Blade had warned her?

She sniffed the air and smelled no smoke. It had to be the security alarm at the gate. And if the person had set it off while trying to leave through the gate, how hadn't they set it off when they'd gotten inside?

What the hell was going on in her house?

She'd had such a close call tonight, on those stairs. If not for Blade, she would have fallen. She reached out and touched her stomach, worried for the child that she could have lost had she fallen. And she might have lost her life as well. Would Blade lose his now in trying to catch her assailant?

She was worried that he might, and that it would be an incredible waste of an obviously hardworking and heroic man. And it would be a personal loss for her because she'd never gotten the chance for him to kiss her and touch her like she'd implored him in her dreams.

And that was all he would remain for her: a dream. Even if he survived the night, she couldn't get involved with him or with anyone else. She had too much to do, too much she needed to finish. And not just for Dr. Pell but for all the other people she could help.

Damn it!

That had been too close. Not her dying; that hadn't been nearly close enough. That should have happened. Priscilla should be dead now.

But that damn bodyguard had appeared again out of nowhere and saved her. How the hell had her falling not knocked them both down the stairs?

And while they'd pulled the gun out of her hand, they didn't know how to fire it. Or they could have finished it there, on the stairs. But when they'd taken it, it had just been so that Priscilla wouldn't be able to use it to protect herself or to protect that bodyguard.

But now... What the hell did they do with the gun?

And how did they make sure that damn bodyguard didn't catch up to them and figure out who they were? Or worse yet, get them arrested?

That would ruin everything. All the plans. All the come-uppance that Priscilla was due.

The bodyguard could not ruin this.

The gun was raised in a gloved hand and studied in the faint light emanating from the house that the would-be killer had escaped. This little slide thing... That had to be the safety.

The would-be killer slid it back just as the bodyguard burst out of the French doors and onto the patio. With the light snow falling again, he might be able to track their footprints and find where they were hiding, like they'd been hiding earlier when he'd come over the wall.

He hadn't found them then. But if he did this time, he would die.

Chapter 7

The sound of the alarm going off drew Blade back toward the house. What the hell had set it off? Had the intruder gone out through the front gate? That was the only place he'd seen sensors and a camera. No wonder Hull had wanted Priscilla to hire the Payne Protection Agency. The current system was woefully inadequate. From what he'd seen of the system at the gate, the camera was just connected to a monitor near the front door at the house, and the alarm would only go off if someone tried to force open the gate.

Was that the person going out, though, or his team or the police coming in that had set it off? And what if the intruder was actually out here?

Blade stared out into the darkness beyond the fountain. And he felt like he had earlier, like someone was out there...

Waiting, like they had earlier.

For Priscilla?

Or for him this time?

That person had a gun now and was even more dangerous than they'd already been. Pushing Priscilla down the stairs hadn't been an accident. That action confirmed what Blade had already begun to suspect, that she was in danger.

Real danger.

And because she was still in that house with the alarm

blaring, he ran back across the patio and through the open French doors. Making sure that she was safe was his number one priority, even more so than the valuables that the insurance company CEO was worried about or even about the research and notes she was worried about. He didn't care about things; he cared about people. And even though he'd just met her, he really cared about her.

There was just something about her, and it was more than her beauty or her brains. Maybe it was her grit. She was tough. And he admired toughness.

But despite how tough she was, she could have died had she fallen down those stairs. She could have hit her head or broken her neck.

He shuddered thinking about that horrible outcome. The tragedy that would have been. And while she was in her room now, she wasn't really safe there either. Someone had tried unlocking that door already, too. And what the hell had they intended to do to her once they'd gotten inside her room?

He ran from the dining room down that long hallway toward the foyer. And when he reached it, he found her standing there at the bottom of the elaborate staircase.

"I'm on the phone with the police," she said to the men standing in front of her. "They're on their way."

"Pris—Dr. Pell," he said, embarrassed that he'd nearly called her by her first name. That was almost as unprofessional as wanting to kiss her. He had to remember that this was just a job, one he was determined to do well.

She turned toward him, and her body visibly relaxed, her shoulders drooping beneath the heavy cloak she wore. "You're back. You're okay."

He nodded and then gestured at the three men standing in the foyer in front of her. "And they're with me. That team

I told you was coming from the Payne Protection Agency." Ivan Chekov and Viktor Lagransky had arrived with their boss Garek. Both Ivan and Viktor were as tall and muscular as he was, just better-looking.

But she didn't look back at them. She barely paid them any attention as she focused on him. "You didn't catch him."

Blade shook his head. "I heard the alarm and headed back."

"What's going on?" Garek asked.

Blade quickly explained the situation, and Ivan and Viktor rushed off to search the house and grounds.

"Mrs. Pell," Garek began.

"Dr.," Blade interrupted, correcting his boss. No matter what her stepfamily thought, she would have had to work hard to earn that doctorate degree. "Dr. Pell, this is Garek Kozminski."

She nodded. "I'm glad you're here," she said. "But I did call the police." She held up the cell in her hand. "Like you told me I should…"

Blade nodded. "Good. They can help us search and see if we can find your gun." Hopefully it had fallen in the hallway or around the staircase, but he didn't put much faith in that hope. Because he had hadn't heard anything drop. And he hadn't stumbled across it on the stairs or in the hallway on the second floor.

"This is a big house," Garek said. "A lot of places to search." He stared up the stairwell, but it wasn't empty now like it had been earlier. The other Pells in the household stood behind Priscilla, like they had on the patio earlier tonight.

Blade stepped forward and reached for her, pulling her closer to his side to protect her. One of them could have pushed her earlier and could have her gun now.

Then Garek glanced behind him, and Blade turned to find the butler and a young woman standing behind him. They'd been on the patio earlier tonight when Officer Carlson had been at the estate. Another man stood a bit farther behind the two of them. He was big like Ivan and Viktor and him.

"Dr. Pell," Garek continued. "We were supposed to meet tomorrow but given the situation Blade Sparks found here tonight, he believed, rightfully so apparently, that it was in your best interest to increase your security tonight."

"What's going on?" the older man on the stairwell asked. "It sounds like all hell's broken loose around here."

"It has," Blade confirmed. He'd been through hell before, so he knew it well.

"All this just started happening since you showed up earlier," the man said. "Interesting timing."

Blade flinched, not over the dig, but over the thought of what could have happened to Priscilla had he not shown up when he had. He was worried that she wouldn't have survived the night. "Good thing that I showed up when I did," he said. "Or who knows what would have happened..."

He would guess that one of them knew because they had planned to get rid of the wealthy widow before he and his team arrived in the morning. But they were here now. And they had to figure out how to make sure that she stayed safe. Viktor and Ivan both returned, shaking their heads. They hadn't found anyone outside.

Was that because Priscilla's assailant had escaped or because that person was still in the house with them?

At Blade's insistence, Priscilla introduced everyone from her stepson, Bradley, to the gardener, Fritz, to the bodyguard and the rest of his team. She had no doubt what would have happened had Blade Sparks not come to the estate to assess the security system the night before her meeting with his agency. Someone would have tried to kill her, just as they'd tried with him present. But if he hadn't been present, they might have succeeded.

But why? Did they hate her that much? Or were they just greedy? Was this all about the inheritance? Her late husband had provided for his family with individual trust funds; they weren't destitute. But she had inherited the bulk of the estate and the things that mattered even more than that: his intellectual property. That was worth far more than any of the artwork or jewelry. And she had control of all of that as well as the estate itself.

Her heart skipped a beat as she considered all those notes and the book she'd already started. "What did you do about the den?" she asked Blade, interrupting his conversation with his boss.

"I secured it before I started looking for you," he assured her. But then he glanced that way, as if he wondered how secure it was. But surely whoever had tried breaking in earlier was the same person who'd tried getting into her room, so they couldn't have been in two places at once.

"I should check it," she said, nerves flitting through her stomach. Or was that the first flutter of the baby moving inside her?

"You're not going anywhere alone until we figure out who's trying to kill you," Blade said.

She gasped. "Trying to kill me…"

"Someone shoved you down the stairs," Blade said, as if she needed a reminder. "They meant to kill you or at least seriously wound you." He glanced at the others that she'd introduced to him, and his gaze went from one to another, as if he was considering them each a suspect.

And they were.

They probably all had a motive to kill her. Maybe even the staff if just out of some misguided sense of loyalty to the Pell family. The staff weren't the only ones who were loyal to the Pells; she saw that when Officer Carlson returned in the way she seemed to treat the family with more respect than which she treated the Payne Protection Agency and Priscilla herself.

"Ah, so you ignored my advice and hired the agency of misfit toys anyways," the officer remarked.

"What?" Priscilla asked. "Who are you calling misfit toys?"

The officer shook her head. "Never mind."

"She's talking about us, Dr. Pell," one of the bodyguards replied. But instead of being offended, the big guy seemed amused. He grinned at the young officer as if he was flirting with her.

And the woman seemed to blush a bit.

Or maybe that was just Priscilla projecting her own attraction to her bodyguard onto them. Maybe if she wasn't the only person attracted to someone from the Payne Protection Agency, she wouldn't feel so foolish and out of control.

But the officer nearly snarled at the man, so clearly she wasn't interested in him, not like Priscilla was with Blade Sparks. Yet her interest was understandable; Blade had probably saved her life. So it was no wonder she might start falling for her white knight.

But he was just doing his job.

As well as protecting her like he had earlier tonight, he was working now with the team he'd called in. They were installing cameras and sensors and new security panels. Securing the estate was clearly his priority. While he answered the officer's questions, he was short with the young woman.

He hadn't seen who'd pushed Priscilla. And she believed him. Everybody else in the house claimed that they hadn't seen or heard anything at all. Priscilla knew they were lying.

They had to have heard her scream. They just hadn't cared. Maybe one of them was even the person who'd pushed her. But they weren't about to admit what they'd done. The officer checked the doorknobs for prints, but she wasn't able to find anything. Whoever had tried breaking into the den and into Priscilla's bedroom must have worn gloves. The officer also asked to search everyone's rooms for the gun that Priscilla had admitted to losing on the stairs. But Carlson didn't find that either. Hopefully the person who'd taken it had run out the French doors that Blade had found standing open. But there were so many other footprints from earlier that night that the officer hadn't been able to track them.

As well as searching their rooms, Officer Carlson had taken a report from everybody in the house. But just as they'd claimed to the Payne Protection Agency, they'd denied seeing or hearing anything. After talking to the officer, they'd gone back to bed, even Thomas, so Priscilla showed the young woman to the front door. Once Carlson was gone, Priscilla passed the guys working on the security panel in the foyer and started slowly up the steps. They must have thought she'd gone all the way up because she could hear the man, who had not flirted with the officer, teasing Blade. "So this is the old widow whose *trinkets* you're supposed to be protecting?"

"Yeah, so I was wrong about her age," Blade said.

"She's not just young," the man said. "She's also beautiful. Are you going to be able to stay focused on your job?"

Blade snorted. "I'm not going to be like you with the

gallery owner, Ivan. I am not like you and Josh. I will not be distracted from my job."

Ivan didn't defend himself. He just asked, "Is that why you're not taking that woman's calls?"

"What woman?" Blade asked the question that nearly popped out of Priscilla's mouth, too.

"Erica or Erin or something," Ivan replied. "She keeps calling the office asking for you."

"There is no reason for me to call her back," Blade said.

And Priscilla released a breath she hadn't realized she'd been holding.

"So she's not your Natalie, like Josh's ex-fiancée who is now his fiancée again?"

Blade groaned. "Not even close. I've never been in love, and I plan to keep it that way. I'm not a romantic schmuck like you and Josh. No falling in love for me."

Love.

Priscilla didn't want that either. She had too much she needed to do for her late husband and for the child she was carrying. She didn't want love from Blade Sparks, at least not the romantic kind. Now the kind she'd been having dreams about...

But her bodyguard was right about not allowing himself to be distracted. Even though she knew he was right, she was a bit offended that he was so convinced he couldn't fall for her. And the part of her that rose to every challenge, to find the correct formula, the right mix of chemicals and compounds, was challenged now, making her wonder what it would take to make him change his mind.

Viktor Lagransky was rewiring the security panel at the only entrance and exit from the estate when the police cruiser drove up. He didn't open the gate for her. A former street kid, he still struggled a bit with authority. While he respected the chief of police and some of the detectives, Officer Carlson hadn't earned his respect yet or even his trust. The feeling was obviously mutual, though. She insulted his team often, and she clearly didn't trust them either.

She lowered her window and asked, "Can you open the gate?"

"I can," he replied but didn't do it.

"What's your problem?" she asked.

"What's yours?" he shot back at her. It was such a shame that she was so damn pretty with her deep blue eyes and delicate features.

"I'm just doing my job," she said.

"So you already figured out who broke in and tried pushing the widow down the staircase?"

"I didn't find any evidence that someone actually broke into the house," she said. "The French doors that your coworker claims he found open weren't tampered with like the lock on the den or her bedroom."

"Blade doesn't lie," Viktor said in defense of his friend. The boxer was honest to a fault, or at least over taking the blame when he probably could have lied his way out of as severe a sentence as the judge had given him. "If he says he found those doors open, they were open."

She sighed as if bored. "That doesn't mean that someone broke into the house. Someone could have left those open."

"To make it look like someone from the outside broke in," he said. "So you think the real threat to Mrs. Pell is in that house?"

"Yes, I do."

"Her family?"

"Or maybe her bodyguard," Officer Carlson replied, her tone sharp.

"Blade would never hurt anyone," Viktor said.

She snorted again. "He went to prison for murder."

"Manslaughter," he reminded her. "He didn't mean to kill the guy."

"Well, he hurt him so much that he died."

"In defense of someone else."

"That's not what she said," Officer Carlson pointed out.

And Viktor groaned with frustration. "I don't know why the dead guy's victim lied at Blade's trial, but I know that Blade told the truth." That was just the kind of guy that Sparks was.

"Do you really know him that well?" Carlson asked. "Your branch of the Payne Protection Agency hasn't even been open very long."

"No," he said. "But, as you know, we've been through a lot in the time that we've been working together." So many of them had nearly lost their lives while trying to protect the people they'd also come to love. "So I know my coworkers well enough to know that I can trust *them*." A hell of a lot more than he trusted her. He knew how corrupt the River City Police Department had been and not that long ago. For decades two crime bosses had ruled the city, and they'd had many officers and prosecutors on their payrolls. Sometimes he wondered if Sheila Carlson was one of them.

The young woman sighed again, but this time she sounded weary. "I don't make that mistake," she said. "I don't trust anyone."

"Why not?" Viktor asked. What had she been through? What drove her to be as ambitious as she was? And what made him so damn curious about her? Sure, she was beautiful, but he was drawn to more than her looks. He liked her snark, too, and he wanted to know what made her tick.

She shrugged. "I just don't. And your friend Blade shouldn't either."

Viktor glanced at the big house sitting behind that stone wall. The place looked like a prison to him. "Blade's smart. He won't make that mistake."

Sheila glanced back over her shoulder, then she leaned farther out the window. "He shouldn't even trust the widow."

On the way over, Garek had filled in him and Ivan about the rumors about the young bride of Dr. Alexander Pell. "You think she killed her husband?" he asked. "Why were charges never pressed?"

"There was no investigation," she said. "No obvious indication of foul play. So I don't know for sure what she did or didn't do," Sheila said. "But I find it highly suspicious that just a short time after their quickie civil ceremony wedding, he dies and she winds up with everything."

"Including a lot of enemies."

She nodded. "Sometimes people earn their enemies."

And something about the way she looked at him chilled Viktor. What had he done to deserve her resentment and mistrust? He couldn't think of anything, so he refused to focus on that right now. He and his team had an assignment to handle, a widow to protect.

"I don't know if she earned them. But there are a lot of people who might want to get rid of her," he acknowledged. Out of revenge or greed or whatever. But it didn't matter what their motive was. They wouldn't be able to murder the woman unless they got rid of Blade first.

Because he'd already proved he would do anything to protect someone, even kill.

Chapter 8

The sun was rising by the time the team from the Payne Protection Agency wrapped up the security upgrade at the Pell Mansion. The place was that big, and despite all they'd done to make it safer, they would probably need to add a few more cameras and sensors.

At least for Blade's peace of mind.

But he assured his boss, as he showed him and his coworkers out, that he had this; he didn't need Vik or Ivan to stay with him for backup. With the security system they'd installed, there were so many cameras and sensors that he doubted anyone would try anything now and if they tried, they would be caught immediately on camera or set off an alarm. So he could definitely manage. He closed the door behind his departing team, and then he leaned wearily against it.

He had this.

As long as that gun didn't come out.

Officer Carlson hadn't found it last night, but he wasn't certain how thoroughly she'd searched. Ivan and Viktor had searched, too, though, and hadn't found it. So maybe the person who'd taken it from Priscilla had left the house with it.

Vik and Ivan had seen tracks in the snow covering the grass, but there had been too many for them to figure out which had been Blade's and Priscilla's from earlier and which might have been from the intruder.

He just hoped like hell that the gun and the person who'd tried to kill Priscilla were gone now. But he had a feeling that they would come back; they would try again to get rid of her and to get into that den. The only way to stop them for sure was to figure out who the hell they were. His boss assured him that they were going to work on that, too, and run background checks on everyone in the house. They would figure out if the threat came from within or outside the house.

Sure, Officer Carlson was supposed to figure out who'd tried to kill Priscilla, but Blade didn't trust her, especially when Vik had shared what she'd told him. That he shouldn't trust the young widow.

Why not?

She hadn't tried to break into her own bedroom and that den, and she definitely hadn't shoved herself down the stairs. Maybe the officer thought she'd staged it, but Carlson hadn't been there. Blade had been there. He'd seen how she'd been thrust forward, toward the stairs, and he'd heard the fear in her voice when she'd screamed. And he'd seen it in her beautiful eyes.

He opened his and found himself staring down into those beautiful eyes. So much for him being able to handle security on his own when she'd been able to sneak up on him.

"Did you fall asleep standing up?" she asked.

"No," he said. "I'm awake. Why are you up? It's early."

"I couldn't sleep." And she was fully dressed now, to his disappointment. She wore loose khaki pants and a bulky black sweater.

"The security is all in place now," he said. "You'll be safe."

She sighed. "I don't think there is enough security to keep me safe in this house, with them."

"I'm here. I will keep you safe."

She smiled. "And who will keep me safe from you?"

He groaned. "So Officer Carlson told you about my past."

"About the woman who's trying to reach you?" she asked.

"She knows about that?" he asked, amazed. What was Erica up to? Trying to get him sent back to prison? That was why he refused to have any contact with her; he didn't want to give her a chance to lie about him again.

"No, I overheard your friend asking you about it," she said, her cheeks getting a little pink as if she was embarrassed for eavesdropping.

But Ivan's deep voice tended to carry, so she probably hadn't been able to miss hearing that. He sighed. "Since I'm going to be staying in your home, you have a right to know."

"Know what?"

"That I was in prison."

She nodded as if she'd already figured that out. "That's why you said that..." She gestured around the house. "About this place reminding you of prison."

He nodded. "Yes. I know what I'm talking about."

"Why were you there?" she asked, and she sounded only curious, not judgmental or frightened as most other people were when they learned about his past.

"Manslaughter," he said.

"Like because of drunk driving or something?" she asked, and now her voice sharpened with disapproval.

He shook his head. "A man was dragging his wife out of a bar by her hair, swearing that this time he was going to kill her. I stopped him."

"You killed him," she said with less disapproval in her tone while her green eyes widened with shock.

He nodded. "I didn't mean to, but I was boxing professionally then. I just…" He sighed. "I should have known better than to…" He trailed off as emotion choked him.

"But if you didn't step in, he might have killed her. Why did you go to prison for that? You were just trying to help a woman in trouble."

He sighed again. "She didn't see it that way. At least that's not what she told the judge."

"Why would she lie?"

He shrugged. "I don't know. There were other witnesses who saw some of it. They helped bring the charge down to manslaughter from murder. And I got a reduced sentence."

"How long?"

"Eight years."

"You spent eight years in prison for helping someone?" she asked.

He shook his head. "For killing a man. Officer Carlson didn't tell you that?"

She shook her head. "No. Did you mean to kill him?"

He shook his head again as that emotion nearly choked him. He cleared his throat. "I just wanted to stop him from hurting her." Like he hadn't been able to stop all the men who'd hurt his mother. He shuddered. "But I punched him so hard that his nose went into his brain." He closed his eyes as he remembered all the blood and how quickly the man had dropped and was just gone.

She gasped.

Probably horrified.

"I should have known better than to hit him that hard," he said. He'd been a professional fighter.

"Like you said, you just wanted to stop him," she repeated. "But you must regret getting involved now."

He released a shaky sigh. "I regret that he died, but I

don't regret getting involved. I couldn't just let him drag her out of there and hurt her. I won't ever turn my back on someone who needs help no matter the consequences." He paused for a moment, then asked, "So now that you know, how do you feel about me? Do you want me to stay here?"

She stepped closer to him and then rose up on her tiptoes and pressed her mouth to his. And he felt sucker punched yet again when desire slammed through him, making his body tense and hot with need. But he was so stunned at the softness and the sweetness of her mouth on his and at the desire rushing through him that he didn't kiss her back.

And before he could even reach for her, to put his arms around her, she pulled away from him. Then she turned and fled through the foyer. He started after her, but his knees were a little shaky. He wanted to blame it on exhaustion, but he knew it was her kiss.

Her...

And he realized that maybe Officer Carlson had been right to tell Vik to warn him about the widow. She was proving to be much more dangerous than any opponent Blade had ever faced in the ring. She kept catching him off guard. And as a bodyguard, he couldn't let that happen again. Or he might not be able to save her if there was another attempt on her life.

And he might not be able to save himself either.

Priscilla should have run back up to her bedroom. But she'd run toward the den instead, which was where she'd been headed when she'd noticed Blade leaning against the front door with his eyes shut. He'd looked so exhausted and vulnerable, too, which, given his size and his muscular build, she wouldn't have thought possible. But he had looked as if he could be hurt, or that he had been hurt.

And now she knew how. He'd tried to help someone and while things had gone terribly wrong, she believed he'd just been trying to save that abused woman from more abuse. And instead of being grateful, the victim had made certain he went to prison. Now Priscilla understood why he was ignoring the woman's efforts to contact him. Even if she was calling to apologize, it was too little and too damn late. He'd lost so many years of his life. And in that moment, sympathy and something else had overwhelmed her, and she'd kissed him.

Her lips tingled from the contact with his. She'd never been so attracted to anyone else as she was to him, the man she'd kept dreaming about even before she'd met him. And she wanted to kiss him again. But he hadn't even kissed her back. He'd just stood there, obviously as immune to any distractions as he'd told his coworker he was. And while she'd briefly considered his statement a challenge, she hadn't really tried to catch his attention because she'd realized he was right that it was smarter to stay focused on staying safe and on finishing the research and the book.

She'd dressed in baggy and comfortable clothes. Despite everything that had happened the night before and her lack of sleep, she'd intended to focus on work. But then he'd told her about himself, about what he'd given up to keep someone else safe, and the attraction she'd already felt for him and his heroism had overridden her common sense.

Even though she was at the door to the den now, she couldn't get inside the room. She didn't have the code for the new digital lock that the Payne Protection Agency had installed last night. She leaned her forehead against the hard wood and tried to cool off the flush of embarrassment that suffused her face. And another kind of heat gripped her body: passion. She wanted him so damn badly.

"I'll give you the code," a deep voice murmured. And he slowly touched buttons on the keypad so she could see what he was doing.

She didn't repeat aloud the sequence of numbers and pound and asterisk signs that he'd entered but committed the code to memory.

"You and I are the only ones who know what it is," he assured her. He turned the knob but didn't push it open. Maybe he was afraid she would fall face-first into the room with the way she was leaning against the door.

She covered his hand with hers, turned the knob fully and pushed open the door. Her skin tingled from the contact with his big hand, just as her lips had tingled. She stumbled inside the room, desperate to get away from him now. But he followed her into the office and closed the door behind his big body. "Can we pretend that never happened?" she asked hopefully.

"I'm a bodyguard, not an actor," he said.

"That's obvious," she said because he hadn't even been able to make himself pretend to return her interest in him.

"What do you mean?"

She shrugged. "Nothing."

"I make a point of always being honest," he said. "I should have been more open than I was about my record. I alluded to it last night, to being in prison, but should I have told you sooner?"

She shook her head. "I should have picked up on it last night when you compared this place to prison. But it obviously doesn't bother me." Or she wouldn't have kissed him.

"I think it does."

"What do you mean? I kissed you," she said, her face heating up along with her body over her audacity in doing it and over her desire to do it again.

"Out of pity," he said. "I don't want your pity. I made a mistake—"

"That was not out of pity," she interjected. She couldn't let him think that. But she didn't want to admit the entire truth either, that she was wildly attracted to him. "That was out of respect and gratitude. You didn't make a mistake. You're a hero. You probably saved that woman's life, just like you saved my life last night. I don't even know if I thanked you for that, for everything you've done…"

"Since you pulled a gun on me?" he asked, his lips curving into a slight and super-sexy grin.

"Since you trespassed on my property," she finished. But she smiled, too.

"I'm glad I decided to assess your security the night before."

"I am, too. You were obviously right that someone might try something last night." She wasn't sure if she'd thanked him or told him how much she appreciated his going above and beyond, working even before she'd officially hired the Payne Protection Agency. She'd been so tired and distracted last night. Maybe that was why she'd kissed him like she had. Or it had just been out of gratitude like she'd told him. She was grateful that he'd saved her life and that for once she felt as if someone had her back. While Dr. Pell—Alexander had supported her career and her future just as her parents had, she'd never felt as safe and protected as she did with Blade Sparks. But protecting her was just his job as her bodyguard.

"Hopefully that was the last attempt they make," he said. "Now that the extra cameras and sensors have been installed, it will be hard for anyone to try anything again without getting caught immediately. I'm going to check the security footage for blind spots, though, and we'll add more if necessary."

She nodded. "Yes, do whatever you think is necessary to protect the estate." She looked around the den then, and she had the odd sensation that something was out of place. Maybe he'd moved something after she'd left him alone in here last night, though.

"I'm more concerned about protecting you," he said, and he stepped a little closer to her then. His gaze dropped from her eyes to her mouth. "That's why I can't let myself be distracted."

"What would distract you?" she asked, and her lips curved into a smile. Maybe he hadn't been as unaffected as she'd thought.

"You," he said. "You might be the most beautiful woman I've ever seen in person."

Once again she knew he was telling the truth and not offering empty flattery or trying to charm her like so many other people had over the years. He spoke too matter-of-factly.

She knew she was beautiful. She'd always been beautiful, but her parents had acted as if that was more of a minus than a plus. They hadn't wanted her appearance to distract her, and anyone else, from what they'd considered her brilliance. Their fears weren't entirely unfounded. People were too often surprised that she was smart, as if she couldn't be both beautiful and intelligent.

"You say that like it's a bad thing," she said with a smile.

"It is. My job is to keep you safe, not fall for you."

"I thought you were in no danger of falling in love," she said.

"You overheard me telling Ivan that?"

She nodded.

"I've never been in love," he said.

"Me neither."

"But you were married."

She sighed. "I respected Dr. Pe—Alexander."

"That's why you do that," he said. "Why you call him Doctor instead of by his first name."

She nodded. "I never called him by his first name."

"He was your husband."

"In name only," she admitted. "He trusted me. He was getting older and not feeling well. He knew he wouldn't be able to go on much longer, and he wanted me to continue his work. We were so close to a breakthrough on some medications for Alzheimer's and cancer."

"Wow..." Blade murmured, and he looked around the office. "So you weren't exaggerating about the lives you could save."

She shook her head. "No. I wasn't." Finishing those drugs meant so much to her. Even though it wouldn't save the ones she'd already lost, it could save so many others that heartbreak. "Dr. Pell wanted to make sure that I would be able to retain ownership of his intellectual property." She gestured around the den. And she nearly touched her stomach, too. She wasn't sure she was ready to tell her bodyguard, or anyone else, about the baby yet. She'd lost those other embryos. And with the stress she was under, there was a chance she might lose this one, too. The last one. "That's why he asked me to marry him."

"But why did you agree?"

"I want to finish that research. I want to make those medications that can save lives," she said.

"But what about your life?" he asked. "The sacrifices you're making?"

She shrugged. "I'm really not sacrificing anything."

"Love?"

She sighed. "I don't think I'm capable of falling in love. That's what some of my exes have told me. That I'm too unemotional and independent to ever need anyone." But she knew they'd been wrong about her. Especially Everett. He'd accused her of being so cold. If only he knew what kind of dreams she'd been having…

But she'd never thought that way about him like she had about the man she'd only imagined until he'd come to life on her property. Blade Sparks.

"You're smart," he said. "That's why you're unemotional and independent."

"I'm not so sure about that anymore," she admitted. She was definitely attached to the baby she was carrying. She was already falling for him, but she was so afraid that she would lose him, too. And he was more than an experiment to her, more even than continuing Alexander's legacy. It had been so important to the biophysicist to have a biological heir. And Priscilla had wanted a child, too. She'd thought a baby would fill that hollow ache of loneliness she'd felt for so long, maybe even before her parents had passed. But each time she'd lost a baby, that ache had intensified.

"You're not so sure that you're smart?" he asked, and he sounded incredulous. "Because you kissed me?"

"That wasn't my smartest move," she admitted.

"Ouch," he said, but he chuckled.

"But it wasn't out of pity," she assured him. "Just gratitude."

"I was just doing my job," he said.

"Ouch," she said, but she smiled at him. "I'm also not used to someone being nice to me."

He tilted his head and touched her face, his rough fingertips sliding along her jaw. "I'm sorry…"

"Now you're pitying me. It's just that everybody in this house hates me."

"Why?" he asked. "Do they think you're a gold digger?"

"You don't?"

He shook his head. "You're smart. You're beautiful. You didn't need to marry for money. You could make your own."

She would have kissed him again if she wasn't already embarrassed over her first kiss. "Wow. That's nice to hear. So if you don't think I'm a gold digger, you must not think I'm a killer either?"

"What?" His eyebrows arched high. "Why would I think you're a killer?"

"If you believe the other people in this house, you're not the only person who should have gone to prison for murder. They think I am responsible for my husband's death. That I killed him for the money and mostly for control of the research we were working on together."

Since Blade had been so honest with her, she needed to be honest with him, too. Her life might very well depend on him knowing everything. So she would have to tell him about the baby, too. But the fatigue and the frustration with being blamed for something she hadn't done had tears springing to her eyes. She blinked furiously to try to hold them back, but one slipped down her cheek.

And he wiped it away with the pad of his big thumb. Then he lowered his head, and his lips brushed across hers like his fingers brushed across her face.

She emitted a soft moan at all the sensations racing through her, all the desire overwhelming her. And he deepened the kiss.

Milek heard doors opening and closing and rushed from his art studio, which was in one area of the renovated warehouse, into the other area where he and Garek had opened their branch of the Payne Protection Agency. Garek, Ivan and Viktor stumbled into the office, bleary-eyed. "You all have a party last night and not invite me?" he asked.

Viktor chuckled. "That was not my idea of a party because I certainly wouldn't have had Officer Carlson on the guest list."

"Officer Carlson?" Milek asked with alarm. "What happened? Are you all alright?" He studied them closer now, looking for injuries, but he saw only the dark circles beneath their tired eyes.

"We're fine," Garek said. "There was a break-in at the Pell Mansion and an attempt on the widow's life."

Ivan snorted. "Didn't look like a break-in."

"More like an inside job," Viktor agreed.

"Are Blade and Priscilla alright?" Milek asked with concern.

"Yes, Blade saved her," Garek said. "He didn't catch the perp, though."

"Is that why you all went over there?" Milek asked, and he was a little stung that they hadn't invited him along.

"We were already on our way," Garek said. "Blade called me with concerns about the place from when he did his assessment. He was worried that somebody was going to try something last night before we were able to upgrade the security system."

"And he was right," Milek said. "He has good instincts." Right away Milek had noticed how intuitive Blade Sparks was. But the guy probably wouldn't have survived as a boxer or in prison if he hadn't had great instincts.

"Hopefully those don't fail him when it comes to the beautiful widow," Viktor remarked. "Officer Carlson is not a fan of hers."

"She's not a fan of anyone," Ivan said.

"Oh, I think she's falling for me," Viktor said.

And everyone laughed. She probably hated him most of all because he teased her so much.

Even though everyone had laughed, the humor didn't quite reach their eyes. Were they tired or worried?

Garek must have figured they were tired because he sent Ivan and Viktor home to get some sleep. Then he stumbled into his office and dropped into the chair behind his desk.

Milek followed him in and asked, "So the system is already upgraded?"

Garek nodded. "Yeah, no need for us to meet with her. She was happy to hire us. In fact she was the one who asked Blade to stay last night."

"Sounds like it was a good thing that he did," Milek remarked.

Garek nodded. "Yeah, she knows she's in danger. I just wonder how that CEO knew how bad things are at the Pell Mansion."

Milek shrugged. "How does he know anything? Maybe he has Penny Payne's sixth sense."

"I don't think that's how he knows."

"So how else could he know?"

Garek shrugged now. "No idea. But we do need to figure out who's out to get her."

"All the suspects are probably right in that house with her and Blade," Milek said. "Is he going to be okay on his own there?"

"We installed a really comprehensive system with a lot of cameras that we'll be monitoring 24/7. And Blade is a damn good bodyguard," Garek said.

"But you're still worried about him," Milek surmised.

"She lost her gun last night," Garek said. "The widow had a gun, but she lost it."

Alarm shot through Milek. "Damn it. We have to get Blade permission to carry a weapon." Amber was working on it, but it was taking too long. And it might wind up costing Blade his life. "Maybe we should pull him off the case and put Ivan on it. Ivan can carry."

Garek nodded. "But I have a feeling that the widow is going to want to keep Blade as her bodyguard. And she certainly has enough money to replace the gun that's lost if she wants another weapon in the house. What she wants right now I think is Blade."

"What do you mean?" Milek asked. "Is there going to be another relationship evolving out of a case?"

"I hope not. We're supposed to be handling security. Not matchmaking. And I think she just let him move in right away because she trusts him."

"She should," Milek said. "Blade is an open book. Honest and straightforward. And he wouldn't hesitate to give up his life to save someone else's."

"He really already has…" Garek murmured, and he looked as worried as Milek was that Blade might wind up giving up his life again. But this time it wouldn't just be life as he'd known it, as freedom; it would be death instead of prison for him.

Chapter 9

Blade lost himself in that kiss, in Priscilla. She was as sweet as she was beautiful. And so damn hot. He'd never wanted anyone as much as he wanted her. That couch hadn't been long enough for him to sleep on, but maybe he could lay her down there and worship her body like he was worshipping her mouth with slow, soft and sexy kisses.

But the creak of hinges jolted him back to reality. He cupped Priscilla's shoulders and whirled her around behind him, so that he was between her and the door that was opening. They hadn't locked it when they'd closed it a short while ago. And they should have.

Priscilla shouldn't be in any room unless the door was locked to keep out intruders. She was in danger, and not just from whoever was trying to kill her but from her bodyguard, too. Because no matter how much he'd claimed he wouldn't be distracted, he had been.

But he braced himself like he used to in the ring, legs apart, feet planted flat, his arms up, fists clenched. He was ready to fight off whoever was intruding now.

The door opened, and a woman gasped.

It was the assistant. Monica something. She might have been pretty with her brown hair and brown eyes if not for the perpetual frown she seemed to wear that had already etched deep lines in her forehead and around her pursed lips. And she was much too young for wrinkles. She was probably just in her early twenties.

Which felt a lifetime ago for Blade, or at the very least a prison sentence ago.

"What are you doing in here?" she asked, clearly startled.

"What the hell are you doing in here?" he asked.

"My job. For her." She pointed beyond him, at Priscilla. "I'm supposed to be here. What about you?"

"You weren't supposed to be here last night," he said. "But yet my camera has a great picture of you coming in here." He pulled out his cell and swiped the screen until he pulled up the photo of her walking into the office last night.

Priscilla stepped out from behind him then and peered at his phone. "When was she in here?"

"Sometime after someone pushed you down the stairs but before the police arrived. I think the alarm going off scared her away."

"I was scared," the girl replied. "I heard all that commotion on the stairs, and I was worried that someone had broken into the house. That's why I was in here then."

"You didn't show up in the foyer where the commotion was? You came into the office instead? Why?" Priscilla asked the question burning in Blade's throat.

"I... I...uh," the girl stammered, "I wanted to make sure everything was safe."

"But you moved things," Priscilla said. "I knew it when I walked in here."

Blade swallowed a chuckle of amusement over how nothing had escaped the brilliant Dr. Pell. He touched the play button on his phone, and it showed Monica taking photos of the formulas and moving some papers around. But she hadn't taken anything. If she had, he would have already addressed it. His phone had alerted him to the movement on the camera he'd placed in this room, but at the time he'd been more concerned about finding whoever had pushed Priscilla down the stairs and taken her gun.

Monica could have done both. Maybe she'd opened the French doors again, hidden the gun and then broken into the den. She'd proved that she wasn't trustworthy.

"I didn't think it was a good idea that you let some stranger move into the house," Monica said. "I wanted to make sure that Dr. Pell's notes were safe."

Priscilla stepped around Blade then, her body that had been so soft and warm moments ago stiff and cold now. "I am Dr. Pell," she said. "And this man is my bodyguard, not a stranger. The chief of police vouched for him. Why would that give you any reason to doubt his integrity?"

"I...uh, the female police officer didn't seem to trust him."

"But the chief of police trusts him, and so do I," Priscilla said. "It's your integrity that is in question now, Monica."

The girl's face flushed bright red, but it might have been more fury than embarrassment because her eyes got dark and hard with hatred. "I have never given you any reason to doubt me. Why are you questioning me now?"

Priscilla pointed toward his phone. "I want those photos you took. And I want proof that you didn't send them to anyone else."

The girl's face flushed an even deeper shade of red. "I... I took them just like an inventory, to show you what it looked like in here. That's the only reason I took them."

"Not to send to someone?" Priscilla asked skeptically.

"Who would I have sent them to?"

"Everett."

"Dr. Fendler?" the girl asked, her dark eyes wide with what looked like fake surprise. Then she shook her head. "Of course not. I work for you."

"Does she?" Blade asked Priscilla. "Or are you going to fire her right now?" That was what he would have recommended. He didn't trust the bitter young woman. And with how she looked at her boss with such hatred and resentment, Priscilla definitely should not trust her.

"I will give you another chance, Monica," Priscilla said. "As long as you let me see your phone."

"I... I...uh, don't have it with me," the girl replied. "But I'll go get it. I'll show you that I've deleted the photos and that I didn't send them to anyone."

Priscilla nodded. And the girl rushed off to retrieve her phone. But she would probably delete those photos and her emails before she returned to the office to show it to her boss.

"Why didn't you just fire her?" Blade asked, and he hoped like hell that the girl was still close enough to hear his question.

Priscilla smiled. "Keeping my enemies close, I guess."

"But all you have in this house are enemies," Blade said with frustration.

"Not anymore," Priscilla said. "Now I have you."

And Blade was afraid that she did. Despite his assurance that he wouldn't get personally involved in his first solo assignment, he was sinking fast. And it wasn't just because of how beautiful she was or how smart she was... but that she needed him.

Even though she had a mansion and a fortune and brains and beauty, she still needed *him*. And he hadn't realized how good it felt to have someone need him. But he didn't want her in danger anymore. He had to figure out how to keep her safe as well as figure out which of the enemies she was keeping too close actually wanted her dead.

"I get why his family might hate you," he said. "If they think you killed him to inherit, but why the staff, too? And this assistant of yours?"

Priscilla sighed. "Alexander's family are actually his late wife's family. He adopted his stepson, but they've never been really close or had anything in common. And the staff..." She sighed again. "They were also closer to Alexander's late wife. She hired them."

"How long ago did she pass?"

"Just a few months before I started working as his research assistant," she said. "So almost two years ago."

"And then he married you when?"

"Six months after her death."

And Blade realized now why his family might resent her.

"His family actually thinks I married him shortly before he died, though." Priscilla's face flushed. "I know that looks bad," she said. "But really, he needed my help with the research. He was desperate to make a breakthrough, even more because his wife passed from Alzheimer's disease."

"Have you lost people to it, too?" he wondered.

She released a shaky sigh and nodded. "Yes, hasn't everyone?"

He really had no idea. The only family he'd had was his mom, and she'd died way before she could have developed the disease. "And what about this Everett?" he asked. "Why do you think Monica would have sent the pictures to him?"

"There are a lot of people who are very interested in this research," she said.

He didn't have to be a biophysicist to understand why. "A drug like that would be worth a lot of money."

She nodded. "And that's all some people care about."

But not her, which made Blade care about her even more than he was already beginning to…

Priscilla wasn't surprised when her assistant's phone came back damaged. "It slipped out of my hand and fell in the toilet," Monica insisted.

"You should fire her," Blade said.

And Monica glared at him. "It was an accident."

"Breaking in here last night? Taking those photos? That was all an accident," he scoffed at her.

The young woman blushed. "I thought I was doing the right thing last night."

That Priscilla believed. Whomever Monica was really loyal to, however, had convinced her that spying was the right thing. "I suspect you think you are, but you're not," she told her assistant. "I'm doing what Dr. Pell asked me to do, what he made me promise I would do. I'm going to finish the research we were working on together that meant so much to him." And to all the people whose lives and whose loved ones it could save. "I'm honoring him. Nobody else in this house cares about what he wanted but me."

Monica pursed her lips. "I'm not dishonoring him."

"You're not helping me like you're supposed to," Priscilla said.

"That's exactly what I was doing," Monica said. "I knew you cared about the notes. I wanted to check on them. I took pictures to make sure they were all still here, and if something or someone got in here, we would have copies of everything."

"But we don't," Priscilla said, "if you're telling the truth about losing them on your phone."

"I am telling the truth," Monica said, her voice nearly shrill as she raised it.

Blade snorted. He clearly didn't believe her.

"Are you going to fire me? Why?" Monica asked. "Because your *bodyguard* told you to?"

Had she seen them kissing? Was that why she'd put the strange emphasis on *bodyguard*. But that was what he was and all that he should be. Priscilla had too much else on her mind, like the research and the book. They both had to get done. There was so much at stake.

"I should fire you," Priscilla admitted. "I can't trust you, so you shouldn't be working for me." But she couldn't trust anyone in this house except for her bodyguard, Blade. He thought she should fire the girl. But because Priscilla had so much work to do, and bringing someone else up to speed would take too much time, she didn't want to waste more time hiring someone else. With her pregnancy, her window to work was limited. She needed to rest, too. And she'd had too little sleep last night to fight right now.

"I'll give you another chance," Priscilla said. "But you cannot come into this room without me. And you will not be allowed to have your phone while you're in here."

"I'll take that phone," Blade said. "Payne Protection has a tech specialist who's so good that the police department uses her. Nikki Payne-Ecklund will be able to recover everything you tried to lose from this phone."

The girl tried hanging on to the cell as he pulled the dripping phone from her hand. "No…"

"It's the phone or your job," Priscilla said. "You agreed to confidentiality when you accepted this position. If you've been sharing any of Dr. Pell's intellectual property, you're in violation of your contract."

The girl let Blade take the phone from her grasp. "It's really ruined."

"Nikki's good," Blade said with confidence.

The color drained from Monica's face. "Uh... I... I... don't feel so well. Can I take the morning off?" she asked. "I need to get some rest."

Priscilla was exhausted, too, so she didn't argue with her. She just nodded.

As the girl fled the room once again, Blade said, "She's probably going to run."

Priscilla sighed over the thought of having to interview and vet someone else for the assistant job. "Why would she run?"

"Because Nikki will find something incriminating on this cell," he said.

She had a pretty good idea what Nikki would find, and it wasn't enough to get her in the kind of trouble she would need to run from. "I don't think Monica is the one who pushed me last night."

"You don't?"

"I think she's a spy," Priscilla admitted. "I don't think she's a killer."

"A spy for whom?" Blade asked.

And she narrowed her eyes at his choice of words.

He chuckled. "Don't think I know good grammar, Dr. Pell?"

"People with doctorates don't always use good grammar, Mr. Sparks."

"I took a lot of classes while I was in prison."

She wasn't surprised that he'd found a way to make the most of a bad situation. "Do you have a doctorate, too?"

He chuckled again. "Not hardly. Just took some criminal justice and psychology courses and some English ones, too."

"So you're more than a pretty face," she said, making the comment she'd heard so often over the years.

He touched his face. "This is not a pretty face. This is a face that took too many hits."

"It has character," she said. And so did he.

"You didn't answer my question. Who has Monica spying on you?"

"Everett."

"Dr. Fendler," he said. "You both mentioned him before, that he's interested in the research. Who is he?"

"Now he's a professor at my alma mater, the university where Dr. Pell also taught and where I was a teaching assistant."

"Dr. Fendler's TA?"

She shook her head and sighed. "No. We were involved...for a while when we were both TAs for Dr. Pell."

"Ah..."

She sighed again. "Yes, it's all a mess. Monica was Everett's TA before she came to work here with me and Dr. Pell. Dr. Pell, Alexander, trusted Everett."

"You don't'?"

She shook her head. "Like I said, he's very interested in the research." And Everett wasn't above claiming someone else's work as his. He'd done that when they were dating and working on assignments together. That was why she'd figured a marriage with clear perimeters and the promise of a child was safer than one with emotions involved. Not that she'd been all that emotional over Everett.

"I'm sure a lot of people are," Blade said, "if it will help with the diseases you've mentioned."

"We won't know for sure how effective it is until after the drug trials," she said. "But I'm hopeful those will go well." That was why she couldn't let anyone distract her from the work she had left to do.

"A lot of people might want to get their hands on this research?"

She nodded. "That's why I really can't trust anyone."

"You trust me."

She smiled. "Yes."

"Why?"

"Because you don't want anything from me."

He stared at her for a moment, his blue eyes darkening as his pupils dilated. "I wouldn't be so sure about that."

"What do you want from me?" she asked. "You don't seem interested in my money or the house that you think is like prison. And none of this—" she gestured around the den "—means anything to you."

"Maybe I took biophysics in prison, too," he said, but the twinkle in his eyes showed he was teasing her.

"You want to be my assistant now? Or you want to steal all the secrets?"

"No," he said. "I just want to protect you and all of these secrets."

"So you don't want anything from me?"

He shook his head. "I learned a long time ago not to want what I can never have."

If she knew that he wanted her, she would have told him that he could definitely have her. But at the moment, he looked so exhausted. And she was so exhausted. "Maybe Monica has the right idea to go back to bed," she said.

His nostrils flared for a moment, making her wonder if she invited him if he would join her in bed. But he clasped that dripping cell phone in his hand. "I'm going to have someone come pick this up, so I can get it to Nikki," he said. "But yes, you should go get some rest."

She doubted she would get any sleep, though, even if she went back to bed. Because she would just keep dreaming about him, about him kissing her, touching her, making love to her. But he worked for her, just like Monica. And while she could trust him, she didn't think it was a good idea to proposition him either. She'd already crossed a line when she'd kissed him. But he'd kissed her back. And maybe she was what he didn't want because he didn't think he could have her.

If he only knew...

Woodrow Lynch wanted to retire and spend more time with his beautiful wife and their kids and grandkids, and that yearning got especially intense right now because of the holidays. He couldn't wait for all the parties with the family gathering around them.

While technically, he and Penny had no children together, it didn't feel that way to either of them. His daughters were like hers, and all her kids, the ones she'd given birth to and the ones her big heart had adopted, felt like his now.

And because of that...

Because there was something going on with the newest branch of the Payne Protection Agency, he had to stay on the job for a while longer. He had to make sure that this branch survived the assignments this mysterious CEO, Mason Hull, had hired them for.

Woodrow was at his desk bright and early the next morning so that Officer Carlson could brief him once her shift ended. He knew she called the Kozminskis branch the franchise of misfit toys or something like that. He'd also heard them called the outlaws. That one was more accurate because some of them had once been outlaws, just not by choice. Circumstances and necessity and an evil man's coercion had forced them to do things they hadn't wanted to do.

And now that they could all choose for themselves, they had chosen to protect others. They weren't outlaws or misfits. They were the good guys, but for some reason Officer Carlson could not see that. While the chief knew everything about the Payne family and their employees because he was close to them, he didn't know much about other people since he was relatively new to River City, Michigan. So he'd had his best detective, Spencer Dubridge, check into Carlson a few months ago.

Dubridge hadn't found any big deposits in her checking or savings accounts. No high-value goods had been gifted to her either. He'd found no evidence of corruption on her part, and Dubridge trusted her. He thought she was a good cop, but the chief thought there was something else going on with her, some secret that not even his best detective had discovered.

"I heard that you went out on another call to the Pell Mansion last night," he said when she stepped into his office.

She looked exhausted with dark circles beneath her blue eyes, and limp strands of dark blond hair trailing out from under her cap. She nodded. "Yes, the widow claims someone tried to push her down the stairs."

"You don't believe her?"

"Nobody saw anything," Carlson replied. "The bodyguard saved her. I'm not sure what's actually going on at that estate."

"Should I bring in Detective Dubridge for this investigation?" he asked. Spencer Dubridge still had a couple of weeks of family leave left to spend with his wife and new baby, but he'd come back a couple of other times to help investigate cases involving the Payne Protection Agency's newest franchise. And to investigate Officer Carlson for him.

"Nobody's been kidnapped and nobody's been killed… that we know for certain," the officer said.

"That we know for certain?"

"There are rumors that Dr. Pell didn't die of natural causes, that his young bride helped him along the way."

"Rumors. There was no evidence. An autopsy showed that he died of natural causes." Because of the rumors, Woodrow had checked into that case himself; Dr. Pell had been so respected and revered in River City.

Her pale face suddenly flushed with color. "Yes, but…"

"We have a lot of real cases to work rather than rumors," Woodrow said.

"I know, sir. I'm not investigating a murder. I just responded to two calls about break-ins last night. The first one was the bodyguard, Blade Sparks, who had trespassed onto the property. And the second…" She shrugged. "It could have been anyone in that house, or maybe the widow just stumbled and started falling. She also lost her gun when she fell. But she was walking around in the dark in the middle of the night. There is no evidence that anyone tried to kill her. Someone did try to unlock her bedroom door and an office door. Did an amateurish job on the locks."

"So you think it's someone in that house?"

"Again. I don't have evidence, just rumors. But everyone in that house pretty much hates her and thinks she doesn't deserve what she's inherited."

And so they could be trying to take it back. "It's a good thing that she hired the Payne Protection Agency, then." They would keep her and her property safe or die trying. That was the kind of people they were, not the outlaws or the misfits that Sheila Carlson thought they were. But she probably wouldn't realize that she was wrong until one of them did die in the line of duty for their client.

Chapter 10

That feeling Blade had had when he'd first seen the Pell estate a week ago was even more intense now. The mansion definitely felt like prison to him. He'd been stuck here in this house, usually in the den with Priscilla like he was now, since he'd started his assignment. And he wanted to climb over that stone wall again but this time to escape. It wasn't because being here was so horrible.

It was because she was so beautiful. He wanted to kiss her again. Hell, he wanted to do a lot more than kiss her, but he was determined to be the professional he hadn't been the morning after his sleepless night. He was determined to have more control and willpower. Letting down the Kozminskis was the last thing he wanted. He didn't want to let himself down either. He'd vowed to be the best bodyguard he could be, and that was a promise he meant to keep to himself.

While she'd kissed him first, it was still unprofessional and ill-advised to get involved with a client, especially a client who was clearly in danger. He needed to stay focused and alert to the next threat against her. But what about the threat against him, or at least against his resolve to not fall for her?

She was as smart as she was beautiful, too. Not only did

she understand what all those equations were, but she kept scribbling away at them, changing them or adding to them. And he wondered how much of this work was her late husband's and how much was hers. She stood over one of the library tables now, staring down so intently at the paper she was scribbling on that there were furrows in her brow and her eyes were squinting.

"If I asked you what you were working on, would you tell me? Or would you have to kill me if I found out?" he wondered aloud. Usually he was quiet when she was working, not wanting to distract her. But after a week spent mostly in this office, he was beyond restless and was about to do something reckless, like kiss her again.

Instead of being annoyed at the interruption, she laughed. "I don't think I could kill you."

"I'm not so sure about that," he murmured. Being so close to her and not touching her or tasting her was killing him slowly. Painfully.

"At least now that I don't have my gun," she said, and her brow furrowed again.

"Officer Carlson searched everyone's rooms. And my team searched everywhere else. It hasn't turned up," he said.

"I know."

"That's a good thing. It probably isn't in the house, and whoever broke in hasn't been able to get inside again."

During the past week, he'd talked to the other people in the house while his team had thoroughly checked them out for prior arrests or complaints, and nobody had raised any red flags. They had no records, and while they were clearly resentful of Priscilla, they didn't seem motivated enough to do more than make snarky comments about her. The Pell family didn't seem motivated enough to even leave the house, but then it wasn't as if any of them had jobs. So maybe inheriting more money in the event of her death would incite them to commit murder. But with all the cameras now, would they risk it?

None of them would survive a prison sentence. "And the security system is doing its job." It was keeping intruders out as well as keeping the people in the house on edge. They were all very aware of those cameras watching them. Of the Payne Protection Agency watching them.

She expelled a shaky breath. "That's good."

It was. It meant the estate was safe. She was safe. Or so it seemed. It was also possible that whoever had made that attempt was just waiting for a better opportunity to try again, like when Blade wasn't around, or when he was distracted. He could not afford to be distracted.

But hell, if he didn't get a break soon he was going to be more than distracted. He was going to be out of his mind. "So I think I'm going to have someone else take over for me today," he said.

She tensed, and her eyes widened. "What? Why?"

"I just..." He tried to think of a reason that wasn't the truth, that he was going to lay her down on that library table and make love to her if he didn't get some distance from her. And as he looked around, he glanced through the bars on the window to see snow falling outside. "I...uh...should do some holiday shopping."

He actually did want to buy something for his coworkers and for Josh's cute little kid and maybe even for Priscilla because he couldn't imagine anyone else in this house giving her a gift. Not that she couldn't buy herself anything she wanted, but she didn't seem like the type who would. She didn't seem to care anything about herself and only about this research and her late husband's book.

"Holiday shopping?" She echoed his words as if she didn't know what he was talking about.

"You know Christmas is just a few weeks away." Wasn't it? He'd been so busy before coming here, helping out with other assignments, that he must have missed Thanksgiving entirely.

"It is?" she asked. Then she flipped a page in a planner on the table and gasped. "I didn't realize it was so close." She looked around the room then, a panicked expression on her face. "I haven't even decorated yet. I really wanted to decorate this year."

"Why? It's not like anyone else in this house will appreciate your efforts for holiday cheer."

Her green eyes glistened as if she had tears in them. But then she blinked. "I just... I haven't been able to before, and I was really looking forward to it."

"Oh, I'm sorry," he said, his heart contracting with the look on her face. "Why haven't you been able to before?"

"My parents were older when they had me, and then they both got sick and didn't have the energy or the inclination to celebrate the holidays. They both died when I was still in college."

"Oh, I'm so sorry," he said, his heart aching for her. She really was as alone as she seemed. Even more alone than he was because at least he had his coworkers and bosses.

"Even if they hadn't been sick, I don't think they would have decorated. I can never remember having a tree or stockings or them ever taking me to see Santa when I was little." She touched her stomach as if she was sick just thinking about it.

He felt sick, too. "So weren't you even allowed to believe in Santa Claus as a kid?" he asked.

She shook her head. "Nope. My parents were very pragmatic and scientific. They wanted me to be the same. I always knew it was just a fairy tale. What about you?"

He sighed. "I think my mom made an effort one year, but I figured out pretty quick that the old man wasn't real, that there are few saints in this world."

"So why do you need to leave to get ready for this holiday you don't seem to really believe in either?" she asked.

He groaned. "I do intend to buy some gifts."

"But?" she asked as she arched a blond eyebrow over one of her beautiful green eyes.

"I just need some air," he admitted. "It's been a long week."

"I'm sorry."

"It's my job."

"But I've kept you in this office with me, with the bars on the window…" She shuddered. "I know how that feels to you. Let's get out of here." She clapped her hands together, her green eyes brightening. "Let's go Christmas shopping. We can get a tree and lights and decorations."

He groaned again. "This is a bad idea. You're safe here. But out there…"

"Despite the new security system, I'm not really safe here," she said. "We both know that."

Just that morning, at breakfast, more comments had been made. Bradley had said something about missing his dad but was sure that she wasn't. Sally had muttered something about the wrong Dr. Pell dying. And Kyle had snickered, acting more like their lapdog than their kid, not that he was a kid anymore. He was in his mid-twenties. Maybe he was their henchman. While he had no record, like the rest of them, could they make him do what they wanted? For that matter, any of them could snap. With the way that resentment and hatred of Priscilla was building inside them, they could forget about the cameras and act on those dark feelings. They could hurt her or worse.

"No, you're not safe here," he said. His presence was probably the only reason that there had not been another attempt on her life. "I'll let my team know that we're going out." And he would make sure that he had backup so that she was safe out there. Because he knew if they stayed in this room much longer, she would not be safe.

He was going to do something they would probably both regret. Or at least he would because he could not risk getting emotionally involved with her or with anyone. While he had just been defending that woman all those years ago, he couldn't help but wonder if he had reacted stronger and swung harder than he would have if he hadn't grown up the way he had. If he hadn't felt so helpless as a kid when all those men had mistreated his mother...

That night, when a man died, was the last time Blade had let his emotions get the better of him. He would not let that happen again.

Priscilla had felt like Blade must have the past week: imprisoned. And it hadn't been just the four walls of the den that had trapped her but also her desire for him. She wanted him so damn badly that her body literally ached for him. And every time she glanced at him, her pulse quickened and her temperature rose. She wanted him in a way she'd never wanted anyone before. But she knew he was determined to be professional.

And she'd vowed to be the same. He was an employee, after all. She didn't want to be like Everett, who had ironically accused Alexander of being inappropriate with her when she suspected that he was now doing the same with his teaching assistant. The girl obviously had a crush on him, and Everett was probably exploiting that to make her do what he wanted her to do, like spy on Priscilla. Why else would he have encouraged Monica to take the job as a research assistant at the Pell estate? Though Monica hadn't been doing much assisting or spying this past week. She'd been *sick* and had spent most of her time in her room.

The young woman was probably sick with fear that Blade's coworker would be able to recover the data from her cell phone. But so far, according to his last update, Nikki hadn't been able to work her usual magic and recover the lost images and text messages.

Priscilla glanced across the console between their seats in the front of the Payne Protection SUV that Blade drove, his big hands wrapped around the steering wheel. The vehicle was long and black with glass windows tinted so dark that she could barely see out them, much less anyone being able to see inside the SUV.

But that was the point, she supposed, for her to be safe in here. But with Blade sitting so close to her, she felt like she was in more danger than she might have ever been. He affected her in a way no one else had, and she didn't think she could keep blaming the hormones. But she could blame him.

For being so heroic and sexy.

He glanced into the rearview mirror, and his grip on the steering wheel eased slightly.

"We're not being followed?" she asked because she had wondered what the family would do when they'd noticed she'd left the estate. Change the locks to stop her from being able to get back inside?

She wouldn't put anything past them, even trying to kill her. But they were the only family Alexander had had, and she wanted to give them grace. Maybe she'd given them too much, though. And now that she was pregnant, her loyalty would have to go to the baby she carried.

The baby she needed to tell Blade about, so that he understood why she was so determined to keep the promises she'd made. She wanted her child to have a secure future and a happy one as well. That was why she'd wanted to decorate this year. While the child wasn't born yet, maybe on some level he would know that his mother had celebrated. He would hear the festive music and feel the ambiance of the season. Or maybe, selfishly, Priscilla just wanted to experience the holidays in a way she'd never been able to before.

"No, we are being followed," Blade said.

And she gasped. "Oh, what are you going to do?" She clasped the armrest, worried that he might start driving fast and erratically.

"Ivan is following us," Blade said. "And that's good. He's armed and will make sure that nothing happens to you."

Blade was making sure of that, too. He'd been like her shadow this week, which had been both unsettling and comforting. She'd felt safe but she'd also felt more frustrated than she'd ever been, to the point that she had considered propositioning him. But that would have been so unprofessional.

And inappropriate.

And somehow very hot as well.

He'd kissed her once, too, so he must feel some attraction to her. But since that day he barely looked at her; he just kept looking around her, as if checking to make sure that nobody was sneaking up to attack her again. So he was as focused on his job as he'd sworn to his friend that he would be. But then, even when he hadn't been a bodyguard, he'd risked everything to protect people. Like the woman whose abusive partner he'd accidentally killed and probably his own mom from her poor life choices. He'd lost his freedom because of one of those women. What would he lose if he got involved with Priscilla? His job? Or maybe even his life if the person who'd taken her gun decided to get him out of their way.

"What's the first stop on your Christmas list?" he asked.

She shrugged. "I have no idea. I've never done this before."

"You, the brilliant Dr. Pell who is working on a lifesaving drug, have no idea where to start Christmas shopping?" he said, his mouth curving into a sexy grin as he teased her.

Her pulse quickened, and she smiled. "Well, I guess I can figure this out. I know I need to buy a tree and decorations."

"Let's start with the tree, then," he said. "Buy off a lot or cut down ourselves? There's a Christmas tree farm not far from here, on the outskirts of the city."

"Uh..." She wouldn't have considered cutting one down herself. But he was so big and strong and the image of him physically cutting down a tree affected her, making her body tingle with appreciation for his strength. "Let's cut one down."

He glanced over at her jacket and fashionable boots. "Are you sure you'll be warm enough?"

Snowflakes drifted down outside those tinted windows, but most of them melted when they hit the ground. "It's not that cold out yet." While she hadn't celebrated the holidays before, she had observed the past few Christmases in Michigan had been green instead of white. Usually the cold front and the blizzards came in January now.

"Okay," he said.

"What about you?" she asked. He had a jacket, but it didn't look that heavy.

"I'll be fine," he said. "I can use the fresh air."

River City was bigger than Detroit but on the west side of Michigan close to Lake Michigan and its sand dunes as well as national forests. So it didn't take long to get out of the city and into the country. He steered into what looked like an open field surrounded by rows and rows of pine trees. But the open field was full of other parked vehicles and people milling around, some with trees already, some heading out to get trees. Once he parked, he stepped out of the SUV and drew in a deep breath.

Priscilla stepped out and did the same, breathing in the scent of pine needles mixed with the smell of roasting cinnamon-glazed almonds wafting from a small red barn that had a service window where people paid for the trees and apparently the almonds and other goodies they carried away. Cups with steam rising from them. Hot cocoa and hot cider that she could smell like the almonds.

Her stomach rumbled a bit at the aroma. Thankfully the morning sickness that had made her queasy had passed now. She was so hungry all the time but not just for food. She was hungry for Blade.

And that hunger only increased when he was so patient with her as she flitted around the farm trying to choose the perfect tree. When she finally settled on one, he tossed off his jacket and then swung the ax, slicing through the trunk in no time. And as he did, his biceps bulged against the tight sleeves of his light sweater. He was so muscular. But even he struggled a bit with the tree as he tried to hoist it up onto the roof of the SUV.

"This thing is a beast," he said.

"It needs to be tall, or it will be dwarfed in the foyer." Which was where she wanted it, near the staircase where everyone would see it. But she would probably be the only one who appreciated it. Maybe part of her held out hope that the Pells would change their minds about her, that they would become the family she didn't have, the family she wanted not just for herself but for her child, too. They'd accepted Alexander even though he hadn't been biologically related; they'd loved and respected him. Could they someday come to realize that she wasn't the gold digger they thought she was? Could they come to love and respect her?

"Hey, looks like you two need a hand," a deep voice remarked, and Ivan stepped forward then from where he'd been lingering close to them. He must have not wanted to make his presence known in case someone else was there, watching them. Had someone followed them from the house?

Occasionally an odd sensation had raced through Priscilla while they were walking around the farm, but she'd thought she'd just been self-conscious because Ivan was watching them. And she'd been worried that the other bodyguard would be able to see how attracted she was to his coworker.

But Ivan just smiled at her as he tried to help Blade hoist the tree up. She would have offered her assistance, too, if she wasn't worried about the baby she carried. She needed to tell Blade about her pregnancy and not just so he wouldn't think she was acting like a princess today. But she was worried that telling anyone would somehow jinx this pregnancy like the others had been, that she would lose this baby, too. And he was the last embryo.

Her last chance for the brilliant child Alexander had wanted to have to continue his work, his legacy. Bradley and Kyle had never been interested in biophysics or even in education at all, and they weren't his biological offspring.

That had mattered to Alexander. To have a piece of himself continue living whether or not they actually carried on his legacy. Because Priscilla had made it clear that she wouldn't force her child into academic pursuits. She wouldn't be the parent that her parents had been. She would be loving and nurturing.

She wanted this child because she had so much love to give and because she'd already given up so much for the greater good, to find ways to save lives. In some ways she felt like having a child would save her life or at least her sanity, like she would finally not feel as alone as she'd felt for so long.

"You need some rope to secure this thing," Ivan said, dropping his end of the tree onto the ground. "And maybe we can use it as a pulley to get this thing up there."

Blade glanced around them and nodded. "Can you grab it?" he asked.

Ivan headed off toward that small red barn, and Blade turned back to Priscilla. "Why don't you get inside the SUV?" he suggested.

She shook her head. "I'm not cold."

He clearly wasn't either since there was a trickle of sweat running down from his temple and a bead above his lip. She wanted to lick it away with her tongue. And she almost involuntarily leaned toward him.

But then an engine revved. She glanced around and noticed an old pickup truck heading toward them, exhaust billowing from behind it. And gripping the steering wheel with black gloves was a Santa Claus complete with the red hat and the white beard covering most of his face.

Blade cursed.

And the next thing she knew, her body was hurtling through the air.

***

The Christmas tree delivery truck had just been sitting there with the keys dangling from the ignition, presenting the perfect opportunity and the perfect weapon to take out both Priscilla and her bodyguard. It was so old that it didn't even have airbags in it to go off once the impact was made.

After hitting them with the truck, the killer drove off toward the field a ways down the street where the getaway vehicle was parked. The accelerator of the old truck was pressed to the worn floorboard because they had to act fast again. They had to get away before the police arrived or before that other bodyguard caught a glimpse of them.

But even if someone saw them, with the disguise that was worn, nobody should be able to identify them. Because of the holiday season, there were so many other people dressed like Santa Claus with the hat and the beard that there was no way anyone could figure out who they were.

And the killer would get away with murder once again…

Chapter 11

Blade had seen that truck idling a short distance from them with the Santa Claus gripping the steering wheel like a racecar driver waiting for the blast of the starter gun. And he'd reached for Priscilla just as it headed toward them. Then he'd hurtled them both as far as he could out of the path of that vehicle. The tree had taken the brunt of the impact, its branches breaking loose from the binding around it when the truck slammed into it. The tree rolled forward, pinning Blade and Priscilla between the SUV and its broken branches. Blade had kept his back between that truck and Priscilla. But she'd hit the ground hard and now she wasn't moving.

"Are you okay?" Blade anxiously asked her. "Priscilla?" He touched her cheek, which bore a little scratch from one of the tree branches that had made it around him. He could feel blood trickling down from his head where a branch had scratched him. Or maybe the bumper of the truck. He was so worried about her, though, that he couldn't feel anything himself.

"Oh my God!" Ivan shouted, and suddenly the tree was jerked away from Blade. "Are you two alright? I called 9-1-1. They're sending an officer and an ambulance."

That was good because Blade was worried that Priscilla

needed one. She was so still, but her eyes were open. She hadn't lost consciousness. That was good. Unless she was in such pain that she'd gone into shock.

"How far out are they?" Blade asked.

"Twenty minutes or so."

"Priscilla, can you wait? Or do you want me to drive you to the hospital?" He cupped her cheek and turned her face until her wide-eyed gaze finally met his. "Priscilla, how badly are you hurt?"

And why the hell had he thought this was a good idea, that even with Ivan as backup that she would be safe?

Obviously this person had just been waiting for the first opportunity to try for her again. So was it someone not inside her household?

Or had someone followed them from the estate to the Christmas tree farm? Was it still a member of her so-called family or maybe even her resentful assistant who wanted her dead?

And how close had they come to succeeding?

How badly was she hurt?

Priscilla had no idea. She'd just known that sensation of hurtling through the air, and then she'd landed. Hard. Half on Blade's body and half on the ground. While he'd kept his arms around her, protecting her as best he could from the truck, branches from the tree had poked her face and her shoulder. And her back had pressed against the SUV behind them. Now she knew what it really felt like to be trapped. Because she had been in those long moments.

She was out of that situation now, away from the Christmas tree farm and even away from Blade, although she suspected he was hovering somewhere close while she was being examined in the curtained-off bay of River City Memorial Hospital's emergency department.

She held her breath, waiting for the ER resident to speak. The dark-haired young woman stood over her, running a wand over the gel on her exposed stomach.

"Is the baby alright?" She couldn't hear anything. Like those times before when she'd listened for a heartbeat that had never sounded.

Then...

Thump. Thump. Thump.

Tears sprang to Priscilla's eyes, and she turned and blinked to clear her vision and focus on the monitor and the little pea-sized collection of cells that was her child. Her child with a beating heart.

"I would estimate that you're ten weeks along, Mama," the doctor said. "And the baby looks healthy."

She expelled a shaky breath. "The accident didn't harm him?"

"Not at all. While you're going to have a bruise on your shoulder and your hip, you're fine, too," the doctor said. "And I assume you're taking prenatal vitamins and getting enough rest?"

Priscilla nodded, but she was really only taking the vitamins. She was definitely not getting enough rest, not with her erotic dreams about her bodyguard keeping her awake most nights.

"Should we let Daddy back to hear the good news?" the doctor asked. "He's pacing outside the curtain."

"He's not..." She swallowed down the emotion rushing up to choke her and shook her head. "He's not the father."

"Oh, I'm sorry," the doctor said, her face flushing. "I just assumed."

"The father passed away," Priscilla said. "Blade is just..."

Her bodyguard. It didn't seem like the right word to describe him. But that was really all he was, and he proved it when he saved her life over and over again.

The doctor cleared her throat. "Uh, he's here…"

Priscilla tore her gaze away from that monitor to see that Blade had pushed aside the curtain and ducked into the ER bay with her, the doctor, the gurney and that portable ultrasound machine. He stared at the screen as raptly as she'd been staring at it.

"You're pregnant?" Blade asked.

Priscilla nodded.

"Ten weeks?"

She nodded again. And she knew he had questions, that he would wonder how that was possible at all when she'd already said her relationship with her late husband had only been platonic. But then, ten weeks ago, Alexander Pell had already been dead for a few months.

She turned to the doctor then. "You said everything's fine with the baby and with me, so that means that I can leave?"

The doctor nodded. "Yes…" She glanced from her to Blade. And then she swallowed hard, as if she was afraid of the muscular man with his tattoos and his scars. "As long as you're comfortable doing that…"

Priscilla felt safe with her bodyguard. She knew he wouldn't physically hurt her, but she was beginning to wonder if he could hurt her another way. Emotionally.

Like her parents had always warned her, emotions were messy, and to them, they were totally unnecessary. All that had mattered to them was science, and they'd thought that was all that should matter to their daughter. They'd had her late in their lives because they'd been getting scared of their own mortality and they'd wanted someone to carry on their legacy. That had been Alexander's motivation, too, for having a biological child. To carry on his legacy.

Priscilla had agreed because she'd wanted someone to love, and maybe more than that, she'd wanted someone who would love her unconditionally. She didn't have to be the perfect daughter or student or wife for her baby. She didn't even have to be the perfect mother; she just had to do her best to love and protect her child and to provide for him. And she had to make sure that his future was secure.

"As long as the baby is in no danger this time, I'm ready to be released," Priscilla said.

"This time?" The doctor glanced from her to Blade again. "What's happened before today's accident?"

"I... I miscarried every other in vitro transfer," Priscilla admitted. "So I'm concerned that it will happen this time." And she would have no more options to conceive the child she'd promised her late husband. She'd also promised herself this baby, too, as someone to love and to love her. And she already loved this baby, as she had the others, so much. To lose him would hurt more than any physical pain.

"I would follow up with your fertility specialist," the ER resident replied. "Just to make sure. But you heard the heartbeat. It's strong. And from the ultrasound, everything looks to be developing correctly."

Priscilla released a shaky sigh.

"But you do need to get rest and take it easy," the doctor advised. "No more close scrapes like today." She glanced at Blade again.

He nodded. "There won't be," he said. "I will keep her safe." But he was looking at that screen with the image of the baby on it and that flicker of that beating heart. He swallowed hard then. "I will keep *them* safe."

She should have been relieved that he wasn't quitting

after that close call and after finding out that she hadn't been totally open and honest with him. But instead of being relieved, she was worried. About the baby. About him and about her heart. Because she was so afraid that something might happen to all of them.

Officer Carlson had techs checking out the crime scene at the Christmas tree farm. They were processing the truck they'd found for any prints or DNA, and they were checking for surveillance footage. The farm didn't have any cameras, though, so there probably wouldn't be any images to recover. Instead she was here at the hospital, pacing the waiting room until she could take a report from Priscilla Pell and her bodyguard. She wasn't the only one waiting for news on their conditions. While Ivan Chekov was back at the scene with the techs and Chief Woodrow Lynch, Milek Kozminski was here, and unfortunately so was Viktor Lagransky.

Of all the bodyguards, he bothered her the most because he thought he was so damn cute. And, unfortunately, he was with his sandy brown hair and green eyes.

But it was his surname that bothered her the most, nearly as much as Ivan's last name bothered her. His father had not been a good man, just as Ivan's paternal uncle wasn't. Until his arrest a few years ago, Ivan's uncle had been the godfather of River City, and Viktor's father had been his right-hand man. The person who'd carried out so much of the godfather's reign of terror and murder. Lagransky had died before he could be sentenced with his boss, but the things he'd done had affected so many people.

While she didn't have proof, yet, she believed he was responsible for a tragedy in her own life. A loss that would always affect her.

And drive her.

Viktor Lagransky's father had been a soulless assassin, so what did that make Viktor? Had he turned his life around like the others claimed they had, or was he just as evil as his hit man father had been?

Instead of avoiding him, like she usually tried, she walked up to him and remarked, "This kind of feels like a professional hit, doesn't it?"

He tensed, and the grin that was usually on his handsome face slipped a bit. "What?"

"The way the perp followed them and then waited for an opportunity to use another vehicle and try to kill them," she said. "And how he got away so easily like a week ago at the mansion." She tilted her head and studied his face. "Feels like a professional job."

Viktor's green eyes narrowed, but he snorted. "Professional? No. If it was a professional job, unfortunately Dr. Pell would already be dead and today Blade would have died, too."

Now she tensed. "What are you saying?"

"Just making observations like you are, Officer Carlson," he replied. "And as you're trying subtly to insinuate, I know professional hits when I see them, and neither of these sloppy attempts on Dr. Pell's life was that. Nope. This is pure amateur. You should recognize that."

She sucked in a breath like he'd slapped her. She tried so hard to be the best at her job, to honor the person who was the reason she'd joined the police department. "Are you calling me an amateur?"

He shrugged his massive shoulders. "Just saying that you're wrong about this just as you're wrong about the Payne Protection Agency."

"I don't have a problem with the other Payne Protection Agency branches," she said. "Just yours…"

"The one with the misfit toys," he finished for her.

But they weren't toys, disfigured or otherwise. They were dangerous men. And maybe this one was most dangerous of all. But then the widow and her bodyguard stepped out into the waiting room and Sheila remembered what Blade Sparks had done. He had killed.

And sure, he'd completed his sentence just as the other ones had for whatever offenses they'd committed. But Blade Sparks's crime had been the most serious. Or at least the others hadn't been caught doing anything more serious than the thefts that had sent them to prison or juvenile detention.

But Sheila didn't trust any of them, especially not Viktor Lagransky. That was why she made sure to take the calls that involved them. She wanted to see what they were up to; she wanted to catch them this time before anyone else got hurt. Or killed. Because every time they were assigned to protect someone, that person nearly died. Eventually someone would.

Chapter 12

Blade felt like he'd been hit by a truck literally and figuratively. As stunned as he was, he'd barely been able to answer Officer Carlson's questions about the attempt on their lives. No, he wasn't able to identify the driver. The person had obviously been wearing a disguise with the Santa hat, white beard and wig. Officer Carlson had admitted that the usual delivery driver had left those items in the running truck because that was how he dressed when making deliveries. They weren't there now. Whoever had tried running them down had taken the disguise with them, probably to make sure no DNA was recovered from it.

She'd promised to do all she could to find the driver, but Blade wasn't going to hold his breath. While he trusted that the young officer would do her best, he didn't think she would find the person in time to stop them from making another attempt on Priscilla's life.

And maybe on his, too.

So he had to be ready, more ready than he'd been at the Christmas tree farm. The entire drive from the hospital to the Pell Mansion, he was on edge and tense. And while he breathed a little easier once the gates closed behind the Payne Protection SUV, he was still tense and on edge.

And a little angry.

And he did not like to be angry. It made him feel as if he wasn't in control of his emotions. So he fought for that control by keeping silent until they were inside the house.

Then he still didn't trust himself to speak to Priscilla. While he showed her to her door to make sure her room was unoccupied and safe, he just left her there to rest. Then he rounded up the rest of the residents and staff and questioned them.

At first they denied leaving the house until he reminded them that all he had to do was check the security footage from the many cameras to confirm their stories. Then every single damn one of them admitted to leaving the house after he did. He jotted down their alibis with the intent of forwarding them to the rest of the team to investigate.

Since Detective Dubridge hadn't been called back yet from his family leave, the attempts on Priscilla's life didn't seem as much of a priority to the police department as they did to the Payne Protection Agency. As they did to Blade, especially. And now, knowing that she was pregnant, he was even more concerned.

About her. About the baby. He had so many questions about the baby. He'd heard and understood what she meant: that she'd become pregnant through IVF. Why? Had she loved her husband so much that she wanted a part of him to live on? While she'd claimed theirs wasn't a real marriage, she had obviously loved and respected Dr. Alexander Pell.

Blade was still edgy when he headed back upstairs from the dining room, where he'd questioned the others. Once the security and lock had been upgraded in the den, Priscilla had upgraded his sleeping quarters to a bedroom across the hall from hers, so that if anyone tried breaking into her suite again, he would know. Hell, he'd know if anyone even walked down the hall on this side of the stairwell because

Priscilla's suite and his and the empty main suite were the only rooms in this wing of the mansion.

Because he hadn't considered that he might be in danger, he never locked his door, so he just turned the knob and pushed it open. But his room wasn't empty. Priscilla, still in her torn red jacket and jeans, sat on the foot of his bed, her shoulders slumped with exhaustion.

"What are you doing in here?" he asked. He'd checked out her room to make sure that it was safe, not his. "You were supposed to be in your suite with the door locked."

"I can tell that you're mad at me."

He tensed. "I'm not mad at you."

"Yes, you are."

He shook his head and sighed. "I'm mad, but not at you. I'm mad at whoever is trying to kill you. And I'm mad at myself for not doing a better job of protecting you."

"I'm alive," she said. "So I think you're doing a pretty damn good job."

He shook his head again. "I shouldn't have taken you out of this house. It was too dangerous."

"We were both feeling trapped and restless," she said. "We needed to get out of the house. And we will need to venture out again. I can't stop living my life, though sometimes it feels like I have."

"Are you really okay?" he asked, and now he was concerned not just about her physical safety but also about her emotional well-being.

She sighed and nodded. "You heard the doctor say that I'm fine. The baby and I are both fine." She released a breath then in a shuddery sigh.

And he sucked in a breath as the knowledge jabbed him again. She was pregnant.

"You're mad that I didn't tell you."

He shook his head. "My job is to protect the house and to protect you. Would it have helped to know about the pregnancy? Maybe, if it goes to motive—"

"Nobody else knows that I'm pregnant," she said. "And I wanted to keep it that way in case having a smaller share of the estate would make one of the Pell family do something to the baby."

"Ah, so it will affect the estate."

"But like I said, nobody else knows about the baby. And I really want to keep it that way."

He understood why if it would cause someone else to try even harder to hurt her. But he was glad that he knew because now he would be even more careful with her when keeping her safe. To think of how she'd nearly fallen down the steps and then how he'd shoved her out of the way of the truck had him flinching. He would be more careful with her, but he would also keep her secret. "That's your personal business, Dr. Pell."

"So now you're going to stop using my first name?"

He nodded. "I need to keep things professional between us." He had even more of a reason to stay focused now, to make sure that she and the baby both stayed safe.

"Why?"

"Because someone's trying to kill you, and it's my job to make sure that doesn't happen," he said.

"So if you call me by my first name, someone's going to be able to push me down the stairs the next time they try, or they'll be able to run me down with a truck and actually kill me?" she asked, her mouth curved into a maddening smile as if she was mocking him.

His mouth twitched because he was tempted to smile back at her. But he just shrugged. "I don't know. But I can't be distracted."

"What's changed?" she asked. "Why are you so upset about my pregnancy?"

"I'm not upset," he said. "I was just surprised."

"I don't know how much you overheard the doctor saying…"

"I'm sorry about that," he said. "I should have respected your privacy for medical treatment." But he'd been so damn worried about her. Too worried. And that had been before he'd found out she was pregnant.

"You are mad that I didn't tell you about the baby," she said. And she touched her stomach again.

He shook his head. "Like I said, it's not really my business. I'm just your bodyguard. But as your bodyguard, it is good that I know now, so that I can make sure we don't take any unnecessary chances again."

"It was necessary for us to get out of this house for a while," she said. "And I do want to decorate for the holidays."

"Hire someone to do it," he suggested. "Or have Monica take care of it. She is your assistant, after all, even though she doesn't do very much for you."

"Not since you arrived," Priscilla said. "I think you make her nervous."

"Because she's afraid I'm going to figure out that she's the one trying to hurt you?"

"Why would she?" Priscilla asked. "If I'm dead, I won't need an assistant anymore."

Blade sucked in a breath at the horrible thought of her dying. A world without her in it just seemed so much darker and hopeless, and not just because of how hard she was working to improve and save the lives of others but because of how she made him feel. Seeing her filled him with warmth and respect and desire. How had she come to mean so much to him in the week that he'd been working for her?

She smiled again as if she was still teasing him and asked, "Did you realize that I won't need a bodyguard anymore either if I'm dead?"

"I realized that I don't want anything happening to you, or to your baby."

Despite how hard he'd fought to stay professional and detached, she had become so much more than just an assignment to him. And that scared him more than anything else in his life ever had. Even prison.

Blade had been so quiet ever since he'd found out that she was pregnant that Priscilla hadn't been able to figure out what was wrong. Was he mad at her?

Was he upset that she hadn't told him she was having a baby? He'd already said that he wasn't going to get involved with her, so she wasn't sure why it would matter to him that she was going to be a mom. Unless he'd changed his mind, unless he was more involved than he'd intended to be.

She wanted to know what the problem was. That was why, after he'd left her in her suite earlier, she'd gone over to his room instead. She didn't like this tension between them, and she really wanted it gone.

She really wanted *him*.

But he stood near the door, as if he was about to leave his own room to get away from her. And long minutes had passed since either of them had spoken.

She released a shaky breath that she hadn't realized she'd been holding. "Don't feel bad that I didn't tell you about the baby. I haven't told anyone. And that's not just because of being worried about how they would react." Although she had been worried about that. "I guess I felt like I would jinx the pregnancy if I admitted it aloud. I've lost so many babies."

"You don't have to explain," he said.

"My parents always said superstitions were ignorant, so I shouldn't have been worried about jinxing it if I said anything. But this was my last chance, the last embryo that Dr. Pell—Alexander and I had frozen."

He pushed a big hand through his dark hair, tousling the thick locks, and his forehead scrunched up. "I don't understand," he admitted. "You said that the two of you only had a platonic relationship."

She nodded. "That's not what anyone else believes, especially my ex, but it's true."

"Then why the marriage? Why the baby?" Blade asked. Then he shook his head. "Never mind. It's none of my business."

"You've risked your life for mine," she said. "It is your business, especially if someone is trying to kill me because of my relationship with Alexander or because they somehow found out about the baby."

Blade drew in a deep breath, as if bracing himself, and then asked, "I know Dr. Pell wanted you to inherit control of the estate so that you could continue with his work, but the baby? I don't understand why he would want you to have his baby."

"You don't?" she asked. "He wasn't thrilled with any of his family. And they're his stepfamily, not his biological family. His late wife had been married before she married him, and he eventually adopted her son. But he wanted a biological heir. He wanted someone to continue his legacy."

"You're doing that," Blade said.

She nodded. "But he also wanted to know if his DNA and mine would create another genius, like he was." She was as well according to her IQ, but sometimes worried that she wasn't as smart as she thought or that she needed to be. She hadn't always made the best decisions.

Blade sucked in a breath. "So this kid is just an experiment?"

She placed both hands over her stomach. "Not to me. I agreed because I want a baby. I want to be a mother." While her work was important, vitally important, it wasn't enough. She wanted more. She wanted family.

"And what if the kid doesn't want to go into research or medicine or whatever it is you're doing? What if she or he—"

"He," she interjected.

"What if he wants to be a truck driver or an electrician or a boxer?" he asked. "Will you let him?"

She nodded. "I know better than anyone what it's like to get pushed into a career in academia. My parents sent me off to boarding schools and college when I was very young. They wanted me to focus only on my education."

"That's why you never celebrated holidays."

She nodded again. "Or much of a childhood at all. I'll make sure that doesn't happen with my son. I'll make sure his life is more well-rounded."

"Is that a promise your husband asked you to keep?"

She shook her head. "No. That's a promise I made to myself and to this baby. I don't want him to grow up like I did. That's another reason I wanted to become a mother while I was still young. I didn't want my child to have to take care of me someday or lose me too soon. But now I have to make sure that nothing happens to him."

Blade stepped away from the door then but not before locking it behind him, like he was worried about someone trying to get inside while they talked. "That's my job.

To make sure that nothing happens to either of you. I was taken by surprise when I found out that I actually have two subjects to protect now."

"Are you up for the job, Sparks?" she asked.

His mouth curved into a slight grin. "I just need to stay focused." But even as he said it, his gaze slipped from her eyes to her mouth. "Which is a little hard with you sitting on my bed."

"What's hard?" she asked.

He chuckled. "Dr. Pell, are you being crude? I thought you grew up so sheltered."

"I did," she said. "But once I got out in the world, I didn't really understand what all the fuss was about…"

"What fuss?" he asked, his forehead furrowing slightly. "What are you talking about?"

"Sex. I understand the mechanics, and the dopamine rush and all that but…" She shrugged. "I never cared that much about it."

His nostrils flared. "Why are we talking about this?"

"Because I want to have sex with you."

His head snapped back like she'd punched him. "I don't think this is a good idea, Priscilla."

"At least you didn't call me Dr. Pell again," she said with a smile. "And I think it's a great idea."

He shook his head, but his jaw was taut, like he was clenching his teeth.

"I know you think it's a distraction," she said. "But maybe it's only a distraction because we haven't done it. And we keep thinking about it. At least I do. I think I was dreaming about you before I even met you. Maybe it's the pregnancy hormones or maybe…" It was just him.

"Hormones?" He repeated the word and chuckled. "It's certainly that."

"So let's just do it," she suggested. "That way we can stop thinking about it. We can get it out of the way, this attraction and tension, and we'll be able to think more clearly about everything." She needed to think clearly, so that she could finish the work she'd promised Alexander and herself that she would complete.

"You want to use me to help with your research?" he asked.

"I don't intend to put it in the book," she assured him. "I just need to be able to focus again, and I can't do that when I can't stop thinking about you kissing me and touching me."

He groaned. "Priscilla..."

"And you might be able to focus more, too, afterward and you'll be able to figure out who's trying to kill me."

He chuckled then. "I have been trying to figure it out," he said. "My team checked out everybody living in this house."

"And you still haven't figured out yet who's after me," she said. "But maybe it will become clearer if our minds are clearer."

"So sex will solve all our problems?"

She nodded.

"I thought you never cared that much about it," he reminded her.

"I didn't," she said. "That's why I can't figure out why it's all that's on my mind lately. Must be the hormones."

"And you think that if we have sex, that you won't think about it anymore?"

She nodded. "I'll get it out of my system. I'll be able to focus again and get my projects done." She touched her stomach. "Then I'll be able to focus only on my pregnancy after that."

He stared at her for a long moment, his blue eyes narrowed. "You really believe that's what will happen?"

She felt a little jab to her heart, like a warning that she might be wrong. Or maybe she was just getting nervous over how bold she was being. But she'd learned long ago that she didn't get what she wanted unless she worked hard for it. So she nodded. "Yes."

He grinned. "Then, okay."

"What?" she asked with surprise. "You'll do it?"

"You're beautiful, Priscilla," he said. "I haven't been able to forget that kiss either. Did you think I would keep refusing you?"

"I... I...uh, you kept saying that you didn't want to be distracted."

"And I don't," he said. "But I am distracted. That's why I wanted to get out of this house and get some fresh air. But that didn't go as I planned either. Life has a way of doing that, of not going how we planned."

She blew out a ragged breath. "Don't I know it..."

"Were you counting on me refusing you?" he asked. "You didn't think I would call your bluff?"

"You think I'm bluffing?"

He nodded. "I don't think that you're really all that interested in me."

"I kissed you first," she reminded him.

"And then you wanted me to forget about it," he reminded her. "So I'll walk you back to your room if you'd rather forget this conversation ever happened, too."

"I can't forget the kiss," she said. "And I can't get this out of my mind. I want to have sex with you."

"Then take off your clothes," he said as if challenging her. As if he didn't believe she would follow through. He didn't know her that well.

And she was fine with that. She wanted him too badly to care about embarrassment or anything else at the moment. She shrugged her coat off and then pulled up her sweater. When she dragged it over her head and dropped it onto the floor, he groaned again like she'd punched him.

He was staring at her breasts that overflowed the cups of her lace bra. Her breasts had gotten fuller with her pregnancy. Her skin was glowing, too, from the hormones and prenatal vitamins.

She didn't care what she looked like, though; she wanted to see him. "Your turn to take off your shirt," she said.

And he dragged his sweater over his head, revealing rippling washboard abs and his muscular chest and arms. The rope tattoo that wound around his neck connected to boxing gloves, one on each pectoral muscle.

Her breath hitched, and her heart seemed to skip a beat. He was so damn sexy. "You're even better than in my dreams," she murmured.

"You've really been dreaming about me?" he asked as if he couldn't believe it.

Did he not know how sexy he was? Still sitting on the bed, she reached out for him, hooking her index finger in the waistband of his jeans that hung low on his lean hips. His erection strained against the fly. "Yes, I've been dreaming about you even before I met you." And she unbuttoned his fly. Before she could pull down the zipper, he jerked back and then he dropped to his knees in front of her.

"I wasn't dreaming about you before I met you," he said. "Mostly because I thought you would be old enough to be my mother or grandmother."

She chuckled. "The old widow whose trinkets you were hired to protect," she said, repeating what Ivan had said to him a week ago. The new security system, with its many cameras and sensors, was protecting all the artwork and safes.

"I definitely want to take care of your...trinkets...and everything else," he said. And then, kneeling at the foot of the bed where she sat, he finished undressing her. As he removed each piece of clothing, he kissed the skin he exposed. Both breasts, his tongue swiping across each nipple. Then he licked his way down over the soft swell of her stomach to the mound between her legs. And he touched her there with his fingers and his tongue.

And she fell back on the bed, a cry slipping out of her lips as she came. She'd needed this release for so long. She'd needed him.

But he wasn't done. He continued to make love to her with his mouth and his hands until she came again. Tears streaked from the corner of her eyes to the blanket beneath her as the passion and the pleasure overwhelmed her. Then he was on the bed beside her, his arms wrapping around her, holding her. "Are you alright?" he asked.

No. She'd had no idea how good sex could be until now. And he hadn't even taken off his jeans yet. She reached for his zipper again, anxious to bring him the same release he'd brought her. But he caught her hand.

"Are you sure this is okay?" he asked.

"What do you mean?"

"I'm...um... I'm a big guy," he said, his voice gruff. "I don't want to hurt the baby."

She smiled. "You won't hurt the baby."

But she understood his concern when he removed his jeans and boxers and she saw just how big he was. She didn't care, though. She wanted him inside her, filling the hollowness she'd felt for so long, which was the reason she'd wanted a baby but maybe that reason was as selfish a one for bringing a child into the world as Dr. Pell's had been. But she would make it up to her son. She would love him so much and make his life so happy.

But right now she wanted a little happiness for herself. She wanted a little pleasure for herself. She pushed her bodyguard onto his back and straddled him, then guided him inside. She couldn't take all of him, but she arched her back and took as much as she could. And as she rode him, he cupped her breasts and brushed his thumbs across her nipples.

And that tension built inside her again. He thrust as she moved, and they found a rhythm like a dance. Then her body quivered as the tension broke, and a powerful orgasm moved through her. She nearly screamed at the pleasure exploding inside her. Then he tensed and groaned as he filled her with his release.

She dropped onto his chest, which was heaving as he panted for breath like she was panting. "That was even better than in my dreams," she murmured. He was even better.

And now she was worried that once wouldn't be enough to make her focus again. That, after making love with him, she might never be able to focus on anything but him.

Garek glanced up from his desk when Nikki Payne-Ecklund tapped on his open door. "Hey," he greeted her. She was his sister's sister-in-law, but she felt like his sister, too. Including Nikki, he had three of them now. One of them he'd just recently met and hired. "How are you?"

She sighed. "Frustrated." She dropped an evidence bag with a cell phone in it onto his desk.

"You weren't able to get anything off Dr. Pell's assistant's phone?"

She shook her head, and her copper-colored curls bounced.

"She really did a number on it."

"It's a burner," Nikki said. "Must have been a spare. There was nothing to get off it. It hadn't been used."

"So she gave Blade a dummy phone."

"She's smart," Nikki said. "And she probably has something on the real one that she didn't want him to see."

Garek groaned. "Damn. I was hoping you'd find something. There was another attempt on Dr. Pell's life today."

"Is she okay?"

He nodded. "But it was a close call. She's in danger."

"Does she have any idea who's out to get her?"

"There's a list of suspects, although none of them have ever done anything like this before," he said.

"Doesn't mean they haven't done it," she said, "just that they haven't gotten caught."

"Well, we're going to catch them. We're currently checking the alibis Blade got from them, seeing if we can place someone at the scene."

"Blade's good," Nikki said.

"Yes."

"But you're still worried about him."

His stomach was knotted. "Yeah, I have a bad feeling that something's going to happen to him."

"Uh-oh, Mom's sixth sense brushing off on you?" she teased.

"I don't know if it's that or just common sense. Someone wants to kill the widow. They're going to have to get rid of Blade first, or they're not going to be able to get to her."

Blade would die protecting her.

Chapter 13

A couple of days had passed since the fiasco at the Christmas tree farm. Leaving the estate had been the first mistake he'd made that day. Making love with Priscilla that night had been the second. She'd claimed that acting on the attraction between them would make them less distracted because they would get rid of the tension and would stop thinking about having sex.

But he couldn't stop thinking about it. He couldn't stop wanting her. And he knew that was another mistake.

There could never be anything but sex between them. He had no idea about her work, about all those equations and formulas she was working on in the den. He'd stepped away from it for a minute, leaving her alone with her assistant.

Monica had recovered from her mysterious illness; maybe because there had been nothing on that cell phone she'd given him for Nikki to find. And when she and Priscilla talked, it was like he was listening to another language. He felt stupid again like he had as a kid who'd missed more school than he'd been able to attend because of his mom's instability.

While he'd taken every class available to him in prison, he hadn't learned enough to be able to understand what Priscilla was talking about or working on.

Medications, she'd said. Some for cancer. Some for dementia. While he could save a life or two as a bodyguard, she would be able to save millions. She was incredible. So brilliant and beautiful. She could have anyone she wanted.

Why did she want him?

She'd come back to his room after that first night. But maybe it was just as she'd said: hormones. That was the only reason she wanted him.

And it seemed to be working for her. After they made love, she slept in his arms while he lay awake, worrying that he was in too deep and too distracted. And during the day, she worked in the den on her research and the book. She'd even managed to order the delivery of a Christmas tree and decorations. He'd helped set up the tree in the foyer. But he was leaving the outside lights for Fritz, the gardener.

Blade didn't want to be too far away from Priscilla because he had a feeling that the person who wanted to kill her was just waiting for a chance to catch her alone and somewhere that didn't have cameras. If they were already a member of this household, that might be relatively easy for them if they could catch her where there were no cameras, like inside her bedroom. But she was spending every night in his bed. So maybe he hadn't made a mistake in crossing the line from professional to personal with her. Maybe the mistake was that he was beginning to fall for her even though he knew they had no future together.

But he wanted to make sure she had a future not only because she was such a good person but also because she could do so much good for other people, especially the baby she was carrying.

So he sat on the bottom step of the staircase with his cell pressed to his ear. "What did you find out?" he asked when Garek answered.

"About?"

"The alibis," he said. "Were you able to confirm all of them?"

"Nope."

"So there's one person who wasn't where they said they were?"

"We can't confirm that any of them were where they said they were," Garek said. "Nikki and her IT team are pulling footage from traffic cams and stuff in the areas they claimed to be, but they haven't found any evidence that they were where they said they were."

Frustration escaped Blade in a groan. "So she's not safe with any of them?"

And he'd just left her alone with her assistant. But there was a panic button inside the room that Priscilla could push if she was in danger. There was also a camera right outside the door.

"No," Garek replied. "I would say the only person she's safe with in that house is you."

But Blade wasn't sure about that. Despite her claim that having sex would remove their distractions, he was distracted. And tired and scared.

He was scared for her safety. And he was scared for his heart.

Priscilla was supposed to be working on the formulas and on the book, on finishing everything up, as she'd promised her late husband. But Dr. Pell's work wasn't as complete as she'd thought and definitely not as complete as Alexander had thought. She had to keep adjusting the equations and compounds. Or maybe she had to keep doing that because she was distracted. Despite assuring Blade that having sex would remove their distractions, she'd been wrong. She couldn't stop thinking about him even when he was right in the room with her. But he'd slipped out a little while ago.

And Monica had taken a break shortly after he left.

But even though she was alone now, she still couldn't focus. That was *his* fault. Blade's. Even after making love with him, she wanted him. He was so generous and protective and not just as her bodyguard but as her lover, too.

He had given up his freedom to save a woman's life, and he'd already saved Priscilla's life twice. He'd done more than protect her, though. He'd given her pleasure she'd never known existed.

She shook her head, trying to knock the images of making love with him out of her mind. But he wasn't just imprinted in her mind; he was in her body, too. She could feel him filling her, filling that hollowness inside her that she'd had for so long. Most of her life she'd been lonely even when her parents were alive and even when she'd been in prior relationships. There had always been something missing. She'd thought it was her fault that she couldn't feel more; that she couldn't feel complete. But she did with Blade.

But right now she felt that hollow ache again, and it wasn't as if Blade wasn't taking care of her every night, giving her more pleasure than she'd even known was possible. But it had been a long, frustrating day with the formulas and with missing Blade even though he'd only stepped out a short while ago.

Maybe he'd needed some fresh air. She understood that need; the bars on the windows of the office were confining her, imprisoning her. Through the bars she could see snowflakes drifting down, sparkling in the faint glow of the setting sun. Lights twinkled around the bushes and some of the trees in the backyard.

And she caught a glimpse of a burly shadow moving around just beyond the patio. Blade? Was he stringing the lights out in the garden? He'd helped set up and decorate the Christmas tree, but she'd been in the foyer with him when he'd done it.

He really hadn't let her out of his sight since the incident at the Christmas tree farm. So she wondered now where he was and if that was him outside. Maybe he hadn't just needed air but also some space from her.

She should have respected that, but instead she found herself slipping out of the den. However, she paused to lock the door. She didn't trust that Monica or someone else wasn't hovering close with the hope that she might leave the den unsecured.

But as she glanced around the hall, she didn't see anyone else. Maybe they were all outside, or they were just so aware of the cameras, like the one pointed directly at the den, that they knew to stay away from any area where they were, which was pretty much every area.

Instead of heading toward the foyer, she cut down the hall the other way and took a shortcut through the dining room. When she opened the French doors, a gust of wind blew snow onto the hardwood floor and into her hair. She should have grabbed a coat. But her red sweater was heavy enough that she shouldn't get too cold if she was only outside for a minute or two.

"Hello?" she called out as she pulled the French doors closed behind herself. She didn't want the snow to damage the floors. "Blade?"

She walked across the brick patio to peer off into the yard where she'd noticed that shadow moments ago. "Blade?"

There were tracks in the snow. Big tracks. A man was out here somewhere. But maybe it was Fritz and not her bodyguard lover.

Lover.

Just the word had her pulse quickening and heat streaking through her. Apparently she didn't need a coat to keep her warm. All she had to do was think about Blade.

Her lover.

Maybe sex had never been a big deal to her before because she'd never been with anyone as good at it, as thorough and generous and gentle as Blade. He always made sure she came, though it didn't take her long. Just thinking about him, about his kisses and his touch, made her nipples tingle and her core pulsate with desire.

"Blade?" she called out again, a little desperately. What had happened to her? Why couldn't she get enough of him? She wanted to blame her pregnancy hormones, but she was beginning to worry that it was something more, that it wasn't just her body that yearned for him but her heart as well. "Blade, are you out here?"

Then she noticed that shadow again just outside the light from the patio. The sun had dropped so quickly or maybe the snow was falling so hard that the sky was dark now. She stepped off the patio onto the snow-covered grass. Her feet sank into the snow, and she could see the other tracks in it, too. She followed them toward the fountain, then stopped and looked around.

Where was he?

Or whoever the hell was out here? Because now it occurred to her that it might not be Blade at all.

This far from the house, the wind was harsher, hurtling snow at her as it began to blow and drift around her. And if there were cameras out here, that snow would probably be all that anyone would see on the monitors. Not people. Not her. Not the person she'd come out here to find.

She shivered and started back across the yard. But she made it only a few steps before something passed in front of her face. Instinctively she reached up for it and wrapped her fingers around the electrical cord of a string of lights. "What the..." The cord snapped tight around her throat and fingers, digging into her skin, cutting off her breath.

That shadow she'd glimpsed hadn't been Blade. It was whoever wanted her dead. And now they were using this string of lights to strangle her.

She had to fight for her life and for her unborn baby's life.

This was how the killer had imagined it would feel to take her life. While she writhed and twisted and tried to fight, the killer just pulled that strand of lights tighter around her throat.

Eventually she would have to stop fighting her inevitable fate.

Then she would stop breathing.

And stop living...

She would die how she deserved to die, cold and alone.

Chapter 14

Knowing that anybody in this house could have been the person who'd tried to run them down at the Christmas tree farm put an urgency in Blade's step as he rushed from the foyer down the hall to the den. He shouldn't have left her alone for even a moment.

What the hell kind of bodyguard was he?

He reached for the doorknob, but it didn't turn beneath his hand. It was locked. He told her to keep it locked, but if she was in the room, she didn't always remember to lock it behind herself.

But she wasn't alone in the room. He'd left Monica in there with her.

He knocked on the wood with one hand while he used his other hand to punch in the code for the door lock. He and Priscilla were the only ones who knew the code to open the door to the den. "Priscilla? Monica?" he called out as he knocked.

Once the code was entered, the lock gave way, and he turned the knob with a shaky hand. He pushed open the door and looked around the room. But it was empty. Both Monica and Priscilla were gone.

Where was she?

She hadn't passed him on the front stairs. Had she

gone up the back? Or into the kitchen or dining room? He reached for his cell to pull up footage from the cameras surrounding the estate. But before he could open the security app on his phone, he glanced at her desk just to see if she'd left him a note. And his gaze caught a glimpse of movement through the bars on the window behind her desk. Priscilla was out there, standing in the snow, in just her jeans and sweater, as she fought against the shadow that stood behind her with something stretched across her throat.

A curse slipped from his mouth, and it felt as if his heart climbed up into his throat. If not for the bars, he would have gone through the window. Through the glass and all. He ran as fast as he could from the den and then down the hall to cut through the dining room. He shoved open the French doors and rushed out into the cold.

"Priscilla!"

She was between the patio and the fountain with that person behind her. She struggled, pulling on the string of lights with one hand between it and her throat and the other on the outside of it, clawing at it, as she gasped for breath.

As Blade started across the snow-covered lawn, the person behind Priscilla dropped the string of lights and shoved her forward so hard that she hit the ground. Torn between racing after the person, who had now turned and was running away, Blade dropped to his knees next to Priscilla instead. He had to make sure that she was alright. That she and the baby were alright. But when he touched her, her body was limp. And when he rolled her over, her face was pale, her eyes closed. The string of lights had chafed her neck bright red.

"Priscilla? Priscilla!"

Had she lost consciousness or was she dead?

* * *

Was she dreaming again? Was this all a dream? Priscilla could feel strong arms wrapping around her, lifting her. Then she floated above the ground as if she was being carried like she was light and delicate. And she was too tall and curvy to be light, not that she'd ever cared. As long as she was healthy, that was all that mattered.

But her throat hurt. And her lungs, too. Suddenly she coughed and gasped, and the burning in her lungs eased a bit. But her throat still ached.

Then she remembered that string of lights wrapping around her neck, cutting off her breath. She had to fight. For her life and more importantly for the baby's. She rallied all her strength and lashed out, swinging her fists and kicking her legs.

"It's me, Priscilla. I've got you," a familiar gruff-and-sexy voice said. "It's Blade. I've got you now."

She released a shaky breath and stopped struggling. Then she managed to drag open her eyes and focus her bleary vision on his face. He wasn't movie-star handsome. His nose was too crooked. His eyes maybe a little too deep-set, but the blue was bright and piercing. His jaw was so square and tough. His lips were soft, too, despite the faint scar trailing from his top lip up toward his nose. His face had character. Blade Sparks had character; he was a hero. Her hero because he must have saved her yet again.

"I called 911. The police are on their way and an ambulance," he said as he carried her through the open French doors.

Thomas and Fritz were standing there.

Thomas said, "The police are on their way." He must have called 911, too.

Fritz said, "What happened? I was just out there."

Had it been him?

Was he the one who'd attacked her?

When she'd looked out the den window, the shadow she'd glimpsed through the bars had been big. Like Blade. Fritz was big like Blade.

Blade carried her through the dining room to the family room that was off the kitchen. It wasn't as formal as the front rooms, and a fire was burning in the hearth. He brought her close to it and said, "Grab some blankets. She's freezing."

And she realized now that her teeth were chattering and her body was shaking. But he was warm. She tried to curl closer to him, but he laid her down on the appropriately named fainting couch. She must have fainted out there.

"What happened?" Monica asked. She must have been in the family room.

"Oh my God," another voice murmured. This one was familiar but Priscilla hadn't heard it in a while. "What happened? And who the hell are you?"

"Who the hell are you?" Blade shot back at Everett.

"This is Dr. Fendler," Monica said. "I have an appointment with him about my thesis. I told Priscilla."

That she had an appointment with him, but Priscilla had assumed that meant she was meeting with him at the university, not inviting him to Priscilla's home.

"And this is Priscilla's bodyguard," Monica said with her usual sneer.

A sneer that was in Everett's voice when he remarked, "He's not doing a very good job. What the hell happened to your neck, Pris?"

"Everybody step back, give her some air," Blade said.

But she didn't want him to step back. She reached up and grabbed his shirt, holding him close to her.

"The police are here again," Kyle said, his voice sounding as bored as always. The kid was just in his twenties, but he acted as if he'd already seen and done it all. But he had actually done very little with his life.

Maybe that was why Alexander had had such hopes for a child they made. He'd thought a baby, with their genes, would be his legacy and maybe a way for him to live on when he'd known his life was coming to an end. Priscilla had admired and platonically loved Dr. Pell, but that wasn't why she'd agreed to marry and have a child with him. She'd just wanted to be a mother while she was young; she'd wanted someone to love and who might love her back. But because of the people who hated and resented her, her baby was in danger, too.

She touched her stomach, worried for the baby, hoping she hadn't lost him.

"The police?" Sally said. As usual she must have been hovering close behind her baby boy. She was the typical helicopter parent, which was probably why Kyle hadn't done much with his life; because his mother wouldn't let him live it. Then she must have caught sight of Priscilla because she let out a little shriek. "What in the world happened to you?"

"Someone attacked her outside," Blade said.

"Someone?" Everett repeated back at him.

"He really isn't a very good bodyguard," Bradley finally chimed in. Had he been in the room the entire time? Or had he just walked in with his son and his wife?

Priscilla saw the look in Blade's eyes, the self-condemnation. He was agreeing with what they were saying. He was blaming himself.

"My fault…" she murmured, but her voice was so hoarse from how raw her throat was that he might not have heard her. She felt so weak that consciousness started slipping away from her again.

"Where the hell is the ambulance?" Blade said.

He might have shouted it, but his voice sounded as faint as hers now. She could barely hear anything but a soft buzzing in her ears. Then she closed her eyes and slipped back into oblivion.

Sheila Carlson knew that the chief was going to call in Detective Dubridge. He'd already told her that when she responded to the call at the Pell Mansion, just as she always made certain to respond first to any call that potentially involved the Kozminskis branch of the Payne Protection Agency. She was supposed to wait for her superior before she started questioning anyone at the scene.

But while the chief didn't trust her, Dubridge did. She'd already been texting with him, and he'd assured her that he didn't have a problem with her starting the interviews while everything was fresh in the minds of the possible witnesses and the possible suspects. So that was what she intended to do, but she couldn't stop the most important witness from leaving in an ambulance. And potentially the most possible suspect might have left with her: her bodyguard.

"When I first saw them, she was trying to fight him off," the gardener remarked.

"She looked very afraid of him," the butler agreed.

"I can't believe that he wouldn't have been right next to her," the assistant remarked. "He's never more than a few inches away from her."

"Even at night," the other Mrs. Pell said with a disdainful sniff. "I'm not sure if he's her bodyguard or her boy toy."

Sheila swallowed a laugh. Blade Sparks had probably never been a boy. The guy was huge with muscles on his muscles. And he didn't have the face to be some rich lady's plaything. Now Viktor Lagransky...

She shook her head. "No."

"What?" Mrs. Pell asked. "You don't think they would have crossed a line like that? She never even slept with her husband, but she shares a bed with that bodyguard."

"How do you know that?" Sheila asked. Just how little privacy did Dr. Priscilla Pell have in her own home? Apparently as little privacy as she had respect.

"You really should get down to that hospital and make sure he doesn't do something to her," the stranger remarked.

Sheila hadn't met him before. "And you are?"

"Dr. Fendler," he said. "I'm an acquaintance of Priscilla's."

"And my mentor," the young assistant said, as she gazed adoringly at the guy who was balding already even though he was probably only in his early thirties, near the same age as Priscilla Pell.

"Well, Detective Dubridge, who is my mentor," Sheila said, "is meeting them at the hospital." That was his reply to the text she'd sent him that the victim was en route to the ER.

"They brought in a detective now?" Mr. Bradley Pell remarked. He was as soft-looking as his kid, like he'd never worked a day in his life. And given how rich his father had been, he probably never had. "The police are taking all this seriously?"

"The three attempts on Dr. Pell's life?" Sheila nodded. "Yeah, they're taking it seriously."

"Are you sure that she and her bodyguard aren't staging these attempts?" Mrs. Pell asked with a little sniffle.

"Why would they do that?" Sheila asked. This branch of the Payne Protection Agency didn't seem to like the police any more than this particular police officer liked these bodyguards.

The woman sniffled again before replying, "To make herself look like the victim in all of this."

"Well, she is," Sheila replied. She'd only caught a glimpse of her before the ambulance doors had closed, but she'd seen the red chafing on her neck. And even her fingertips had been bleeding. Sheila doubted anyone would have willingly done that to herself.

Bradley sighed. "That's what she wants everyone to think. Then everyone will forget who the real victim is in all of this."

"Who is?" Sheila asked.

"My father," Bradley said. "But the police will not take our claims about his death seriously. He wasn't that old, just early seventies."

"And he was in good health," the butler added. "To just not wake up one day like that…" He shuddered as if reliving the moment when he must have tried to wake up the corpse. So even the butler didn't think his former employer had died of natural causes.

"The coroner didn't find anything suspicious in the autopsy," she reminded them and herself. Because she'd wondered, too.

The new guy, Fendler, chuckled. "You do know what Alexander did, right? He created medications. Some were lifesaving, some were failures, though he did not like to admit to those." Clearly he had not idolized the late Dr. Pell like his student idolized him.

The young assistant stared at him with awe, and the professor waited, as if he expected Sheila to react the same way, or at least follow where he was trying to lead her.

Sheila was too cynical and too smart to let anyone manipulate her.

He sighed then, as if he was disappointed in her. Then he continued, "You don't think that the good doctor created something that could kill him and go undetected? There could even be a sample of it in his den. If you haven't considered that, then you are quite naive, Officer."

Sheila was a lot of things. Bitter. Resentful. Ambitious. She was not naive. She hadn't been since her father died when she was still a kid and his killer had never been brought to justice. Maybe that was why she'd been so quick to believe the Pells' claims about Dr. Pell being murdered because her dad had been, too.

But now it seemed like they and Dr. Fendler were trying too hard to get her to believe that and to suspect the doctor's young widow. Yet Priscilla was the one that someone was obviously trying to kill.

But she nodded, humoring the guy. "That is certainly a possibility, then, and I'll bring that to Detective Dubridge's attention. But I'm here about the recent attempt on Dr. Priscilla Pell's life," she reminded everyone. "I'm not here to discuss a death that has not been ruled a homicide."

But she couldn't help but wonder if the doctor's death and the attempts on his widow's life were related somehow. Was someone trying to kill her out of revenge? Or was the same person who'd killed her husband trying to kill her now?

Chapter 15

The red marks on Priscilla's neck were making Blade see red, so he stepped out of the ER bay for a moment to draw in a deep breath. The doctor was checking her out, making sure that she was alright and running some tests to find out why she'd lost consciousness.

He breathed deeply, trying to calm his rage and his fear over nearly losing her. If he'd been just a bit later, he might not have been able to save her.

This had been too close. He wasn't doing a very damn good job. And he overheard a conversation that reinforced that. Officer Sheila Carlson had arrived at the hospital, and she stood near the doors to the waiting room, filling in Detective Dubridge on her interviews at the house.

Of course the Pell family had cast blame on him and on Priscilla. As if she would risk her baby and her own health to play the victim…

"That's all ridiculous," he said.

And the two law officers glanced over at him.

"What's ridiculous?" Dubridge asked. The guy was tall and dark-haired and always seemed serious. Maybe that was why he was so good at his job, though, and also the reason he was rumored to be the chief's first pick as his replacement when Lynch retired.

"The fact that Priscilla would hurt anyone for any reason," he said. "She idolized her husband and is working hard to honor his legacy and to complete the work he started, making drugs that could save lives."

"Is she honoring his legacy or trying to claim it?" Carlson asked.

"It's already hers," Blade pointed out. "She doesn't have to do anything, but she's working hard to complete his work." She was determined to keep the promises she'd made to her late husband, even if it put her own life at risk. But maybe that was more about her own parents and how they'd died than about Alexander Pell. "Now you need to find out who keeps trying to kill her."

"You really didn't see anything?" Carlson said, repeating what he'd told her when she'd tried stopping the ambulance from leaving earlier that evening.

He shook his head. "I saw Priscilla struggling, but the person was behind her, wearing some dark clothes. And they were just outside the light from the house and the fountain. I couldn't see them. I couldn't even tell you if it was a man or a woman." He wouldn't put anything past Priscilla's assistant or her stepdaughter-in-law.

"The family doesn't think you're doing a very good job as a bodyguard," Carlson said, her lips pulling into a frown of disapproval.

Blade couldn't argue with that. He didn't feel like he was doing a very good job either. He shrugged. "I guess that's what you get with the misfit toys, huh?"

"Misfit toys?" Dubridge repeated. Then he nodded and chuckled, "Oh, yeah, that's what you call them…"

"Not all the Payne Protection bodyguards," Carlson specified. "Just this branch of…"

"Misfits?" Blade finished for her.

"I was thinking more like ex-cons," she said.

"You clearly don't think people deserve a second chance," Blade said.

"It's more about not knowing if people can really change or ever be trusted again."

"All I know is that you can't trust anyone in that house," Blade said.

"So you want me to believe they're lying about you and the victim struggling just before the police arrived?"

He snorted. "What?"

"They said she was fighting you off when you carried her in," Carlson said.

"She didn't know it was me," he said. "She was fighting for her life when I found her." Her life and her baby's life. He knew how much that child mattered to her; it meant more to her than a promise to her late husband. It meant the family she'd never really had and obviously wanted more than anything.

"Stop," a female voice said, and he turned to find Priscilla standing next to him in her hospital gown. "Stop interrogating him like he's a suspect," she said. "He saved my life once again."

"Yeah, but if he was better, you wouldn't be in danger in the first place," Carlson said.

And once again Blade couldn't argue with her. He saved his argument for later. After Priscilla gave her statement, that she hadn't seen her attacker, and after the doctor released her to go home, Blade argued with her.

"You can't go back there," he said even as he drove the Payne Protection SUV Ivan had dropped at the hospital back toward the Pell Mansion.

"I have to," Priscilla said with a heavy-sounding sigh.

"No, you don't," he said. "Let me take you to a safe

house. The Payne Protection Agencies have a few around River City and a few in other states and even countries. Let's get out of here until the detective or my team figures out who's trying to kill you." He glanced across the console to find her shaking her head.

"I can't go anywhere," she said. "I have so much work to do."

"Screw the work," he said. "You're in danger, Priscilla, because of those damn promises your husband manipulated you into making. Everybody thinks you killed him, and yet he's the one who's killing you."

"What? He's dead, you know."

"But because of all of his manipulations, you're the one in danger now," he said. "And it's not just you. It's the baby you're carrying, too. Alexander might have figured the kid was just an experiment and didn't care about what that child will want to be or do. But I think you care." He hoped like hell that she did, or he'd been very wrong about her. "I think you care a lot."

Her breath hitched, and he glanced over to see a tear slide down her cheek and she held her hands against her stomach. "Of course I care. I love this baby so much. I want to be a mom. I want to be his mom. And I want him to be whoever he wants to be, whatever he wants to be, and I will support him in that." Her voice cracked as more tears streaked down her face.

He let a curse slip out. "I'm sorry, Priscilla. That was out of line. I've been out of line." He was losing himself in this assignment, losing his focus just like he'd vowed he wouldn't. "I should turn over your protection duty to someone else." Someone who wasn't in danger of falling for her like he was. While he was scared of falling for her even though he knew they had no future, he was more afraid of losing her completely, of her dying.

"No," she said, and she reached across the console to grab his hand. "I need *you*."

His heart skipped a beat, and he wished for a moment that was true, that she needed him not just as a bodyguard but as a partner. But partners were equals, and Blade was not her equal. She was too smart, too rich and too driven while he was happy just keeping people safe the best he could. But he couldn't keep her as safe as he wanted. "Ivan can carry a gun. He'll be more protection for you than I will be."

"But I trust you," Priscilla said.

And while his heart warmed, he was honest enough to admit, "*I* don't trust *me* anymore."

Because he couldn't think clearly around her, or her assailant wouldn't keep getting so damn close to her. Blade wanted to keep her from harm and figure out who the hell was after her.

"Please," she said. "Stay until I can figure out..."

He waited after she trailed off, then asked, "One of those damn formulas?" He felt a pang of guilt over his resentment of them; he knew those drugs could save so many lives. But right now he was most concerned about her life and her baby's life.

She shook her head. "Which one of them is trying to kill me. That's the only way I'm going to be safe, is to figure out which one of them it is."

"Is that why you haven't kicked them all out of the house? Or did Alexander set up his will so that your hands are tied, and you're stuck with them?"

"They are all entitled to stay in the mansion," she said. "But I do have certain grounds where I can evict them."

"I would assume attempting to kill you is one of those grounds."

She chuckled. "Yes, but I would need proof of that. And I don't want to kick them all out if it's just one of them or none of them."

"But what if it's all of them?" he wondered aloud. Maybe they were all working together to get rid of their common enemy, though he couldn't imagine anyone hating Priscilla. Loving her. Now that was something he could imagine all too well.

She shook her head. "No. I don't want to think that they're all capable of murder."

"I think anyone is capable of murder," Blade said. Even himself. "That's why I want to take you to one of the safe houses. Why don't you want to leave the estate, Priscilla? You inherited money as well as the house. You could buy another house where you wouldn't have to live with people you can't trust."

"That house meant a lot to Alexander."

"He's dead," Blade said, his resentment of her late husband surging through him again.

"The house meant so much to him that he specified in his will that the work he started needed to be completed at the house. All of his notes for the book and the formulas he started have to be finished there."

"Damn, he was controlling," Blade said, his resentment growing even more.

"I think he was just concerned about things getting lost or stolen if they were moved from the estate," she said.

"We can ensure that won't happen."

She sighed and shook her head. "I can't. The will is ironclad. And even if I could fight that part of it, I'm not willing to risk it either, not when so many lives can be saved with that work. I have to stay and finish it."

Blade sighed, too, with resignation and concern. He was worried that she wasn't going to be able to finish anything...because her would-be killer was going to keep trying until they succeeded.

Priscilla had been insistent on coming back to the mansion. But as the SUV drove through the gates that opened when Blade punched in the code, she drew in a deep breath to brace herself to go back inside that mansion, back into the den of possible suspects.

She wanted to finish her work on the drug formulas, but she also wanted to figure out who was trying to kill her. And being here, with the suspects, might be the only way to figure out who kept attacking her.

But at what cost?

She touched her stomach. The ER resident had confirmed that the baby was, thankfully, okay. Priscilla's blood sugar had been too low, though, which was why, after her struggle with her assailant, she'd passed out. An IV of nutrients and some hospital food had revived her enough to be released, but now she was wondering if Blade was right.

If they should just go someplace else...

That safe house he'd talked about, although anywhere with him was safe. Even here?

He'd parked the SUV and had come around to the passenger door. He held it open for her. "Did you change your mind? Did you realize that I'm right about this? That it's too dangerous to be here?"

"I know you're right," she said. "But I can't just walk away."

"Those damn promises you made, they're going to be

the death of you," Blade said, his voice gruff with frustration. Then he reached out and covered her hands, which were cradling the soft swell of her stomach, with one of his enormous hands. "And that means the death of him, too, Priscilla. If you don't care about your own safety, what about his?"

Tears stung her eyes. "I do care about him," she insisted. She loved the baby. And she cared about Blade, too, and didn't want him or the baby to get hurt. "But I can't just run away. This is his future. His family." And to someone who'd never had a real family life or a home, that was important to her. But since they hated her, they would undoubtedly hate her child, too. Unless they could come to understand that she wasn't a gold digger or a killer...

Maybe they would actually start to care about her and her son.

Blade sighed and stepped back, then he helped her down from the SUV. When she put her hand in his, a tingle shot all the way up her arm to her heart. But if he was affected, too, he didn't show it. He just guided her inside the front door and into the foyer where the glittering Christmas tree reached beyond the second story. It was so beautiful.

She wanted to experience Christmas here, not just this year, but for her baby's future. This was his legacy now just as it was Alexander's. She wanted this to be his home and hers.

"There you are," a male voice remarked.

And she looked away from the tree to where Everett stood with Monica in the archway that led to the hall to the den. The new security measures and lock would have kept them out, though. "You're still here," she said with disappointment.

"There was no way I could leave until I knew that you

were alright, Pris," he said, sounding appalled that she would have thought he would.

"I'm fine," she said. "Monica can show you out now."

"You have no vehicle parked outside," Blade said. "How did you get here?"

"A driver from the university," the professor replied, his tone as haughty as ever. "I came by earlier to make sure you were going to attend the fundraiser next week."

"I didn't intend to," she admitted. Because of him.

"But the university is honoring Alexander," he said. "If you don't attend, it will look as though you're not."

Monica sniffed then, something she'd probably picked up from Sally to indicate her disapproval of Priscilla.

"Everything Priscilla does is to honor her late husband," Blade said.

She didn't know if he was defending or condemning her. Was he jealous of Alexander? She'd told him so many times that her marriage had been platonic. Unfortunately, her relationship with Everett had not been, just as she doubted that his relationship with Monica was platonic. Poor girl. She was going to be as unsatisfied as Priscilla had been.

"Of course," Everett said to Blade. "Pris owes him so much." Then he turned back toward her. "That's why I thought you would be able to overlook whatever awkwardness you must feel over our breakup and show up for Alexander's sake."

"The man's dead," Blade said. "He's not going to know if she shows up or not."

But she would. And she truly did owe Alexander a lot. He'd trusted her with his groundbreaking work and with his home and his child. His work, their work, meant as much to her as it had to him. He'd lost his first wife to dementia just as she'd lost her mother. And her father had died of cancer. She had to complete the work as much for them as for all the other lives that could be saved and for the families that could be spared the loss and heartbreak. And Alexander was the one who'd taught her what she needed to know to finish his work. She had to honor him privately by finishing it, but maybe if she honored him publicly as well, some of his family would change their opinion of her. They would see that she had really loved him, as a mentor, as a friend, even though not as a spouse.

Everett had been ignoring Blade, but he looked at him now. And even though Blade was a foot taller than him, he arched his head back so that he could look down his perfectly straight nose at him. "I would not expect *you* to understand the obligations of the world of academia," he said. "But Pris does." He walked past her then toward the front door with Monica stumbling over herself to follow him like a puppy that couldn't contain its adoration.

Priscilla could have told him what she'd told him during their *breakup*, but he would just accuse her of being crude and immature again. So she didn't say anything. She just started up the stairs while her ex and his new admirer walked out the front door.

Blade hesitated for a long moment, staring at that closed front door, before he went up the stairs after her. What Everett had said must have bothered him. Or maybe what she hadn't said bothered him more. That she hadn't said no. Or maybe he was just frustrated that she hadn't taken his advice. That she wouldn't leave for the safe house he'd offered to bring her to. But all she really needed was him to feel safe. But that wasn't all he made her feel; he gave her so much passion and pleasure, too.

* * *

Instead of dying like the killer had intended, the merry widow was back home safe and sound. For now…

But that was just because of her damn bodyguard. He had to go. In order for her to die, the bodyguard, Blade Sparks, had to die first.

Chapter 16

Blade had never been a jealous person in his life. He'd never envied anyone else for having more than he had or for being better-looking or smarter. Until now.

Now jealousy simmered in his chest like heartburn. But he breathed his way through the irritation just as he'd breathed his way through the pain during a bout. He could not let emotion get the better of him ever again, especially negative emotions. But seeing that polished and pompous guy and knowing that Dr. Fendler had once been in a relationship with Priscilla reinforced what he'd already known. Blade had nothing in common with her. The professor was right; he didn't understand their world and he sure as hell would never fit into it.

But, at the moment, Blade was the only thing keeping her alive in her world. So he unlocked the door to her suite and checked it out to ensure that it was safe. But when he started to head back out the door, she grabbed his arm.

"Don't go," she said.

"That's what I want to say to you about that damn party," he remarked. "But we both know that you're going to go no matter what I think. Is it to honor your late husband or to spite that condescending ass of a professor?"

She laughed. "He is a condescending ass."

"I can understand why you broke up with him," Blade said. "But I can't see why you ever dated him in the first place."

"When we were both students, he wasn't as pompous as he is now. We were study buddies and friends."

Blade shook his head. "Friends? I don't think that guy has any."

She tilted her head as she scrunched up her beautiful face for a moment. "Actually, you're right. I don't think he does. And he actually broke up with me."

"What?"

"Well…" She tilted her head again. "It was my fault, I guess. He gave me an ultimatum. If I took the job as Dr. Pell's teaching and research assistant, we were done."

Blade chuckled. "And you took the job."

"My parents instilled in me from a very young age that I could never let anything or anyone get in the way of my education and contributions to society."

"Ah…" He'd been blaming her late husband, but now he understood that Priscilla's sense of duty went back even farther than her marriage. To her childhood, which didn't sound like any more of a childhood than his had been.

Her face, which had been so pale, flushed nearly as red as those marks around her neck. "What? Are you psycho-analyzing me, Blade?"

He shook his head. "I'm not educated enough to do that."

"Bullshit," she said. "You're every bit as smart as Everett, and I hope you realize that."

"The guy's a doctor."

"The guy's a narcissist," she said. "He was actually surprised that I didn't let him control me. That I didn't pass on Dr. Pell's offer so that he could take it."

"Would he have given it to Fendler if you'd turned it down?"

She laughed. "No. He was well aware that Everett is an idiot. That he has more bravado than he has knowledge. He was not a fan."

"Of course he wanted you for himself, so he would say that," Blade pointed out.

She shook her head. "He just wanted me to work with him. And because he was my mentor and my teacher, he knew that I could finish the work he'd started."

"Why couldn't he finish it?" Blade asked. "Did he know he was dying? I thought it was a heart attack or heart failure or something."

"He died from heart failure," she said. "Or maybe a broken heart from losing his wife. But I also think he was getting dementia like his wife. That might have been why he was so lax with some things like the security on the estate but then so paranoid about other things, like moving anything from it. My mother got like that with her early onset Alzheimer's."

"I'm sorry," he said.

She shrugged. "I can't remember what she was like before it. My father insisted he could handle everything on his own and made me continue my studies at boarding school and college. But I think taking care of her is what wore him down and he got cancer. That's how I lost them both." Tears glistened in her beautiful eyes.

And he wanted to wrap his arms around her and pull her close. But he was too worried. "You can't bring them back," he said. "This research you're working on, it can't bring any of them back. Not your mom or dad or even Alexander."

"I know," she said, her voice cracking. "But it can save other lives."

"Not if you don't live to complete it. And you won't if you stay in this house and go out to that fundraiser. You need to go somewhere until it's safe for you to come out again."

She shook her head. "I can't stop now. There are so many other people with these diseases. I can't bring back my parents, but I might save someone else's."

"You don't even know if your formulas will work," he said.

"No," she admitted. "I don't. But I will keep working on them until they do."

She was determined, too determined and too exhausted for him to continue trying to reason with.

Regret squeezed his heart. "I'm sorry," he said. "I don't want to upset you. You've been through hell today. You need to get some rest. I'll let you go to sleep." And he started for the door again. But her grasp on his arm tightened.

"Don't go..." she said.

He closed the door then and locked it, locking himself inside with her. He knew it wasn't a good idea. That every time he was with her, he wanted her more. But the last time he'd been separated from her, she'd nearly died.

And he couldn't risk her life again.

But he was scared that he was risking his...at least his life as he'd known it, as he'd envisioned it. Because now he knew that no matter how this assignment ended, he would never be the same.

Blade was right; Priscilla saw that now. He was right about the reasons she'd made all the promises to Alexander. While she wanted to save other lives, she wanted most to help the people she'd already lost. Her mom and her dad and even Alexander. But she couldn't bring them back. And she couldn't help anyone if someone killed her.

But she couldn't let this person scare her away from work that mattered or from honoring Alexander. If she went into hiding, the would-be killer might never be found. She had to trust that Blade would catch the person.

"I should go," Blade said even though he'd locked the door. "You're exhausted."

She'd been standing there, just staring at him, probably looking as vacant and clueless as she felt. "I'm stunned," she admitted.

"By the attack earlier?"

That had stunned her, too. "By you."

His mouth curved into a slight grin. "That I'm not as stupid as you thought I was."

"I never thought you were stupid," she assured him. "I am stunned that you see me." She'd thought Alexander had when he'd chosen her over Everett to help him with his work, with his legacy. But with the disease already affecting him, she couldn't trust Alexander's judgment just as she shouldn't have trusted Everett at all.

To be a bodyguard, Blade had to be observant, but his skill was next-level. Maybe that was why he'd saved her life so many times. "Thank you."

"For seeing you?"

She shivered a bit. "No. I think that scares me," she admitted. She was used to people looking at her surface and not bothering to peer any deeper. But Blade had. He'd seen through the surface to her very soul.

"I won't hurt you," Blade assured her. "I just want to keep you safe."

"You have," she said. "You've saved my life. Again. Thank you for that." But she wasn't convinced that he wouldn't hurt her emotionally and that was because he saw her so damn clearly, even more clearly than she saw herself.

And while she trusted him to keep her safe, she wasn't sure she should trust him for more than that. She'd been wrong about Alexander and Everett. Why was she so convinced she was right about Blade?

But he didn't seem to want anything from her but to keep her safe. And maybe that was why she was falling for him.

"Is that why you want me to stay?" he asked.

She smiled. "To thank you?"

"Because you're scared?"

Those moments when that strand of lights had wrapped around her neck flitted through her mind again. And she shuddered.

Then his arms closed around her, and he pulled her against his chest where his heart beat hard and fast. "I was so scared for you," he said.

"Me, too," she murmured. But he'd saved her as he had again and again since trespassing over the wall more than a week ago. He'd only been in her life for little more than a week, but she couldn't imagine him not being part of it now. She couldn't imagine the hole he would leave in it when he moved on to his next assignment.

While she wanted the threat of danger gone, the person trying to kill her caught, she didn't want Blade gone. And she held on to him now as if he was being ripped away from her. And she kissed him with all the passion burning inside her.

Her lips moved over his, and he deepened the kiss, their mouths mating. But it wasn't enough for her. She wanted nothing between them. She tugged at his buttons and zippers, frantically undressing him as she wriggled out of her own clothes.

Then, finally, they were naked, skin rubbing against skin. He groaned.

She moaned, sensation and desire overwhelming her. She needed him so badly. He lifted her as easily as he had earlier that evening and carried her to the bed, his arms barely straining. He was so damn strong.

So sexy...

So protective...

And so gentle.

He settled her softly onto the bed. And then he worshiped her body with his fingertips and his lips. He stroked every inch of her body until she was nearly sobbing with the need for release.

Her nipples and her core throbbed as her heart pounded fast and hard. "Blade..." She writhed against the blankets, aching for him to fill her. And she reached out, closing her fingers around his erection.

He groaned again. And then finally he was inside her, moving gently. But she locked her legs around his waist and arched up, taking him deeper. She moved fast and frantically, seeking her release.

He reached between their bodies, stroking first her nipples and then the most sensitive part of her. And she came, crying his name as the power of the orgasm rocked her body, her very existence.

Then he tensed and his big body shuddered as he joined her in release. As gently as he'd carried her to bed, he carried her into the bathroom. Cradling her body with one arm, he reached his other arm into the walk-in shower to turn on the faucet. The water heated quickly, steam filling the space. He stepped inside with her, letting the water wash over them as he soaped up her hair and her skin. He washed every inch of her body before dropping to his knees.

Then he lifted one of her legs over his shoulder and made love to her with his mouth, his tongue flicking against her before dipping inside her. Her other leg weakened, and she leaned against the slate wall of the shower.

He held her with one arm around her back as his other hand reach for her breast. He stroked the nipple as his tongue stroked her.

And she shuddered as she came again.

Then he stood and brought her with him, wrapping her legs around him as he slid inside her. And he made love to her against the shower wall. Despite thinking she was satiated, desire swept through her again, and her body quivered as she came.

He groaned like a man in pain, his body tense, the cords in his neck and at his temples stretched taut. Then he came, pumping inside her. And his legs seemed to shake a bit from the force of his release or maybe from the exertion of holding her up. He washed them again and then dried them before carrying her back to bed.

She had always been so fiercely independent, but she didn't protest his taking care of her. She enjoyed it as much as she enjoyed him. And she was definitely falling for him.

But could she trust her own judgment when she'd been wrong so many times before?

Even if she could trust him not to hurt her, she couldn't promise him the same. While she felt safe with him, being with her put him in danger.

Eventually it might even get him killed. And she knew that she'd done the wrong thing. She should not have returned to the estate, and she should have fired Blade.

Garek played the voicemail that had been left on his cell late last night. Actually early this morning, but he hadn't noticed it until now. And he was playing it for himself and for Milek, who sat in his office with him.

"This is Priscilla Pell," she said. And Garek was glad that she identified herself since he hadn't recognized the number or the voice. She was whispering, "I appreciate all that your agency and Blade have done to keep me and the estate safe. However, I think it might be better if you replaced Blade with another bodyguard."

"Why?" Milek asked as if she was actually on the phone with them and could hear his question.

After a slight pause, the voicemail continued, "I am just concerned that the attempts on my life are going to get more dangerous, and since he can't carry a firearm to protect himself that he's going to get killed."

"Wow..." Milek murmured. "She's more worried about him than she is herself."

Garek nodded. "Yeah, the rumors about her were certainly off base. She's not a dangerous murderess since she's so worried about him." While she'd been in the hospital the previous night getting checked out, Blade had called to fill him in on what had happened. "No matter what her late husband's family thinks."

Dubridge and Carlson had also talked to him. Carlson was actually lobbying to have the dead man's body exhumed and another autopsy performed on it.

"We should know better than anyone to make assumptions about someone's guilt or innocence," Milek said.

Their father had died in prison serving a sentence for a murder he had not committed. And one of their bodyguards, Josh Stafford, had also served time for a theft he hadn't done. But he'd willingly taken the blame. Their father had had it foisted on him by a dirty cop.

"So should we take him off the case?" Garek asked.

"Should we reassign it to someone else? Ivan who can carry a weapon?"

"I think we should figure out who the hell is behind these attempts on her life," Milek said. "That way both she and Blade will be safe."

"Dubridge and Carlson told me last night to back off," Garek reminded him. "To let them handle the investigation."

Milek snorted. "Like we've ever done that before."

Especially when one of their team was in danger.

They would do whatever necessary to keep him safe.

Chapter 17

She wanted him gone. That was the message Blade got the next morning from his bosses. The text said: The client wants to replace you.

As her bodyguard or as her lover?

She hadn't seemed to have any complaints about either of his positions last night. About any of the positions they'd been in, actually. But then he'd fallen asleep before she had. And maybe she'd had time to think, to realize that her ex was right. Blade would never fit into her world.

Into *their* world...

When that text vibrating his phone woke him up, he found that she was already awake and out of bed. Maybe she'd sent the text that morning before he'd awakened.

Instead of texting back, Blade called his bosses. "So she wants another bodyguard?" he asked when Garek picked up his cell.

"She doesn't want you getting hurt," Garek said.

But it was already too late for that; Blade knew this one was going to hurt whether he remained her bodyguard or not. "If that was the case, she should have let me bring her to a safe house after last night's attempt on her life," Blade said. "Instead she insisted on coming back to the mansion."

"Yes," Garek said. Of course he was aware of everything that was going on; he probably had some of the team watching the footage from the security cameras they'd put all over the estate.

Unfortunately, the one in the backyard hadn't picked up any clearer image of her attacker than Blade had seen with his own eyes. He'd asked his boss that last night when he'd filled him in on everything that had happened.

"What do you want?" Garek asked.

"I want to find out who's trying to kill her," Blade said. "But are you taking me off the assignment?" Priscilla was the client after all, and wasn't the client always right?

"No."

"But she's the one paying the bills."

"And if she wants to keep her valuables insured, she's going to have to follow the recommendations of the company insuring those valuables. And Hull leaves it up to us how to handle security."

While there was quite an extensive collection of artwork and jewelry, all the material things were safe.

"Nobody tried to steal anything," Blade said. But her life. That, however, was the most valuable thing on this estate.

"We're going to send Viktor out for backup," Garek said. "As long as you're sure you want to stay."

"I'm going to see this through," Blade said. Just as she'd made promises to her late husband, he had made promises to himself. He wanted to be the best bodyguard Payne Protection had. So he needed to step up his game.

He needed to figure out who the hell was trying to kill her. That was the only way to stop them from trying again and succeeding.

Worried that there already could have been another attempt, Blade hurriedly dressed and sought her out. She had to be in the den. That was where she always was. But the door was locked. She didn't respond when he knocked; maybe she was avoiding him and the awkwardness she might feel over wanting him fired. Why did she really want him gone?

Because she was worried about him getting hurt like she'd told Garek? Or because he was getting too close?

Maybe some of the things he'd said last night had been insensitive or too accurate. But if her only concern was him, getting rid of him wasn't going to prevent him from getting hurt. He would just go on to another assignment, one that might prove just as dangerous as this one. He unlocked the door with the intention of pointing that out to her. But he found the den empty.

Scared of a repeat of the night before, he looked out the window, but nobody was in the yard, where snowflakes drifted down onto the bushes and trees that twinkled with the lights someone had finished stringing around them after someone had strung one around Priscilla's neck.

With all the cameras around the estate, whoever was monitoring the security footage would have called him or set off alarms if she was in danger. But he was still frantic to find her. As he ducked out of the den, he took a moment to lock the door, knowing how important it was to her to secure the space. Then he headed toward the dining room. For once it wasn't empty. The entire family, including Priscilla, was gathered around the table. Even the gardener was in the room, leaning against one of the walls as he sipped from a coffee mug.

Her green eyes widened with surprise when he walked into the room. Had she expected him to be gone already? To leave without talking to her?

Was that what she'd wanted?

"Ah, so here's the bodyguard," Kyle Pell remarked. "Slacking on the job again?"

Blade's patience with these people was wearing thin. "What would you know about jobs? Have you ever had one?"

The kid's face flushed bright red. "That's...you're..." he stammered.

"You can't talk to my son that way," his mother rushed to his defense. "You're just the hired help."

Out of the corner of his eye, Blade noticed the gardener's big body tensing, and he shot a glare at Sally Pell. Was there something going on between them?

"And...and you're just here because you're sleeping with her," Sally added.

"You would know about people sleeping with the help," Bradley Pell remarked.

Priscilla's eyes widened again as she must have come to the same conclusion he had, especially when Fritz opened the patio doors and stepped outside without even bothering to grab a jacket.

"I'm here because someone is trying to kill Priscilla," Blade reminded them. "And it's pretty obvious that it's one of you."

"Priscilla..." Sally muttered with a disparaging sniffle. So she was well aware that Blade's relationship with his boss wasn't just professional anymore.

"Why would anyone want to hurt her?" Monica asked the question now but with feigned innocence.

"Because they're greedy and spiteful," Blade said. "And they want a bigger piece of the inheritance and control of the estate."

"Or maybe because she killed a good man and shouldn't

get away with it," Bradley remarked, and tears actually glistened in his dark eyes.

Had he loved his adoptive father?

Blade had never gotten the sense that there was much love at all in this family, just some weird codependency. "So you're the one going all vigilante justice with her?" he asked Bradley. "You're the one trying to kill her?"

The older man's face flushed, and he shook his head. "Of course not..."

"And you're the one with a criminal record," Monica said. "For murder, right?"

Blade had wondered when one of them would dive deep on him. Of course it would be the research assistant who had. Or had the professor done the search or maybe just ordered her to do it?

"Manslaughter, actually," he said. "I stepped in to save a woman from getting abused."

"Hero complex much?" Monica said with a smirk.

"Don't-like-seeing-anyone-being-hurt-or-abused complex," he said. "Which is a complex every person should have. And if you can stand by and watch someone trying to hurt or kill somebody, you're as bad as the killer himself."

Her face flushed. "I'm not sure if that's hypocritical or profound," she admitted with a slight chuckle.

"It's very ironic that a killer is protecting a killer," Sally remarked with one of her sniffles.

"Dr. Pell's death was declared natural causes," Blade reminded them. "You're all going to have to let that go. But the attempts on Priscilla's life are criminal, whether vigilante or not. Whoever has been trying to hurt her will go to prison or worse..."

Monica shuddered. "Are you threatening to kill that person?"

"Well, you said he's a killer," Kyle reminded her. "So apparently he intends to kill again."

"He's threatening our lives," Bradley said to Priscilla. "Why are you just sitting there? Why aren't you firing him?"

"Is he that good in bed?" Kyle asked.

And Blade had to curl his fingers into his hands, clenching them so that he didn't reach for the scrawny kid and shake him. "Show your grandfather's widow some respect," he said through gritted teeth.

"I'll show my grandmother the respect she deserves for sleeping her way into a fortune."

Blade stepped toward Kyle then, but Priscilla jumped up and grabbed his hand. Then she tugged him out of the room. And he felt sick that she was actually worried about what he would do to the kid.

"I was not going to hurt him," he assured her as she tugged him toward the den. "If that's one of the reasons you want me gone, because you don't trust me, you're going to have to fire the Payne Protection Agency to get rid of me. Why do you want to get rid of me that badly, Priscilla, that you would put your life and that baby's life at risk?"

It was ironic that she'd pulled him out of the dining room as if afraid he was going to hurt Kyle, but he was the one hurting that she couldn't even wait until whatever they had came to its inevitable end.

She wanted him gone now. Clearly she didn't trust him, or she was worried that she was getting in too deep with him. And while she didn't mind sharing her bed with a convicted killer, she probably did want her baby growing up around one.

She was so glad that he hadn't left yet. In those vulnerable moments after they'd made love the night before, she'd been so afraid for him. And maybe of him as well, of how he saw her more clearly than anyone else ever had.

Priscilla closed the door behind them and leaned against it, her knees a bit weak with relief that he was still here. And she was also rattled from the ugly scene in the dining room. "I didn't want you fired," she assured him. "You're a wonderful bodyguard. This is what you're meant to do."

"Then why did you ask my boss to take me off this assignment?"

"Because I don't want you getting hurt." And she didn't want to get hurt either, in case her judgment was as wrong about him as it had been about Everett.

"And you don't think I will get hurt on my next assignment or the one after that? You said I'm meant to be a bodyguard, but don't you understand that means putting myself between whoever I'm protecting and the threat against them?"

She was glad she was leaning against the door because her knees trembled again at the thought of him putting himself in danger over and over again. Which was another reason to protect her heart from him. "But I don't want you getting hurt over me," she said. "That was why I sent that text last night. I don't want to be responsible for you getting hurt."

He shrugged. "So you'd rather it be someone else that I get hurt over?"

"I don't want you getting hurt at all."

He sighed. "It's too late for that, Priscilla."

Her heart ached with the thought that she might have hurt him. That was the last thing she'd wanted. But she was determined to protect herself from getting hurt, too.

He touched his nose. "I've been hurt many times. But I always survive. You're the one I'm worried about. You shouldn't have snuck out of your bedroom to join those jackals in the dining room. You're not safe with them."

She closed her eyes as tears burned her eyes. "I know." Her hope of a happy, loving family for her son was never going to be realized. Even if they weren't trying to kill her, they thought she was a killer and a gold digger, and they all hated her. "And you're right about Dr. Pell—Alexander still controlling me from beyond the grave." She'd been indignant and embarrassed when he'd first pointed that out to her. Sure, Alexander had been suffering from his own ailment and fears, but she should have known better. About him. About Everett and maybe even about Blade.

Now she was mad. Her spine and legs stiff, she straightened away from the door and then turned and opened it. "I'm not letting that happen anymore."

He followed her out of the room, pausing only to lock the door behind them. "What are you doing?" he asked as she started down the hall. Then he ran to catch up to her as she stalked back into the dining room.

Everyone but Fritz was still there, lingering over their breakfast. But it wasn't as if any of them had anything to do. Not even Monica, really, because there was so little that Priscilla trusted her to do.

She didn't actually trust any of them. And for her baby's sake, she had to get them away from her. Away from them.

"I've had it with the disrespect," she said. "I'm not going to live like this."

"So you're leaving?" Sally asked with a wide smile.

"No, you're leaving," Priscilla said. "All of you."

"What?" Bradley asked, and he jumped up from his chair. "You can't do that. You can't throw us out of our home."

"My home," she said. "Your father left you each with

a trust. You have money to buy your own place and fund your own lives."

Bradley shook his head. "You can't do that. Father made sure of that in his will."

"There are stipulations around you living here," she said. "One is that you not threaten me or make me feel unsafe." She touched her neck that was still sore from the strand of lights. "And I don't feel safe with any of you in this house. You have to go."

"You bitch!" Sally hurled at her. "You can't do this. It's Christmastime."

Priscilla snorted. "And you've all been so nice and charitable to me?"

"Why would we be?" Bradley asked. "You came into this house and took it over, marrying and then murdering an old man."

"The next person who accuses me of that will be sued for slander," Priscilla said, and she shot each of them a warning glare. "I'll give you until after the holidays to find a new place. But you're all leaving. All of you." She looked at the butler and Monica, too.

The young woman gasped and touched her own chest. "Why me? I've not been insulting you like the rest of them."

"Because I can't trust you," Priscilla said.

"And you think you can trust him? That bodyguard?" Monica asked with a glance at Blade, who stood stoically next to her. "He's probably using you to get some of your money, to live in this mansion."

She didn't think Blade wanted anything from her. But then she'd thought the same of Alexander, too, and Everett and had wound up giving up so much of herself to them. But was she just using them as an excuse to back away from the powerful feelings she had for Blade?

"That's poetic justice if he is," Bradley remarked. "She deserves to be used like she used my father."

"Keep it up, and you can leave today," Priscilla said. "I was trying to be understanding, thinking that you were just grieving. But it's clear that you're just horrible people. That's why Alexander married me, and why he made sure I would give him another heir. One that wouldn't be the disappointment you were." She patted her stomach then.

"You're pregnant?" Sally asked, as she shot up from her chair. "What the hell? You whore—"

Blade started forward, but Priscilla grabbed his arm. "It's fine. They're all leaving."

"You can't do this," Bradley said. "Father's will protected us. I'm calling the lawyer. You're going to regret this."

"Threatening me is grounds for eviction," Priscilla said. "You just guaranteed your removal from this estate."

She'd thought the earlier scene in the dining room had been ugly. But this was far worse because for the first time she clearly saw how hateful these people were. No wonder Alexander had wanted a do-over.

She wanted one herself. But it was too late now. She'd sealed her fate and her child's fate. And maybe Blade's as well because he wasn't going anywhere unless she fired the Payne Protection Agency. After the gauntlet she'd thrown down, she wasn't going to do that.

Even though she'd tried to get Blade removed from the assignment, she really didn't want him gone. She just wanted him.

Viktor had walked in on the last part of that conversation in the dining room. And he could see and feel all the hate in that room.

While the widow walked past him without even noticing him, Blade stopped. "I'm damn glad you're here," he said.

Viktor nodded. "You're definitely going to need backup." Because these greedy, hateful people were going to do whatever they could to get rid of the widow now before she could get rid of them. He thought for a second about being preemptive and calling Officer Carlson.

Because he had no doubt something was going to happen. But Sheila wouldn't be able to do anything until after it did. Until there was another attempt on the widow's life or until someone died. But Viktor had a horrible feeling that she was going to have to come out soon.

That someone was definitely going to die.

Chapter 18

Once Blade had Viktor's assurance he would be patrolling the property and the house, he rushed up the stairs after Priscilla. He wasn't surprised she was going to her suite. After that confrontation, she had to be exhausted. But the minute he opened the door to her room, she launched herself at him. Winding her arms around his neck, she pulled his head down for her kisses. And her lips devoured his mouth, her teeth nipping and teasing, her tongue swiping out to soothe away the hurt she might have inflicted.

But she'd inflicted worse pain on him than those little nibbles. And even as his body hardened with need for hers, he tugged her arms loose from his neck and stepped away from her. "I thought you wanted me gone," he reminded her. Yet here she was kissing him, making him want her again, making him fall for her even more than he already was.

"I told you why I asked your boss to replace you," she said. "I was worried about you."

"I'm worried about you," he said. "And I don't think you're being entirely honest either with me or with yourself."

She let out a slightly hysterical laugh. "I probably do seem like I'm losing my grip on reality right now. I would like to blame my pregnancy hormones, but I think I've already blamed them for enough things."

That was the reason she'd once given for sleeping with him. Maybe he would have been offended that hormones were the only reason she was attracted to him, but he couldn't think of any other explanation himself. They had nothing in common. With how different their careers and pasts were, it was like they spoke two different languages.

Maybe he should just shut up and let her have her way with him because she was going to tire of him eventually. He would never tire of her, though.

But he was afraid that he was going to lose her. "What did you just do in the dining room?" he asked. "Was that hormones, too?"

"That was long overdue," she said. "I thought you would agree with me. You didn't understand why I've let them stay."

"No, I didn't," he agreed. "They treat you horribly and one or all of them might be trying to kill you."

"So you got what you wanted," she said. "I'm tossing them out."

He had a feeling that it wasn't going to be as easy as he'd thought. "They're going to get lawyers involved." He didn't trust lawyers. His hadn't saved him from a long prison sentence like the public defender had promised. And the district attorney, Amber Talsma-Kozminski, hadn't gotten him a permit to carry yet either despite her assurances to her husband that she was working on it. "They're going to fight you tooth and nail to stay. The Pells and the staff."

"So. Maybe a lawyer and a judge will drag out their eviction a bit." She sighed and shrugged. "But they have threatened me. You can be a witness to that."

"I'm sure the security cameras will back that up, too," he

said. "They will have to leave. And hopefully that will be sooner than later because I'm worried that you're in even more danger now."

Because the only way those freeloaders would be able to stay would be if they got rid of her and that new heir she'd told them about.

"You and the baby are in even more danger," he said.

And he wasn't sure that, even with Viktor's help, he would be able to keep them safe from harm. The thought of losing her, of them, scared him more than anything else in his life ever had.

And now he was the one reaching for her.

Priscilla knew that what she'd done was like taking a pin out of a live grenade and hanging on to it. It was going to blow up, and she was the one who was going to end up getting hurt. But she was getting hurt anyway. Her neck was sore and red from the string of lights that had nearly strangled her. She'd survived that attempt.

Because of Blade rushing to her rescue.

He held her now, his strong arms wrapped around her, her head on his muscular chest. When he'd first come into her room, she'd flung herself at him, kissing him.

But he'd pushed her away to warn her about what she'd done, about how she'd put both herself and her baby in more danger.

She knew that he was right about that just as he was right about so much else. But instead of belaboring the point, he reached for her. And as always when they touched, the passion ignited.

He kissed her as hungrily as she'd kissed him. And somehow her clothes and his dropped away, leaving them naked. Despite how often they'd made love the night before, she was even more needy and desperate for him. The tension inside her unbearable.

And every touch and kiss raised her temperature and her need until she was burning up for him. "Blade..." she murmured.

He lifted and spun her around to the bed. But when he lowered her onto it, he didn't join her. Instead he knelt next to her and made love to her with his mouth.

The orgasm rushed through her with such intensity that tears burned her eyes. Then he gently joined their bodies, filling her, filling that hollow ache inside her that nobody else had ever been able to fill.

She locked her legs around his waist, taking him deeper, matching his rhythm. And the tension built inside her again.

His chest, with those boxing glove tattoos, moved with his harsh breaths. And his arms that he'd braced on the bed beside her were tense, the muscles bulging. She ran her fingertips over his chest and lower, between their bodies.

He lowered his head and kissed her, his mouth mating with hers like their bodies mated.

The tension inside her broke, pleasure spiraling through her, making her cry out again. His big body tensed, then shuddered, as he joined her in the release.

In the pleasure.

He rolled to his side, taking her with him, holding her against him. And his fingertips touched her neck. "I don't want you getting hurt again..." he murmured, his voice gruff with his worry. "You came so close last night. That killer got so close..."

She owed him her life. And she'd wanted to make sure that his stayed safe. But he was right. His job was a dangerous one. If he wasn't risking his life for her, he would be risking it for someone else.

And the thought of losing him scared her. But keeping him safe wasn't the only reason she'd wanted him taken off this assignment, taken away from her.

Because the thought of losing herself scared her even more. And until he'd pointed out to her how the promises she'd made were affecting her, manipulating her, putting her behind prison bars, she hadn't realized how much of herself she'd lost. And she'd lost faith in her own judgment now, too.

She could be wrong about him.

But she wasn't wrong about how much she'd tolerated. And finally instead of being scared or distracted, she'd gotten mad. So she'd gone into the dining room to toss all the haters out of her house.

"I don't regret throwing them all out," she told him. But like he'd warned her, it wasn't going to be that easy. They would lawyer up. And Alexander's will might not protect her as much as she thought it did.

Obviously, he'd put her in a horrible position with the promises he'd pressed her into making. But she'd respected him so much, had been so in awe of his success and brilliance that she'd been honored he'd trusted her. But maybe she shouldn't have trusted him as much as she had, especially given his medical condition. And maybe she shouldn't have so readily trusted Blade either.

"Trying to get rid of all of them is going to put you in more danger," he said, and his arms tightened around her, holding her closer to his madly pounding heart.

His concern for her touched her heart. But then she had to remind herself that he was just doing his job. She was the one who'd let it get personal. Who'd started to care about him.

And she'd even considered sacrificing her safety for

his. That was how she was all over the place, not thinking clearly at all. While she would like to keep blaming hormones for her erratic actions and emotions, she knew it was him. And how she was beginning to feel about him.

Too much.

He cared about her. She knew that or he wouldn't make love to her as gently and thoroughly as he did. But like Monica said, he had a hero complex, probably because he hadn't been able to save his mother from her bad choices, so he was determined to save every other woman that he could.

He'd already gone to prison over one. He'd already proved he was willing to give up his freedom. And he would probably give up his life as well.

She just didn't want that to be over her. He was right; she had made everything worse.

And so much more dangerous.

Not just for his life and hers and the baby's as well.

But for her heart…

The killer was getting fed up. Security was getting increased around the estate. There were more cameras to avoid. More people around watching and waiting for that next attempt on her life.

Some of those cameras and some of those people had to go.

Predictably, when one of the cameras, on the stone wall near the back of the property, was damaged, a bodyguard came out to fix it. He was all bundled up in a coat and hat. But he was big.

Maybe it was Blade Sparks himself.

Or the other guy who'd arrived today.

But either way, that person was a dead man.

The killer had the gun that had been taken from Priscilla so long ago. But a gunshot would draw too much attention. That was why the killer hadn't chosen to use it yet.

Though it would have been easier and more effective than that string of lights. But that would have worked had Blade Sparks not rushed to Priscilla's rescue like he had.

He wouldn't be able to rush to her rescue again. The killer pulled out a knife. It was long with a sharp point and a sharper blade. It cut easily through the big man's jacket and into his flesh. The man tensed, then cried out with the pain. But he didn't move, as if frozen in place near that wall.

Maybe the blade had severed his spinal cord.

The killer drew it out, sending droplets of blood spattering across the snow. Then the blade was plunged in again. Deeper. But the bodyguard didn't let out even a moan this time. He was already dead.

Chapter 19

Blade was worried about Priscilla venturing out of her room again. If only he could keep her in bed, in his arms, forever. But she had work to do. And even though she'd admitted to realizing how some of the promises she'd made had put her in danger, he knew she was still going to honor them. Because she was honorable. That was one of the things he admired most about her and proved how wrong her late husband's family was about her.

Once they were dressed, they stood just inside her locked bedroom door. "Aren't you going to open it?" she asked. "Or are you afraid that they're all waiting outside it to pounce on me?"

He shrugged. "I really don't know." He could have pulled up camera angles on his phone and checked. But instead he just clicked the contact for Viktor. "I'll find out."

But while Viktor's deep voice answered, it was a prerecorded message. "Lagransky. I'm not available right now, but leave a message and I'll get back to you. If it's an emergency, contact the Payne Protection Agency..." And he read off the main number for their office.

Was this an emergency?

Blade didn't want to believe that it was, but Viktor was supposed to be patrolling the house and the grounds. What about that would make him unable to take a call?

A chill raced down Blade's spine. "This isn't like Vik not to answer his phone."

"Maybe he's on another call with one of your bosses," Priscilla suggested.

Blade nodded. "Yeah, that makes sense. But still, if he saw I was calling..."

"He'd take your call because he would be worried," Priscilla finished for him. And her forehead furrowed with lines of concern. "We need to look for him. He was staying here, right?"

Blade nodded again. "Yeah, he was going to patrol the house and the grounds."

"Let's split up and search for him," she said, as she reached for the doorknob. "I'll take the house, and you can look outside."

He caught her hand in his. "No. You're not the Payne Protection bodyguard. I am. You need to stay inside this suite with the door locked for your safety." He would call in the rest of his team to help protect her and find Vik. But first he would make sure he wasn't overreacting. Maybe the guy had just lost his phone or something.

"Blade..."

"You're the one who just poked every bear in this house, and you don't think they're going to snap at you the next chance they get?"

"You're the one who told me that I shouldn't be letting them live here," she said, arching one of her blond eyebrows.

A groan of frustration rose from his throat. "I still think that, but I see now that getting rid of them won't be as easy as I thought."

They were definitely lawyering up. And with the rumors circulating, because of the Pell family viciously spreading them, that Priscilla was a gold digger who'd killed the well-respected doctor, a judge might side with the late doctor's family over his widow no matter what the will said. From experience, Blade knew that judges weren't quite as impartial as they were supposed to be.

But he wasn't as worried about them right now as he was about his coworker. He hit the contact for him again, and again, it went directly to his voicemail.

"We need to find him," she said.

"I need to," he said. "You need to stay here, so I know you're safe."

"But how will you know that if we're not together?" she asked. "Someone could break in here or I could think I'm needed somewhere else and unlock the door."

"Damn it," he said with another groan. He would call in backup, but if Vik was in trouble, they might not get here in time to help. He had to look for him right away. "You can help me look, but we're not splitting up."

Ever.

He wanted to add that word, but he knew it wasn't true. For one thing, they weren't even really together. He was just working for her, and his job was to keep her safe. He couldn't do that if he was off looking for his coworker and she ventured out on her own.

He drew in a deep breath and turned the knob, but before he opened the door, he said, "You need to stick close to me."

And he wished like hell that he had that gun she'd lost even if legally he wasn't supposed to have it. The Kozminskis branch of the Payne Protection Agency was supposed to focus only on preventing the theft of valuables. Most of the time to do that they only had to upgrade security systems.

But this assignment, like the others they'd taken on for

the insurance company CEO, Mason Hull, had proved to be much more dangerous than it had seemed.

How dangerous?

Was Vik okay?

Blade was worried that he wasn't because if Lagransky was alright, he would have answered his cell, if not the first time, at least he would have the second time.

Priscilla was worried, too, about Blade's friend and about Blade. Something happening to his coworker proved to her that she'd been right to be concerned about his safety. But his job was a dangerous one no matter where he was doing that job, for her here at the estate or for someone else.

The thought of him protecting someone like he protected her had jealousy jabbing her heart for a moment. But he'd been determined to be professional with her. She was the one who'd kissed him first, who'd crossed the line between professional and personal.

And now everything about her bodyguard was personal to Priscilla. She wanted to help him find his friend, and she wanted to help clear his name of the manslaughter conviction that should have been dismissed instead of prosecuted. While he hadn't been acting in self-defense, he had been acting in the defense of someone who'd needed protection whether she'd wanted it or not.

Priscilla hadn't wanted to admit she needed protection either. But after the attempts on her life, she knew how much danger she was in, and unfortunately anyone who tried to protect her was in danger, too.

They searched the house for Viktor Lagransky but found no sign of the man. He was as big and broad and larger than life as Blade was, so he wouldn't have been easy to miss or overlook. He wasn't in the house.

Blade must have concluded that, too, because he stopped in the dining room and stared out the French doors to the patio. Snow was falling hard today, blocking out the sun in the sky and making it look much later out than it was.

"You said he was patrolling the house and grounds," she reminded him. "He must be out there."

Blade nodded. "I'll look out there, but I'm going to bring you to the den or upstairs. I want you to stay locked in somewhere in the house."

"But why? We didn't see anyone else when we were looking for your friend," she said.

Blade nodded again. "And that's what worries me. Where is everyone? I highly doubt that they moved out already."

"Me, too," she agreed. While she and Blade had been in her room for a while, it hadn't been long enough for anyone in the house to pack up and leave, let alone for everyone to have done it.

And she doubted they would go that easily or quietly.

"We didn't search their rooms," she said. "They might all be in them."

Probably plotting how to get rid of her or talking to their lawyers. Or both.

"And they could all come out of their rooms while I'm outside," he said. "That why I want you locked in one of the rooms that they can't access." Just as they could not access those people's rooms. While they were still living in the house, they had a right to privacy.

Unless there was a search warrant issued, but then the police would be the ones searching their rooms. And it might be too late for Viktor Lagransky.

"We can't waste any time if Viktor's out there," she said. And instead of heading toward the den or the staircase, she walked through the butler's pantry to the mudroom behind it. In there was the cloak she'd grabbed that first night she'd found Blade trespassing on her property. She pulled that around her as she stepped into her tall rubber boots.

Blade looked at the hooks by the door and pointed toward an empty one. "My jacket was hanging up there," he said. But it was gone. He didn't have boots or a jacket. But he didn't seem to care. He was focused on her. "You think you're going out there with me?"

"I am," she said. "He could be like I was…" She touched her throat that hurt yet from that damn strand of lights. If someone had done the same to Lagransky, he might need CPR… If they found him in time. "And if he is, we need to find him right away."

Blade nodded and opened the back door. The patio was covered in snow, making it tough for them to slough through it. She had the boots that protected her pants while Blade's jeans got dark from the snow melting on them and wicking up nearly to his knees.

Viktor was not on the patio.

"Where the hell is he?" Blade asked, but he didn't sound annoyed. He sounded a little scared.

And that scared Priscilla.

"I called for backup, but like I thought, they're taking too long to get here," he muttered as he started across the yard.

There were dips in the snow. Not quite footprints anymore. But maybe they had once been only for the heavy snow filling them back up again.

Someone had passed through here. On their way away from the house or toward it?

Blade headed away from it. And Priscilla followed him, closely.

He skirted the fountain, which still trickled water through the swans' mouths. Fritz must put something in the water that tinged it blue and kept it from freezing. The snow that fell into it melted instantly, disappearing.

Priscilla had felt as if she'd done the same for a while in this house. As if she'd disappeared. Even before Alexander died, she'd spent so much time in the den with him that she hadn't had a life of her own.

She wondered now if she ever had. Or if she'd just been trying to make first her parents happy and then Alexander. The only thing she'd ever done for herself with no thought or promise to anyone else was Blade. But what if she'd been wrong about him, too?

Even if she was, she still wanted him. Would she ever not want him? Maybe once she got through the first trimester or the second or had the baby, maybe then her hormones would level off again, and she wouldn't be so needy and emotional. Those feelings had irritated her when she'd first started having them and the dreams about that faceless, muscular man, but now, knowing how good sex could really be, she was enthralled rather than irritated. Too enthralled. And that was probably affecting her already faulty judgment.

She shook her head to clear it and focus, and snow rained down around her. It had fallen so fast and hard that it had already covered the hood of the cloak she wore. "Where are you going?" she asked Blade.

He was walking even faster than he'd been despite how deep the snow was, and she was struggling to keep up with him. The snow brimmed over the top of one boot and slipped down inside, dampening her sock as it melted.

"I'm following the tracks."

So those dips in the snow were tracks of some kind. Human, though? But how would an animal have made it over that stone wall?

Blade once had that first night she'd met him. The night

she'd stuck a gun in his back. Where had her gun gone? Who had it now?

The person who'd tried to kill her?

Then why hadn't they used it instead of that strand of lights? Because they hadn't wanted anyone to hear the gunshot and catch them. Because they were someone who wanted to get away with murder like they all accused her of getting away with murder. She never would have hurt Alexander or anyone else. But she was afraid that she had hurt Blade when she'd asked his boss to replace him as her bodyguard, which she'd only requested because she hadn't wanted him to get hurt.

She slammed into Blade's back when he stopped suddenly. Deep in thought with her head down to keep the snow off her face, she hadn't noticed that he'd stopped moving. "What's wrong? Why did you stop?"

But when she peered around, she noticed that they were near the stone wall. So they couldn't go much farther. But Blade wasn't looking at the wall. His head was bent down, too. And then he dropped to his haunches, and she saw why he'd stopped.

A man lay in the snow, half-buried in it. But the snow wasn't white when it fell on him. It turned red when it struck the blood that had saturated his jacket.

No. Not his.

The man wore Blade's jacket. And he was big and muscular like Blade.

A cry slipped through her lips, and she reached for her bodyguard, not for her protection, but to make sure that he was here with her.

That he was alive.

He reached through the snow and touched the man's neck, his fingers probing for a pulse.

"Is he..." She couldn't bring herself to finish her question.

"He's dead," Blade said, his voice gruff with emotion. And he pulled out his cell phone, his hand shaking as he punched in the emergency contact for the 9-1-1 dispatcher.

"Oh, my God..." Priscilla murmured.

She was upset that this man had died. But she was even more upset that the person who'd killed him probably thought they'd killed Blade because he'd been wearing a hat that covered his head and Blade's coat. Even now, with the snow covering his face, Priscilla couldn't see who it was.

Just that he could have been Blade.

She'd been right to worry about him losing his life trying to protect her. But this time the assailant hadn't even tried to kill her, just the person they'd probably assumed was Blade.

"So nobody touched anything?" Officer Carlson verified as she approached the area of the yard where Blade Sparks and Dr. Pell had discovered the body. They'd stood out there, waiting for her to arrive, and both of them were shaking either from the cold or the discovery of the murder.

Detective Dubridge was on his way, but Sheila was first on the scene. If a call involved the Payne Protection Agency, at least *this* Payne Protection Agency, she always made certain she was the first to respond.

One of the bodyguards or the bosses in this agency was going to slip up someday. And she would have proof that leopards, or at least criminals, could not change their spots. And maybe she would be able to get the truth out of them about the past, about what had really happened to her father.

She hadn't expected Viktor Lagransky to be the one who slipped up. But this slipup wasn't going to land him in jail but in the morgue. And for some reason she had a strange feeling in her chest, like a hollow feeling. Maybe it was just that she wouldn't be able to get the answers she wanted, the ones that she was pretty sure Viktor Lagransky, of all of this team of misfit toys, probably had for her.

"I touched his neck to see if there was a pulse, and there wasn't. He was already cold," he said, his voice gruff with emotion.

And from the amount of blood around the body, it was clear that the man had bled out quickly. An artery must have been severed.

"Then I called 9-1-1," Sparks continued, "and we haven't moved from this spot." He'd also given Dispatch the code for the gate, so she'd let herself into the estate.

He glanced at Dr. Pell. "You should go back into the house," he said. "Warm up."

The widow reached out and clasped his hand. "I'm not leaving you out here..."

With his dead friend.

"What's going on?" a deep voice asked. "You all having a party without me?"

Sheila gasped and turned to find Viktor Lagransky standing behind her.

"Vik!" Blade exclaimed with obvious relief. "I thought you were..." He gestured at the body. "I thought that was you."

"Who the hell is it?" Lagransky asked.

Sheila stooped down next to the body and brushed some snow from the cold face of the deceased. He looked vaguely familiar to her.

"Fritz," the widow identified him. "That's the gardener."

Sparks swore, then repeated to his friend, "I thought it was you. Why the hell weren't you answering your cell?"

Lagransky cursed now. "I was trying to get all the cameras to come up on my cell, and I wasn't able to. That assistant of yours, Dr. Pell, tried to help but somehow managed to drop my phone into a bowl of soup instead."

"But we looked for you," Blade said. "You weren't anywhere in the house."

Lagransky nodded. "Yeah. I met Nikki outside the gates, on the street. She had one of the vans with equipment in it and was trying to get my phone working again and the cameras up on it. The cameras were still being monitored by other team members, though, or I would have let you know. I was outside with Nikki when Carlson here rolled up and let herself inside. I figured she was looking for me. She just can't stay away from me."

Sheila glared at him even as a smile tugged at her lips. For some reason she was relieved that he was alive. But maybe it was just because she might have a chance to get the answers she'd wanted for so long. That had to be it; it wasn't as if she actually enjoyed seeing or talking with this arrogant, impossible, funny man.

But his grin slid away when he looked down at the body again. "Don't know how you all mistook him for me," Lagransky said. "He looks more like Blade. Hell, he's even wearing your jacket."

"So whoever killed this gardener meant to kill Sparks?" Sheila wondered aloud.

Blade shrugged. "I don't know. He might have been the intended target."

"Why?" Sheila asked.

"Because we discovered earlier today that he was having an affair with Bradley Pell's wife."

"Who else discovered that?" she asked.

"Everybody at breakfast, including Bradley Pell and his son. Fritz took off right then and nobody saw him again."

"He must have come back inside, though, because when he walked out he wasn't wearing your jacket," the widow said. "I think it's more likely that whoever killed him thought they were killing my bodyguard."

Bodyguard?

Was that all the man was to her? The way she clutched his hand in hers indicated that Sally Pell probably wasn't the only woman in the house having an affair with the hired help. But Sheila wasn't here to judge; she was here to solve a murder. This one…

And another one from long ago…

Chapter 20

A week had passed since Fritz Parker's murder. As far as Blade knew, the police had found no evidence to implicate his murderer. A knife had been found buried in the snow beside his body, but the killer had worn gloves. There were no prints on the handle, no way of proving who had plunged it into his back. The other thing they didn't know and that bothered Blade the most was if Fritz had been the intended victim, or had the killer thought they were plunging that knife into Blade's back?

He imagined there were a few people in the house who would have been happy to do that. Monica was gone; she'd had no way to fight her termination. But the others were fighting their evictions and termination.

The butler had been mentioned in the will, with a guarantee of living quarters and employment unless Priscilla could prove he was actively trying to harm her. She couldn't prove it. The same went for the family; they were allowed to live in the mansion as long as they weren't trying to hurt her. Since they had made threats, there was a court hearing pending, but a judge wouldn't hear either side of the argument until after the holidays.

They had two weeks to stay.

And Blade...

He had no idea how much longer he would be here. Surprisingly, Priscilla hadn't tried to have him replaced again even though she really believed he had been the intended target and not Fritz.

Blade wasn't so sure since Sally couldn't stop sobbing over the loss of her lover. Her husband and her son seemed to be enjoying her reaction with the little smirks that crossed their faces.

Blade stared back at his own face as he tried to tie the bow tie that had come with the tuxedo Priscilla had rented for him. No matter how much she dressed him up, he was still going to look like a thug. The boxer he'd once been, a bodyguard, not the handsome, successful, intellectual she should be with.

Not that Blade wanted to be anything other than he was. He was happy with his life, happy to help people without having to suffer any consequences for helping. The image of Fritz, half-buried in the snow with his jacket, flashed through Blade's mind again.

That would have been a hell of a consequence. He had a horrible gut feeling that there would be consequences for what they were about to do tonight.

Attend that damn fundraising gala.

"This is a bad idea," he told Priscilla.

She was in the en suite bathroom getting ready while he stood before the full-length oval mirror in her walk-in closet.

"I am not doing this because Everett goaded me or Alexander is still controlling me," she said. "I am doing this because Alexander was a great man who did a lot of amazing things for medicine and for the field of biophysics. And in his will he set up scholarships at the university for students who would not be able to afford an education without his help. I was once one of those students. When my parents got sick and the medical bills mounted, I couldn't have afforded my education without scholarships like this."

"So you talked him into this?" Blade asked.

"Maybe he wasn't the one doing all the controlling," she admitted. "But everything that both of us wanted is going to benefit many more people than either of us. Alexander really was a good man, and as his widow, I should be there to represent him."

"But you're in danger," he reminded her.

"Nobody has tried anything the past week."

"Because the police keep coming around," he said. "And we haven't gone anywhere but this suite and the den."

"I need to do this."

He sighed because he understood. And he had backup in place for the ride there and for the party itself. It wouldn't be just him protecting Priscilla. "I know." He sighed again and tugged at the tie, but the bows were lopsided.

She chuckled as she walked up behind him. "Here, let me." She tugged on one end of the tie, pulling loose the knot he'd made.

He turned around to face her and felt as he had so many times before with her, like he'd been sucker punched. Her beauty took his breath away.

Her shimmery blond hair was bound up on the top of her head with a few silky tendrils curling around her heart-shaped face. Her makeup highlighted her beautiful green eyes and added color to her delicate cheekbones and full-lipped mouth.

Then he looked down, his gaze sliding over the silky red dress that clung to her curves. "You are…stunning," he murmured.

"Ditto."

He chuckled. "Not me."

"You look like James Bond in that tuxedo."

He shook his head. "Like James Bond after he's been in a few too many fights maybe."

"You are too hard on yourself, Blade Sparks," she said. "You're a good-looking man."

He chuckled again. "You need to have your eyes checked, Dr. Pell." But he didn't need to be handsome. He just needed to be helpful.

She reached for his tie again, but instead of tying it, she used the ends of it to tug his head down to hers. And then she kissed him the way she usually kissed him, like she wanted to devour him. Her lips moved over his, and her tongue sneaked its way into his mouth. Then her hands moved to his shirt, undoing those difficult little studs that it had taken his big fingers so long to maneuver. But he didn't care.

"We're going to be late," he said.

"I don't care," she said as she pulled his shirt apart. Then she lowered her mouth to his chest, kissing it.

And his control, tenuous at best around her, frayed away. He clutched her hips and lifted her up. He carried her back into the bathroom but stopped at the vanity, settling her onto the edge of it.

Then he dropped down between her legs to pull off her panties and push the long hem of her dress up. He touched her first with his fingers, stroking her while he kissed her mouth. She gasped as he rubbed his thumb against her clit. Then he felt the rush of heat as she came, her body quivering.

His body was tense with need. But he also didn't want to rush. He liked giving her pleasure first. He liked how wild he could make her with just his fingers or his tongue. He pushed down the bodice of her gown and moved his hands to her breasts, stroking and cradling them in his palms. She could have been a swimsuit model or movie star with her figure and face, but she'd chosen instead to go into biophysics. She wanted to save people, too. Maybe she wasn't as different from him as he thought she was.

She threw back her head and moaned as he closed his lips around one of her nipples. But she reached for him, tugging down the zipper of his tuxedo pants. Then she released him, sliding her hand up and down the length of his engorged cock.

"Priscilla..." He ground her name out between clenched teeth.

Unable to wait a moment longer, he slid inside her. In and out. She matched his rhythm like this was a dance they'd done many times.

And they actually had. Just as he couldn't get enough of her, she couldn't seem to get enough of him. They came together, their bodies shuddering in reaction to the power of the orgasm, the power of the pleasure.

But then a sudden chill rushed over Blade's perspiration-slick skin. He wanted to just stay here, safe in her suite, because just as he'd told her, it was a very bad idea to go to the fundraiser.

Even with the backup he had in place, he was worried that she wouldn't be safe. That if the killer tried again, he might not be able to save her.

Moments ago in her bathroom, Priscilla had felt that chill pass through Blade. And it passed through her, too, even after she was dressed again with a long wool trench coat over her gown. She felt it the moment they stepped outside the mansion and walked toward the long black SUV idling outside.

This probably was the mistake that Blade had warned her it was. She had never been one for parties or speeches. But she was supposed to give one here, to talk about Alexander's work, about his legacy. It was also her legacy now, and she was proud of the part she was playing in it and that Alexander had trusted her to finish it.

"Did you change your mind?" Blade asked hopefully as she hesitated outside the back door he held open for her.

The driver's window rolled down and Viktor Lagransky grinned from behind the steering wheel. She was so glad that he hadn't been the one they'd found dead, not that she was happy that it had been Fritz.

But Viktor was quite the character and he was kind, like Blade. He cared about people and wanted to protect them just like Blade. He was good-looking, too, but he didn't make her heart beat faster like Blade.

"It would be safer to stay home for once," Viktor said. "The rest of your family has already left for this event."

"They're going?" Blade asked, his voice thick with dread.

She sighed. "It's to honor Alexander," she reminded him. "Of course they will be there."

"Not to honor him, though," Blade said. "Or they wouldn't keep spreading rumors about his death and calling you a gold digger. That makes him look as bad as it makes you look."

She sucked in a breath.

"I'm sorry," he said. "I'm not saying you look bad. You look beauti—"

"Smooth, Sparks," Viktor teased his friend.

"I know what you mean," she said. "I know that they

have people believing I'm at the very least a gold digger, at the very worst a murderer."

"And that makes Alexander look like an idiot," he said. "Like he didn't know how smart you are and that you were the only one he trusted to continue his work when he'd realized that he couldn't."

She sighed again, her heart aching for her former mentor. "Knowing that he was getting the disease he feared and wanted to fight the most was devastating to him. I have wondered sometimes if his death wasn't natural…"

"You think he might have killed himself," Blade said.

She shrugged. "I don't know. I just know that getting dementia was his greatest fear."

"To lose his mind," Blade said. "I can understand how hard that would be for a man who was that brilliant, who had so many groundbreaking ideas and discoveries."

"You do understand him just like you understand me," she said with a smile. Blade was so much smarter and insightful than he realized. She drew in a breath and climbed into the back of the SUV. "I need to do this. I'm ready."

"I hope we are, too," Blade said to his friend and climbed in next to her.

Viktor nodded. "Yeah, we've got this. We'll keep Dr. Pell safe."

Priscilla wasn't as worried about herself as she was about Blade and his coworkers. She knew that they would do anything to protect her, just as they'd promised.

But their promises might get them killed. They might have to lay down their lives to save hers. And her baby's. And she didn't want any of them to have to make that sacrifice. Especially not Blade. Even if she wasn't entirely certain she should trust him with her heart, she didn't want anything to happen to him.

***

Christmas music played. And lights twinkled from all the trees and garlands strung around the massive ballroom. The lights reflected off the many windows and the marble floor. Conversation flowed like the champagne and the guests danced and mingled.

Except for her.

Where was she?

This was the killer's best chance to get rid of her. And if her bodyguard got in the way, he would have to die, too. He should have already been dead. That sharp knife should have severed his spine and spilled his blood.

But instead some hapless gardener had died.

What the hell had he been doing out there?

It didn't matter now. It was too late for him. And soon it would be too late for Priscilla. She was going to die tonight. No matter what or who was here to try to protect her, she was going to die.

Chapter 21

Blade knew that the tuxedo hadn't made a difference. It didn't fool anyone at the fundraiser into thinking he actually belonged here. He should have dressed as a waiter like Viktor and Ivan. Nobody spared them a second glance as they moved around the ballroom. But he felt like everyone was staring at him.

Maybe that wasn't just because of how out of place he looked at a university fundraiser wearing a tuxedo. Maybe it was because of Priscilla holding on to his arm as she walked around the room.

They probably wondered what the hell Dr. Pell's widow was doing with any man, let alone one who looked like him. Or maybe they knew he was her bodyguard.

The Pells were here, glaring at her and speaking loudly to the people around them. "I can't believe she had the nerve to show up here," Sally said with one of her sniffles.

"Especially with that goon boyfriend of hers," Bradley added.

"Probably the only time he's ever been on a college campus," Kyle added with a snicker.

Blade had gone to an entirely different kind of school when he'd been about Kyle's age: prison. He'd been schooled on how to survive. Kyle wouldn't last a minute behind bars that weren't on the windows at the mansion.

"Ignore them," Priscilla said.

"That seems to be what everyone else, besides the Pells, is doing to you," Blade remarked.

Nobody had rushed up to greet her. And while they looked at her, if she turned toward them, they quickly looked away.

"You were right about this," Priscilla said.

"You want to go home now?" Blade asked hopefully.

She smiled. "You were right that everybody thinks I'm a gold digger and a murderer now. But that's why I need to be here, to show that those rumors aren't true. To give my speech and show them who I really am."

Strong. She was incredibly strong.

"Yeah, Sally, Bradley and Kyle have been spreading their lies," he said. "And if anyone is foolish enough to believe them, they don't deserve to know you."

She smiled at him, her green eyes bright as if tears were in them. "You're sweet."

"People usually cross the street when they see me," Blade said. "They don't think I'm sweet." He cocked his head toward a couple that were scrambling to get out of their way as he and Priscilla walked toward one of the banquet tables.

"They don't know you," she said.

"And these people don't know you if they think you could hurt anyone," he said. "You're the sweet one."

She smiled. "I'm the hungry one right now."

One of the waiters, Viktor, picked up a plate and handed it to her.

"Thank you," she told him.

"Quite a turnout tonight, isn't there?" a male voice remarked, and Blade turned to find his boss Milek standing behind them. He wasn't alone. A beautiful redhead held on to his arm like Priscilla had been hanging on to his. Now she was filling her plate with food from the banquet table.

Viktor and Ivan were both close, so he was able to relax a bit.

"Are you talking about the guests or the staff?" Blade asked with a slight grin.

"The staff, of course," Milek said. "We're ready for anything. Amber, you remember Blade Sparks from our opening ceremony."

District Attorney Amber Talsma-Kozminski smiled at him. "I remember Blade Sparks well. I've been talking to everyone associated with your old case. I think I can get the—" she looked around and then lowered her voice "—conviction overturned."

He shrugged, refusing to let his hopes get built up again. "What does it matter now? I already served my sentence."

"A clear record matters," Amber said. "You'd be able to carry a weapon. And you might even get restitution for that judge not allowing other people to testify about how much that man had been abusing his wife."

Blade shrugged again. "It was hearsay," he said, repeating what the prosecutor had told the judge then. "And the victim wasn't on trial."

"Her abuser should have been," Amber said. "I want to make this right for you just like Josh's case."

"I appreciate that," Blade said. But he wasn't going to get his hopes up. Anytime he had in the past, he'd only been disappointed. Like about his career. And that trial...

And now Priscilla.

He was falling for her, but he couldn't see a future between them. He didn't fit into her world, and all the tuxedos in the world wouldn't fool anyone into thinking that he did, least of all him. And what kind of role model would he serve for the son she was having? He was an ex-con.

The professor had sidled up beside her at the banquet table. He wore that smarmy, condescending little smile as he spoke down to Priscilla. Or Pris, as he was probably calling her.

And Blade's hands clenched into fists. He really didn't like that guy, and it wasn't anything to do with jealousy. Really. Sure, this pseudo-intellectual had been involved with Priscilla. But he hadn't been any more deserving of her than Blade.

So he wasn't jealous of the man. In fact, he pitied him, because it was clear Dr. Fendler was still obsessed with her. Blade didn't think it was love, but it was something. Something darker and more insidious than love.

Resentment. Jealousy...

The professor wasn't the only one feeling those emotions because Blade caught someone else staring at them. Monica stood a short distance away, her face scrunched up in a scowl of displeasure.

She was obsessed with old Everett. And if she considered Priscilla her competition, she might do anything to get her out of her way. Even try to kill her.

But would Monica have been strong enough to nearly strangle Priscilla with that string of lights? And to plunge that knife into Fritz's back?

But sometimes jealousy and hatred made a person stronger than they were. And the string of lights hadn't managed to strangle Priscilla. And the knife had been ridiculously sharp so it might not have been hard to stab the unsuspecting Fritz.

Monica could possibly be the killer.

Really anyone could be the killer. And that made Blade

very nervous. Even with the team they had in place, he wasn't sure they would be able to keep tabs on all of them and keep Priscilla safe.

"Uh-oh, Pris, the district attorney is talking to your boyfriend," Everett said, his voice in Priscilla's ear as he leaned way too close to her. "Think she's about to have him carted back to prison? Has he violated his parole or something?"

Priscilla studied the little man through eyes narrowed with suspicion. "How do you know about his record?" she wondered aloud.

Everett shrugged his shoulders, and one of the pads in his tuxedo shifted so that it looked like he had a growth on the back of his thin shoulder blade. "I've always done the research, Pris. Something you should have done. He is a convicted felon, you know. A killer."

Priscilla sighed. "He's a hero. He saved a woman's life."

"That's not what the woman said in court."

He really had investigated Blade. And that unsettled Priscilla. But instead of making her doubt Blade, it was making her doubt Everett. "Why would you so thoroughly check out Blade Sparks?"

"He's supposed to be protecting you, and he's probably more dangerous than whoever is after you," Everett said. "You really need to be more thorough."

"I know everything about Blade," Priscilla assured Everett and even winked at him to let him know what she meant.

He grimaced. "I can't believe you're sleeping with the help. But then maybe I should. I hope you enjoyed yourself because if the DA is after him, he probably won't be free to be your boy toy much longer."

"The district attorney isn't after him," Priscilla said. "She's married to Milek Kozminski."

"The famous artist," Everett said and bobbed his head, with his thinning brown hair, in a quick nod. "Everyone in River City knows who he is."

"He's Blade's boss and his friend," she said. "They both are." She knew that the DA was trying to get his conviction overturned but that Blade wasn't about to get his hopes up at the possibility. Growing up as he had, he had learned to not expect too much. That way he wasn't disappointed. She understood that, too.

She had learned to not expect much from her parents; that way she hadn't been disappointed when they hadn't picked her up from boarding school or college to spend any holidays with her. But that had been because they were sick. If they'd had the drugs she was working on, everything might have been different. She focused now on the lights and the decorations since she had lost her appetite for the food on her plate when Everett joined her at the banquet table.

"The ballroom looks beautiful," she said to him.

"Monica was working with the caterers and decorators."

"No wonder she was doing so little for me in her role as my assistant," Priscilla remarked. "It appears she was really working for you." And she felt a sudden chill at the thought. Just what all had Monica been doing for Everett?

"Jealous, my little Pris?" Everett said, his voice low and full of innuendo just as he had always been so full of himself.

"No," she said. "Just a little annoyed with myself for not firing her sooner than I did."

"You always did give everyone second chances that they don't really deserve. Like that bodyguard."

"I didn't give you a second chance," she reminded him,

and she managed a grin as annoying as the one usually on his weasely face.

"And I am actually deserving of one," he said. "Think about it, Pris. We could do so much for the world of biophysics if we got back together."

"I could do so much, and you could take the credit for it," Priscilla said. "Dr. Pell—Alexander told me what you tried to do. The credit you tried taking for the work I actually did."

Everett snorted. "Alexander was a senile old has-been with a schoolboy crush on you. That's the only reason he chose you over me, because he wanted you in his bed, Pris."

Fury was bubbling up inside her now. She slammed her plate down on the banquet table. "He wanted me to work with him because he knew I was the better person for the job, that I am smarter than you are and work harder than you will. And you can't deal with that."

Everett's face flushed. "Wow, you're full of yourself now. What? You think you won because you got the estate? Because you have more money now? I still have more power, Pris. And you're going to find out just how much. You shouldn't have come here. I think it would be better if you left now and if I gave the speech for the scholarships Alexander bequeathed for the school. I was always the better public speaker."

"That's you, Everett," she agreed. "You're all talk and no action."

Everett made a tsking noise and shook his head. "You've gotten so crude, Pris, hanging out with lowlifes like you are now. Poor Alexander. He would be so disappointed if he could see you now."

"You didn't know Alexander at all," Priscilla said. "And you're not giving the speech. I will be doing that. I am the reason Alexander included those scholarships in his will in the first place."

The lights flickered for a moment and the music stopped playing only to start up again.

Monica rushed up to Everett. "We seem to be having electrical issues," she said. "There's a blizzard outside—"

"No, there's not," Priscilla interjected. "It was barely snowing when we drove up just a short while ago."

"It's bad now," Monica snapped at her before turning back to Everett. "The wind is blowing and it's snowing hard, and I think the power might be about to go out. Is there a backup generator?"

"I am not the janitor," Everett said. "You should take care of this, like we discussed. You know what your job is, Monica. You know your place." And he glared at Priscilla as he said it, as if she didn't know her place.

"Wow," she murmured. "Not only are you a pompous ass, but you're a misogynist, too." She sighed and shook her head. But she also felt nauseous that she had ever been involved with such a man. What was wrong with her judgment? How could she be so smart about some things and so stupid when it came to others? Like people.

Feeling ill, she started off toward the restrooms. The light indicating them was starting to blink as the lights flickered off and on again. Maybe the weather had taken a turn for the worse suddenly.

Blade stopped her before she walked inside. "Priscilla, where are you going?"

"To the ladies' room," she said with a smile.

"Are you alright?" he asked with concern. "Was old Everett giving you a hard time?"

"He's an ass," she said.

And he chuckled. "Yes, but are you okay?"

She nodded. "Yes, just queasy. I'm going to take a moment."

He nodded. "Let me check the room first, make sure that it's empty." He ducked his head into the restroom door.

An older lady shrieked. She sat on one of the padded chairs in front of the vanity mirrors, reapplying her lipstick, which was a little smeared now. "Excuse me, this is not the men's room."

"He knows," Priscilla assured her as she followed Blade inside.

"I need to make sure nobody else is in here," he said.

"Why?" the older woman asked. Then her face flushed. "You need to leave, young man, or I'm going to call security."

"I am security," Blade said.

"You are not with the university," she said. "They have uniforms."

And he was wearing a tuxedo. "He's my security," Priscilla said as he checked the stalls in the other part of the bathroom.

"It's clear," he said. But he stared at the older lady.

Priscilla guided him back out the door. "I will be fine. You don't have to guard me in here."

He released a sigh. "I just don't like to let you out of my sight, especially here where I know you're in danger."

"I'll be fine. You have bodyguards all over the place. Nobody's going to try anything here."

But she knew that she was in danger. In danger of falling irrevocably in love with him. But what if she was wrong about him like she'd been wrong about Everett and Alexander and even Monica?

The woman must have been concerned that Blade was going to come back into the restroom because she rushed out, leaving Priscilla alone. She sat down on one of the soft chairs in front of the vanity mirror. And she breathed in and out, trying to calm herself.

The confrontation with Everett had been ugly. But it hadn't upset her as much as realizing that she'd fallen in love with Blade Sparks.

Was she wrong to even doubt him? Putting his safety at risk for others should be enough to prove that he was a good man. But what if he just had some sort of hero complex like Monica had said?

What if he did things to make himself look good like Everett had done? What if he cared more about his own image than the lives of others? And what if she was letting Everett mess with her head and being unfair to Blade?

If that was the case, she didn't deserve him.

The lights flickered again and then went out, plunging her into the darkness.

Priscilla sat still for a moment, waiting for the lights to come back on. But they didn't so much as flicker again. And while the music had stopped, voices called out frantically to each other. And for a second they got louder as the door opened, then shut again.

"Blade?" she called out. He would have stayed close, wouldn't he have?

But nobody answered her, and if it was him, he would have.

"Who's here?" she asked.

She might have thought the door had opened and closed without anyone coming inside the room, but she could hear breathing. Someone was in the restroom with her, someone who didn't want her to know who they were.

And she knew that her bodyguard had been right to worry about her. She wasn't safe here.

And she probably didn't need to worry about her future anymore. Because she had no doubt that whoever had tried to kill her before was in this room with her.

And they intended to try to kill her again.

She needed to get away from them. But she couldn't see anything. And they stood between her and the door. She couldn't escape.

She just had to fight. For herself and for her baby and for Blade…because she realized now that he would never forgive himself if he wasn't able to protect her.

Chapter 22

Once the old lady left the restroom, Blade breathed a little easier. Priscilla was alone in there now. Not that he suspected that the older lady was the one trying to kill her. But he breathed a little easier knowing that nobody was near her.

And he verified, through the earpiece he wore, where all the actual suspects were. "Eyes on everyone?" he asked.

"The assistant is heading downstairs for some reason," Viktor replied. "I'm following her now."

"Good. What about Sally?" he asked. Since Priscilla was in the ladies' room, he was most concerned about where the ladies were. Not that a man couldn't walk into it. But people would notice, just like that older lady had noticed him.

"She was just flirting with me," Ivan replied. "And her son and husband were glaring at me like it was my fault."

"It is," Viktor teased him. "You're too damn good-looking. Blade and I don't understand what a burden that must be for you."

Blade chuckled. Then the lights flickered. "What's going on with the power?"

Viktor let out an oomph. "Son of a…"

"What's going on?" Viktor was the one who'd been following Monica downstairs. Where? He started toward one of the stairwells. "Vik?"

The lights went out, plunging the ballroom into darkness. First there was an eerie silence because the music stopped. But then people started exclaiming and complaining over the power outage.

Blade didn't think it was because of the weather; it hadn't been snowing all that hard when they drove up. And now, with the lights out, he could see outside the many windows where only a few flakes drifted down from the dark sky.

Somebody deliberately shut off the power. Because they didn't want him and his team to be able to see them, to be able to stop them.

Priscilla...

He had to get back to her because he knew that she was in danger. But the darkness was so complete that he was disoriented for a moment. When Vik had made those strange remarks, Blade had instinctively taken a few strides toward one of the stairwells, but he couldn't even see that now. Weren't the exit signs supposed to stay lit up even during a power outage?

Someone had planned this, had made certain that the darkness would be as complete as it was and that people were unable to see anything or anyone. And, like the older woman in the restroom had said, the university had security, and that security had confiscated cell phones at the entrance with the excuse that usage of them was prohibited during the gala. So nobody could use them to see their way around the room right now, not even Blade.

He bumped into other people as he tried to move through the crowd back to that restroom where he'd left Priscilla. But she might have stepped out of it now, especially when the power went out.

He had no way of knowing where she really was. But the one thing he knew for certain was that she was in danger. Mortal danger.

Priscilla wanted to call out again or scream. But that would only give away her location. She needed to hide, at least until the lights came back on. Or Blade came back.

He would come back for her.

If he was able...

But had whoever was in the room with her already attacked Blade?

She was worried about him as well as herself and her baby. She had to find a weapon, something to fight off whoever was stalking her in the darkness. But when she reached out, all she found was a box of tissues.

That wouldn't protect her or help fend off whoever was in here with her. If only she could get around them to the door...

But maybe she would be smarter to lock herself into a stall. She felt her way along the counter where she'd found the tissues until she found a wall. Then she moved along that toward the archway that led back to the stalls.

But before she could step into that area, gloved hands wrapped around her neck, squeezing just as the string of lights had wrapped around her throat, cutting off her breath not so long ago. Her neck still sore and bruised, she flinched at the pain.

But she'd fought then, and she intended to fight now, too. She reached behind her, swinging her hands through the air until she touched skin. Finding the person's face, she clawed at it. And as she clawed, she shoved herself back against their body. Then she stepped back with her stilettos, slamming them down again and again. The heels dug into the shoes of whoever was holding her, choking her.

But instead of letting her go, the gloved hands tightened around her, squeezing harder. Her lungs burned for air. But she couldn't stop fighting.

For herself, for her baby...

For Blade.

Blade...

He was strong. She had to be, too. So she kept fighting. Clawing, stomping and kicking...

She wasn't going to stop fighting until she drew her last breath. But she knew, if help didn't come, that might be soon.

Viktor had thought he had the easy job, watching the mousy little assistant. But the woman was young and fast. And sneaky as hell.

Why the hell was she going downstairs when everyone else was in the ballroom?

There were no bathrooms down there. And if she was the one trying to kill Priscilla, why wouldn't she go into the same restroom that the widow had?

No. She wasn't the killer. And he was probably wasting his time following her.

But he'd been assigned to watch the assistant, which was probably the easiest one. She seemed so preoccupied that she didn't notice him watching her.

She'd been watching that slimy professor instead and Priscilla Pell. It was easy to see that she was jealous of the beautiful widow. And Monica was obsessed with that professor, too. So much so that she wasn't even mooning over Ivan like most women did.

While Ivan had the other Pells in his sight, Viktor kept

Monica in his. He followed her down the stairs into what must have been the mechanical rooms of the building. The pipes and the ductwork were exposed. He had to duck under it to avoid hitting his head.

Then the lights flickered and went off, plunging him into the dark. He didn't move for a moment, waiting to get his bearings, or for his eyes to adjust to the darkness.

But before he could move, something hit him. Hard. Something like a pipe, but he hadn't walked into it. Someone was wielding it, swinging it at him.

"Oomph..." Pain radiated from his stomach that had taken the first hit. When it swung toward him again, he grabbed it, jerking it from his attacker's grasp.

He tried to swing it back at whoever had struck him, but he hit only air. The person was running away from him; he could hear the footsteps growing quieter as they escaped from the mechanical room.

From Viktor.

"Are you okay?" a voice asked from his earpiece.

Ivan.

"Yeah, yeah, I'm fine," he said, then rallied and rushed after them. But he was running blind, so he had to duck low so that he wouldn't hit his head. So that he wouldn't knock himself out like the person wielding the crowbar nearly had.

He heard the footsteps on the stairs now, heading back up to the ballroom. There had been no hesitation with those footsteps.

And with the way they had so easily struck him even in the dark, it was clear that this person had been prepared for a blackout.

"They must have night vision goggles," he said into the small mic on the lapel of his dress shirt. "Beware. They can see us."

"They?" Ivan asked. "Is there more than one?"

"I don't know," he said. "I was following Monica." But he didn't know if she was the one who'd struck him. "Do you have eyes on the Pells yet?"

"I can't see anything," Ivan replied.

Neither could Viktor as he stumbled around and felt his way along the wall, trying to find the door handle for the stairwell.

"Blade?" Viktor asked. "Where's Blade? Does anyone know where the widow is?"

Blade would know.

"I left her in the restroom," he said. "And I'm trying to find my way back to it. Back to her..."

But he couldn't see either.

Whoever had planned this was smart; they'd figured out how to take out Priscilla's security team. They'd effectively blinded them with this blackout.

"I'm going back to the mechanical room," Viktor said as he turned around. "I need to get the power up again." That was the only way to save Priscilla.

If they weren't already too late...

He hoped like hell for Blade's sake and for the widow's that there was still time to save her. That she wasn't already dead.

Chapter 23

Blade concentrated hard on retracing his steps back to where he'd left Priscilla. Was she still there?

She'd been alone in that restroom. But he doubted that she was now. He'd heard Viktor in his earpiece.

They had night vision goggles.

They?

Was there more than one person after Priscilla? It was damn likely. He'd already been worried that everybody in that house had been working to get rid of her. Maybe they'd worked together on a plan to get rid of her here at the fundraiser.

Panic had his pulse racing as he fumbled around in the dark. He found the archway to the hall he'd gone down to the restroom. He ran his hands down the wall of it until he found the door and pushed it open.

"Priscilla!"

She didn't answer him, but there was some kind of struggle happening. He could hear heavy breathing from one person as another person flailed. The sounds drew him toward them, and he reached out.

His hands ran over the sleeve of what felt like a tuxedo jacket. And he jerked on that arm, trying to pull the person away from Priscilla.

He kept pushing and shoving at the person in the dark, trying to break them loose from their hold on Priscilla. Then suddenly there was a gasp, as if someone had been holding their breath for entirely too long and was just now able to breathe again.

He'd been strangling her. Just as she'd nearly been strangled before. He flailed around in the dark, and he grabbed the arm of the person again. They were wearing gloves. One of those gloves swung at him and connected. But he didn't even stumble back. He was too enraged.

He pushed and shoved.

But there was another gasp. A weak one.

"Priscilla?"

He dropped to his knees, fumbling around on the floor to find her. And the person they had both been struggling with scrambled around him. The door opened and closed.

The killer was gone.

Was Priscilla gone, too?

His hands, patting the ground, touched silky hair and then silky skin. "Are you alright? Can you breathe?"

She gasped again.

"Help!" he yelled. "We need an ambulance. Priscilla is hurt."

But she was breathing.

She wasn't dead.

But once again he'd come too damn close to losing her.

She reached out and grasped his hands. Hers were wet.

The lights suddenly flickered and came back on, and he could see her. Her throat, which was still bruised from that string of lights, was red and swollen again.

And her hands weren't wet with water. They were smeared with blood. Had she been stabbed like Fritz?

"Where are you hurt?" he asked, and he ran his hands

down her body, checking for stab wounds. "Where are you bleeding?"

She rolled her head back and forth against the floor. "Not mine…" Her voice was just a weak rasp. "Not mine…"

"You got him, Priscilla," he said, tears stinging his eyes with pride. "You fought him. You marked him. We'll be able to find him."

The door opened behind Blade, and he tensed. If the person realized like he had that they would be caught, maybe they'd come back.

With that gun they'd taken from her.

To protect her, he leaned across her body. He would willingly take a bullet for her and for her baby. He would be happy to give up his life for them. He'd already given them his heart.

Priscilla knew why Blade had covered her body with his. He'd been protecting her in case her would-be killer had come back with the gun they'd taken from her. He'd been willing to die for her. And that wasn't for his image or for show but just because he was a truly good man. A hero.

God, she loved him. And she wanted to tell him so…

But when that door opened, the others rushed in to check on her. Ivan and Milek had run into the restroom.

"Are you alright?" Milek anxiously asked. "Are you both alright?"

"We need an ambulance for Priscilla," Blade said. "Is one on its way?"

Ivan nodded. "Carlson is, too."

Just a few seconds after he uttered her name, the young officer rushed into the restroom with them. She must have been close; maybe she'd been expecting trouble just like Blade had been.

Blade.

Priscilla looked for him in the room that was suddenly crowded with other people. Where had he gone?

The paramedics arrived, but Carlson held them back for a moment. "You're okay for now, right?"

Priscilla nodded. Her neck hurt, but her throat hurt more. She could breathe now but talking was hard.

"You've got DNA under your fingernails," Carlson said as she put plastic bags over Priscilla's hands. She taped them around her wrists. "We have to preserve this for evidence."

"It's going to be easy to find and identify your attacker this time," Ivan said. "You must have left some serious scratches on them."

"Blade..." she whispered.

Where was he?

"Sparks is who attacked you?" Officer Carlson asked.

Priscilla shook her head.

And Milek said, "No way that he would hurt her."

"He saved me," Priscilla whispered. "Where... Where is he?" She needed him. But more importantly she needed to make sure that he was okay.

"I think he went out to find the paramedics," Milek said. "To get them back to you."

The paramedics were here, waiting for Carlson to get out of their way. But there was no Blade. Even if he'd showed them where she was, he hadn't stayed.

And Priscilla needed him more than she needed medical attention. She could breathe again, and she started breathing harder with fear. "He's looking for..."

"For the person who attacked you," Carlson finished for her. And she jumped up then. "Damn it. He better not interfere. I was going to round up everyone..."

"Gun..." Priscilla whispered.

"What?"

"Killer...has my gun," Priscilla reminded the officer. She didn't want her getting caught unaware by a weapon.

Blade knew about the gun; that was why he'd covered her body with his. He expected that person to use the weapon they'd taken from her.

Because they had nothing left to lose.

Just as Carlson had vowed, she was going to find the person. And the DNA under Priscilla's nails would be enough evidence for a conviction.

Not a single one of the people she and Blade had suspected of wanting to hurt her would be able to survive prison like he had. Knowing that, knowing how desperate that person would be, Blade must not have been willing to wait for Carlson to find them.

He was seeking them out.

And he might not survive when he found them.

He had to get to the gun. He knew he would need it to get the hell out of here. Those damn bodyguards were everywhere, blocking exits, making sure that nobody left the building. Moving around in the dark, with the night vision goggles on, he'd overheard one of them saying that they'd blocked the exterior doors.

But he would shoot his way out if necessary. And it was necessary.

Because of that bitch.

She'd clawed the hell out of his face. Blood oozed down his cheeks and dripped from his chin, staining the bright white of his tuxedo shirt with red splotches.

Fortunately, he'd managed to get out of the ballroom before the damn lights had come back on. He'd been half-way down the hall toward his office when they flickered back on.

Monica couldn't do anything right.

He should never have trusted her. She hadn't managed to carry off anything she was supposed to do, that she'd promised to do.

She hadn't managed to steal Alexander's notes. And the few pictures she'd sent him of the formulas had made no sense. She didn't know what she was looking at.

She wasn't smart like Priscilla.

But that was why she'd been so easy to use.

Not only was his face bleeding, but his feet were swelling up within his dress shoes. She must have broken bones with the way she'd kept stomping on his feet. Bitch.

When he finally got to his office, he grasped the knob and found that it turned easily. And when he opened the door, he found her in his office.

Her face was red from the tears trailing down it. Then her dark eyes widened when she saw him. "Oh, my God. Everett, what happened to your face?"

He blinked against the sting of the blood running into his eyes. "That bitch...that damn bitch clawed me up..."

Monica gasped. "Why? What did you do to her?"

"What do you mean? What the hell do you think I did?"

The color left her face. "Did you kill her?"

"No, damn it!" But he'd been so close, so very close again. He'd locked his gloved hands around her neck and squeezed so hard. But the bitch had kept fighting him. And he hadn't been able to squeeze the life out of her like he'd wanted.

"You...that's what..." She gasped again, and her eyes widened. "You've been trying to kill her..."

"What did you think I've been doing all this time, you imbecile?"

"The notes... Dr. Pell's notes," she said. "I just thought you wanted to finish the research you started with him. That you didn't want her taking the credit for your work again."

He snorted. "You are so stupid, little girl."

"Oh, my God," she murmured. "It was you. Everything. Fritz? You killed Fritz?"

"I thought I was killing that damn bodyguard. You were supposed to get rid of the other one while I took care of Sparks."

"I ruined his phone. And while I was doing that, you were killing Fritz." Tears were flowing down her face again, and she dashed them away with trembling hands. "I hit that one bodyguard...downstairs...with a crowbar. Oh, my God, I'm in this, too."

"Yup, honey, you're going to prison with me unless we can get the hell out of here."

"The bodyguards are everywhere," she said. "And the police. I heard the sirens when I ran in here. The police are out there." Her shoulders bowed. "We should just turn ourselves in. I... I need to explain..."

"Explain what, Monica?" he asked as he walked closer to her. "What are you going to explain?"

"I... I didn't know what you were doing. I thought it was your work." She shook her head. "But you didn't even understand it. While she... It was all her. Maybe even more than Dr. Pell, it was her work."

"She's smart," Everett admitted though the words nearly stuck in his throat like Pris's breath had been stuck in hers. "She wouldn't have been the fool you've been, Monica."

He reached for her then, closing his gloved hands around

her throat. She stared at him with her dark eyes full of terror. Even though Monica had to die so she couldn't testify against him, he didn't see her face as he tightened his hands around her neck.

He saw Priscilla's.

She was the one who was supposed to die.

He had to kill her if it was the last damn thing he did. And it probably was. Because he heard the door behind him open.

He hadn't even been smart enough to lock it behind him. Maybe Alexander had been right about him. That he wasn't good enough to be his research assistant. Or even a professor.

But the old man was dead now, killed by one of the drugs he'd created that Everett had slipped into his drink the last time they'd talked. It had been one of the failures, just like Pell had considered Everett. And while the drug had been controlled, Everett had been able to make some more of it, just enough to kill Pell.

"Let her go," a deep voice told him.

Of course it was the bodyguard. He had that whole hero complex Monica had accused him of having. He saw the hope in her eyes. She actually thought Sparks was here to save her.

He was just here to stop Everett.

But it was too late. Too late for all of them. He was close to his desk, close to the drawer where he'd stashed that gun. He just had to get to that now. But his hands were locked so tightly around Monica's throat that he couldn't release them. He couldn't release her.

He wanted to make sure that she died. And again, her face morphed into Priscilla's. He had to kill her. That was the last thing he wanted to do.

Chapter 24

Blade rushed forward and pulled Everett off the girl just like he'd pulled him off Priscilla a short while ago. But this time he could see. As he dragged the man's hands off her throat, he said, "You don't want to do this, man. You don't want to kill anyone."

The professor snorted as he whirled around and flung Monica at him.

Monica grabbed at Blade, hanging on to his arms as she gasped for breath.

"God, you're an idiot," Everett said as he ducked around his desk, putting it between him and Blade. "Are you so stupid that you didn't figure out that I killed that damn gardener and the esteemed Dr. Pell?"

Voices emanated from Blade's earpiece, but he ignored them to focus on the professor. "There's no evidence that you killed anyone, Fendler. This isn't that bad yet. You need to not make it any worse."

"He tried to kill me," Monica murmured. "And Priscilla..."

Blade was well aware of that. He gently shoved her toward the door. "Get out of here. Go!"

"No!" Fendler shouted and then he shot the gun he pulled

from a drawer. The kickback of the weapon had him flinching and he nearly dropped it.

The bullet had gone wide, missing Monica's head but splintering the doorjamb as she ran through it.

"You're damaging your office," Blade said. "You don't need to do this, Fendler."

"I know you're talking to the others. I saw your earpiece!" Fendler shouted. "Pull it out! Pull it out or I'm going to kill you now."

Blade pulled it out. His coworkers were too far away to help him anyways. He had to figure this out on his own, or he was going to die.

But he wasn't as worried about his life as he was Priscilla's. He had to make sure that Fendler posed no threat to her or to anyone else.

The professor wasn't a good shot. He didn't know how to hold the gun. And with the blood trickling into his eyes from the scratches on his high forehead, he probably couldn't see clearly.

Maybe Blade could duck and dodge enough that he wouldn't lose his head or his life as he rushed the professor to get the gun away from him.

"What's your plan?" he asked.

"I know what you're doing!" Fendler shouted. "You're trying to get me talking. You're trying to stall so your friends can get here."

Blade shrugged. "I was just wondering how you intend to get out of here. Or are you giving up? You going to kill me and then yourself? Is that the plan? Were you going to kill Monica and then yourself?"

"Monica..." he murmured. And he took one glove off the gun to wipe the blood from his face.

"You nearly strangled her."

"You and your hero complex," Fendler muttered. "That's what Monica says you have."

"I'm a bodyguard. I'm just doing my job."

"You're doing Priscilla! You're sleeping with her! You don't deserve her."

"No, I don't," Blade wholeheartedly agreed. "She's beautiful and brilliant."

"And you're a nobody."

Blade nodded. "I know."

A sob slipped out of the man's lips. "I'm a nobody, too."

"No, Fendler... Everett, you're not," he said. "You're smart."

"Don't patronize me, you idiot! I had a plan. I was going to take that research..."

"And claim it as yours," he said. "That's why you had to kill Priscilla. Because she would have known the truth."

"You screwed everything up!" Fendler shouted. And he put his other hand back on the gun, holding it as he pointed the barrel right at Blade's heart.

The sound of the gunshot energized Priscilla. Using all her strength, she ran down the hall toward Everett's office. Officer Carlson was beside her, Ivan and Viktor right behind her.

When they'd left the restroom earlier, the Pells had been waiting right outside the door. They were all fine. No scratches on their faces. And in that moment, Priscilla had realized who it was.

And where Blade had gone. So she'd led the others to Everett's office. But as they'd started down the hall, a gunshot rang out. And now a girl ran toward them. She was crying hysterically and shaking.

Officer Carlson grabbed her. "Are you hurt?"

Monica shook her head, but her neck was red like Priscilla's.

"He tried to kill you, too," she said.

The girl nodded. "The bodyguard saved me. Blade..."

"Fendler has the gun?" Carlson asked.

Monica nodded.

"Of course he does," Priscilla snapped. "Blade can't have a gun."

"That doesn't stop some of these convicted felons," Carlson remarked.

Ivan and Viktor pushed around them. "We're going in there."

"No," Carlson said. She was holding her gun, and she started down the hall. "I've got this."

But then another gunshot rang out.

And Priscilla knew she was too late.

The officer ran, and Viktor and Ivan were right behind her. Priscilla took another minute, her legs trembling, before she rushed after them. But Viktor stopped her at the door, as if he didn't want her to see what had happened inside.

"Is he...is he..." She couldn't even say the word. She couldn't imagine Blade not being alive, part of the world, protecting it, protecting her and her baby.

She gasped as pain gripped her. And she dropped to her knees, holding her stomach that suddenly cramped. The baby.

Oh, God, she couldn't lose the baby, too.

Not Blade and the baby.

Sheila Carlson had fired her weapon before. She'd even shot someone. But she'd never killed anyone the way she had Professor Fendler, with a bullet through the brain.

But she knew it was the only way the guy was going to stop. He'd shot the bodyguard once. His friends were leaning over him now, trying to stop the bleeding, trying to save him.

And the woman...

Priscilla Pell lay on the ground outside the door. Had she been hit?

Had Fendler fired more shots before Sheila had taken him out?

Had she hesitated too long?

Was she the cop she'd always wanted to be? The cop her father had been?

Or had she failed him again and all the people who'd been counting on her?

"Are you okay?" Viktor Lagransky asked her.

And the question, and the concern in his deep voice as he asked it, snapped her back into action. She used the radio on her collar to direct the paramedics down. "The scene is clear," she said. "It's safe."

The threat had been eliminated. She'd killed the killer. But she might have acted too late.

Blade Sparks might not make it and neither might Priscilla Pell.

Chapter 25

Blade flinched as pain exploded in his stomach. Burning. He pressed his hand to the wound and felt his blood bubbling out between his fingers. Then his legs buckled beneath his weight, and he dropped to the floor of Fendler's office.

He could hear voices. Shouting. Crying.

"Hang in there, damn it!"

"Hang in there..."

Viktor.

Ivan.

They were here.

Where was Priscilla?

He tried to speak, but his voice was gone. He cleared his throat and rasped out her name, "Priscilla..."

"Priscilla?" Someone else repeated the name back to him. A female voice.

Carlson? Was that the officer?

She'd been there, too, when Fendler shot him. Where was she now?

Where was anyone?

Blade couldn't see. And he panicked for a moment, and something beeped. That beep and the voice drew him back to consciousness.

And he opened his eyes to find a woman leaning over his bed. Her face was vaguely familiar. He'd seen her somewhere before. But it had been years ago. Many years.

"Mom..."

But she was dead. He remembered that last boyfriend beating her up. A rib broke, punctured her lung, and she aspirated on her own blood.

Was Blade dead?

Was she leading him to wherever he was bound to go?

"It's Erica," the woman said. "It's... I've been trying to talk to you."

He blinked and cleared his vision. "What? Who...?"

"You saved my life," she said. "All those years ago, you saved me." Tears ran down her face. "I'm so sorry that I didn't do anything to save you."

"Am I dead...?" he murmured.

"No, buddy," Viktor said, and he jumped up from a chair next to the bed. "You're good, man. Belly wound, but you're tough. It missed all your organs. Well, it got your spleen. But who needs a spleen anyway?"

Blade chuckled. "Priscilla?" he asked.

And Viktor's grin slipped away.

"What happened?" Blade asked, his voice still raspy. "How is she?"

"She's here," he said. "She's getting checked out."

"Her throat...?"

Viktor tensed.

And Blade knew. "The baby?" Oh, God, no... She couldn't lose that baby. She wanted him so badly, already loved him so much. Tears stung his eyes. He'd failed her after all.

"Fendler is dead, though," Viktor said. "Who knew Sheila Carlson was such a damn good shot?" He whistled.

Then he glanced at the woman standing there, watching them. "Erica works in the ER and saw you come in. She wanted to talk to you, buddy. I think you should hear her out."

"Priscilla..."

"I'll check on her," Viktor assured him, and then he slipped out of the hospital room, leaving Blade alone with that woman.

"You can take your revenge now," he told her. She was wearing scrubs so knew what she was doing and could probably pull out one of the tubes or wires going into him. He wasn't as sure as Viktor was that he was alright. His head was foggy, and his body throbbed with pain.

"Revenge?" She repeated the word back as if she didn't understand it. "You're the one who should want revenge on me. I failed you. You were just trying to help me, and I failed you."

"What?"

"I should have told the truth when I testified," she said. "I should have admitted that Kirk was going to kill me. He would have. If not that night, another night."

Blade cleared his throat. "Why did you lie?"

She sighed. "I was scared."

"But Kirk was dead."

"His family wasn't," she said. "And neither was mine. And I was pregnant and suddenly all alone. I didn't know how to be alone, how to take care of my baby or myself."

He reached out for her hand that was twisted around the railing on the side of his bed. And he patted it. He remembered then how young she'd been. How alone. He knew how that felt; so did Priscilla. "It's okay," he told her.

She shook her head, and her tears spattered the sheet covering him. "No. It's not okay. I told the DA the truth.

I should have done it years ago, but I was worried that I would go to prison for lying. And I had my son to think of, to take care of..."

"I understand," he said.

"I don't," she said. "I don't know how you can."

"It's okay," he said again. "I understand." He swallowed hard, swallowing down old resentments and frustrations. "And I forgive you."

She sobbed and leaned over the railing. "I'm so sorry. So sorry..."

He patted her head. "It's okay."

"The DA said she will fix this," Erica said. "She'll overturn the conviction or something."

For the first time, Blade felt a little flicker of hope. But then it slipped away. He didn't care about the conviction or anything else right now. He just cared about Priscilla and her baby. He needed to make sure they were alright. Both of them. He couldn't imagine losing either of them.

But now that Fendler was dead, there was no threat to her life. She didn't need him, not like he needed her.

"Can I bring my son to meet you sometime?" Erica asked.

Blade blinked. "What?"

"He wouldn't be alive if it wasn't for you. Neither would I. I want him to meet the man I named him after."

"You named him Blade?" he asked.

She nodded.

"Thank you," he said.

"For naming him after you?"

"For not hating me," he said. "I thought you hated me."

"I was young and stupid and scared. It wasn't until my son was born that I realized how wrong I was about everything. But then I was scared of going to prison for perjury, and I didn't want to lose my son."

"It's okay," he told her again. "It really is."

She drew in a shaky breath and nodded. "Okay..." She glanced behind her. "Oh, I'm sorry. You must be Priscilla. I'll leave you two alone." She ducked out of his room then.

But Priscilla didn't come any closer. She just stood there, a couple of feet within the door. And he could see the tears streaming down her face like they had Erica's.

And his heart broke for her. And for him. She must have lost the baby. Tears rushed up on him, stinging his eyes and burning in his throat. "Priscilla, I'm sorry," he said. "I'm so sorry..."

He'd failed her. He hadn't protected her like he'd promised. While she was alive, she'd lost what mattered most to her.

Priscilla stared at the man she loved, unable to believe her eyes. That he was alive. She was also unable to believe what she'd just heard.

He'd forgiven the woman who'd sent him to prison despite his saving her life. How could he be so forgiving? But that was good; maybe he would forgive her for having doubts about trusting him with her heart.

Priscilla was tempted to go after the woman and slap her for costing Blade his freedom. His life.

"I'm sorry," he repeated.

"What?" she asked. "Why are you sorry?"

"The baby," he said, his voice gruff with emotion as tears brimmed over and slid down his face. "I'm sorry you lost the baby."

She instinctively clutched her stomach and sucked in a breath. "What?"

"Viktor told me—"

"I didn't lose the baby," she said. And she stepped forward now, rushing toward the bed. "He's fine."

"But you were getting checked out."

"Yeah, I had some cramping," she said. "Turns out something from the buffet was not good." She touched her stomach again. "But I'm fine." She'd probably reacted more to his being shot than she had to whatever bite of food she'd taken. She hadn't eaten much. "And I hear that you're going to be okay, so I'm even better than fine."

"Yeah, apparently I don't need a spleen," he said. "Though I'm going to need a second opinion on that. Viktor's no doctor."

"I think he wants to play doctor with Officer Carlson," Priscilla joked.

And Blade laughed, then grabbed his stomach and groaned.

"Oh, I'm so sorry," she said.

"I forget how crude you can be sometimes."

"Everett hated that."

"He was an idiot," Blade said. "I love it."

Did he love her?

His smile slid away. "If you didn't lose the baby, why were you crying when you walked in?"

She touched her heart then and had to clear her throat. "I was crying because I was relieved that you were conscious. And I was crying because I heard what that woman was saying to you."

He shrugged, then winced. "Yeah, apparently she's already talked to Amber, the DA."

"That's the least she can do after what she stole from you," Priscilla said.

"She was in a horrible situation. And she was scared,"

Blade said, as if that excused what she'd done to him, what she'd taken from him. Nearly a decade of his life.

"She should be scared now," Priscilla said. "I'm thinking about chasing after her."

He reached out and grabbed her hand and pulled her closer to his bed. "You're fierce. And so very strong and smart and beautiful. And you understand what she felt because you felt it, too, that fear of being alone."

She sighed and nodded. "Blade..."

"And even though I know I don't deserve you, I have to tell you that I love you. You deserve to know that and to know that you're not alone. You and your baby can have me. If you want me..."

"You don't deserve me? I don't deserve you."

"What?" he asked. "You have a doctorate. You're doing such important, lifesaving work."

"You're literally a lifesaver," she said. "You've saved my life. And Monica's, too. You're the amazing one. I don't know how you forgave that woman. You're so kind and incredible. And I love you." And she never should have doubted her feelings or him.

"You sure that's not just the hormones talking?" he asked.

She smiled and shook her head. "That's my heart talking," she assured him. "It's yours. I'm yours, if you want me."

"If I want you?" he asked, sounding incredulous. "Of course I want you."

"I'm carrying another man's child," she reminded him. "You're not taking on just me but my baby, too."

"Our baby," he said. "I want to be a father to this child. I want to be a family for this child and for us."

Tears stung her eyes, and she had to furiously blink

them away. "Speaking of family... What if I don't get rid of mine?"

He groaned. "They're not your family, and we'll make sure that they leave."

She touched her stomach. "They're my baby's, our baby's, family. And they're actually here."

"What?"

"They were worried about me, about you, and came to the hospital to check on us."

"The Pells?" he asked, and he sounded incredulous again.

She had been, too, until she'd talked to them. "Apparently, just before Carlson took Monica off in handcuffs, she filled in the Pells on everything that Everett had done."

"He killed Alexander," Blade said, as if just remembering himself.

She nodded. "She told them all of it. They actually apologized to me."

He snorted. "Yeah, because they want to stay on the estate."

She shrugged. "We'll see."

"You're a forgiving person, too," he said.

She smiled. "I guess that's another thing we have in common."

His smile slid away again. "Do we have enough in common to make it forever?"

She nodded. "We have a lot in common. We're both smart and hot and forgiving. And we're really good in bed."

He chuckled, then grabbed his stomach again as he grimaced with pain.

"I'm sorry," she said. "I wasn't joking, though, because it's true. We actually have a lot in common, Blade. We have the same values, and we want the same thing for this baby and for ourselves. Family."

He blinked and nodded. "Yes, we do. I love you so much."

She leaned over the bed railing and kissed him. "And I love you so much."

"It's like Christmas already happened," he murmured. "I have everything I could want and more."

"Me, too," she said. "But I hope you can be home in time for Christmas."

"Home..." He touched her face. "You're home, Priscilla. You're my home."

"And you're mine."

"You're a little overdressed for the waiting room," Garek remarked as he dropped into a chair next to his brother.

Milek wore a tuxedo, the tie undone. There was some blood on his shirt and on his hands.

"You okay?" Garek asked.

He nodded and sighed. "Yeah, it didn't look good for a while there. But Blade is going to be alright."

Garek released a shaky breath. "I know. He's tough."

"The toughest," Viktor Lagransky said as he joined them.

Garek wasn't sure which of the bodyguards was the toughest. They'd all been through so damn much and had survived. But Garek had a feeling that they were going to have to endure a lot more.

While Everett Fendler was dead, there would be another assignment. He'd already ignored one call from Mason Hull. But he'd been more worried about Blade than anything else.

But what if Hull had figured out that Garek was investigating him? What if he'd figured out which person was investigating him?

Garek had to make sure that his "man" on the inside at Hull's Midwest Casualty company hadn't had her cover blown. He shouldn't have put her in there, so close to the CEO. But he hadn't thought she would be in as much danger there as the others were on the outside.

While Milek and Viktor talked, Garek texted her. Okay?

All he got in reply was a thumbs-up, but it was enough. He expelled a sigh.

"She's okay," Milek said.

They weren't twins like Logan and Parker Payne, but Garek and his brother were so close that sometimes they were like twins in that they instinctively knew what the other one was thinking or feeling.

Milek was now watching Viktor, who'd jumped up to meet Officer Carlson, who was just stepping inside the room. "He's the one I'm worried about."

A chill raced down Garek's spine. "And now I'm worried, too."

Ever since they'd opened their branch of the Payne Protection Agency, he'd had this uneasy feeling, this fear that something bad was going to happen to one of their bodyguards. Because of that feeling, he probably shouldn't have hired the half sister they'd just met.

But she'd given the thumbs-up. Sylvie was okay.

Was it Viktor who might be in danger?

And who was that danger from?

Officer Carlson?

She'd come through this time. She'd stopped the professor before he'd been able to shoot any other members of the team or any other innocent people. But Garek still didn't trust her. She was always around, always watching them.

Why?

What was her problem with their agency?

What did she have against them?

It was past time that they figured it out. And Garek knew that the one person who could probably get the truth out of her was Viktor Lagransky.

Clearly he got under her skin. But she was under his, too. Would he be able to figure out the truth without getting hurt or worse?

Garek did not want another member of their agency winding up in the hospital again. Or the morgue...

* * * * *

Get up to 4 Free Books!

We'll send you 2 free books from each series you try PLUS a free Mystery Gift.

FREE Value Over **$25**

Both the **Harlequin Intrigue®** and **Harlequin® Romantic Suspense** series feature compelling novels filled with heart-racing action-packed romance that will keep you on the edge of your seat.

YES! Please send me 2 FREE novels from the Harlequin Intrigue or Harlequin Romantic Suspense series and my FREE gift (gift is worth about $10 retail). After receiving them, if I don't wish to receive any more books, I can return the shipping statement marked "cancel." If I don't cancel, I will receive 6 brand-new Harlequin Intrigue Larger-Print books every month and be billed just $7.19 each in the U.S. or $7.99 each in Canada, or 4 brand-new Harlequin Romantic Suspense books every month and be billed just $6.39 each in the U.S. or $7.19 each in Canada, a savings of 20% off the cover price. It's quite a bargain! Shipping and handling is just 50¢ per book in the U.S. and $1.25 per book in Canada.* I understand that accepting the 2 free books and gift places me under no obligation to buy anything. I can always return a shipment and cancel at any time by calling the number below. The free books and gift are mine to keep no matter what I decide.

Choose one: ☐ **Harlequin Intrigue Larger-Print** (199/399 BPA G36Y) ☐ **Harlequin Romantic Suspense** (240/340 BPA G36Y) ☐ **Or Try Both!** (199/399 & 240/340 BPA G36Z)

Name (please print)

Address Apt. #

City State/Province Zip/Postal Code

Email: Please check this box ☐ if you would like to receive newsletters and promotional emails from Harlequin Enterprises ULC and its affiliates. You can unsubscribe anytime.

Mail to the **Harlequin Reader Service**:
IN U.S.A.: P.O. Box 1341, Buffalo, NY 14240-8531
IN CANADA: P.O. Box 603, Fort Erie, Ontario L2A 5X3

Want to explore our other series or interested in ebooks? **Visit www.ReaderService.com or call 1-800-873-8635.**

---

*Terms and prices subject to change without notice. Prices do not include sales taxes, which will be charged (if applicable) based on your state or country of residence. Canadian residents will be charged applicable taxes. Offer not valid in Quebec. This offer is limited to one order per household. Books received may not be as shown. Not valid for current subscribers to the Harlequin Intrigue or Harlequin Romantic Suspense series. All orders subject to approval. Credit or debit balances in a customer's account(s) may be offset by any other outstanding balance owed by or to the customer. Please allow 4 to 6 weeks for delivery. Offer available while quantities last.

Your Privacy—Your information is being collected by Harlequin Enterprises ULC, operating as Harlequin Reader Service. For a complete summary of the information we collect, how we use this information and to whom it is disclosed, please visit our privacy notice located at https://corporate.harlequin.com/privacy-notice. Notice to California Residents – Under California law, you have specific rights to control and access your data. For more information on these rights and how to exercise them, visit https://corporate.harlequin.com/california-privacy. For additional information for residents of other U.S. states that provide their residents with certain rights with respect to personal data, visit https://corporate.harlequin.com/other-state-residents-privacy-rights/.

HIHRS25